EVERYTHING
THAT WAS

K.R. HANSEN

Book Cover by Debbie O'Byrne of JetLaunch

Hardcover: 979-8-89079-071-2
Paperback: 979-8-89079-072-9
Ebook: 979-8-89079-073-6

First edition 2023

Dedicated to everyone who has
lost someone special.

Chapter Playlist

1

Darklands ~
The Jesus and Mary Chain

One perk for members like me of the Dead Sibling Club? Dreamless sleep spent hovering within a gloriously empty void. A void where everything's numb, where everything's safe. Technically, I have no one to compare experiences with to know if nightmares or dreams of loss should be my norm. I am the sole constituent of this hellish society at my way-too-small-for-comfort high school. Lucky me.

It's fine though. I have a plan: slog through my senior year with as little effort as possible, graduate, and move to the city. Leave behind all my classmates, who can't relate, and my parents, who are too wrapped up in their own grief to remember I exist. Say goodbye to this dinky, Podunk town full of bad memories and people who know everyone else's business. And most importantly, escape the guy who ruined my life in the first place.

Maybe then I can breathe again.

I squeeze my eyes shut, the hard knot that greets me every morning locking into place in the pit of my stomach. Pulling the covers tight over my head, I sink into the mattress. This time last year, the days were filled with tangle-free bellies, laughter, love, and my very best friend in the world. Everything was perfect.

"*Wasss…*" I hiss the word, morning breath rank beneath the sheets, drawing out the *S* until my lungs empty entirely. Everything that was? I want it back.

I want it back much more than I want to draw another stupid breath.

I consider not getting up at all and spending the entire day in bed. The parental units wouldn't notice. BD—before Davis—they sure would have known. But now, in AD times, everything's changed. If not for the alarm disintegrating my brain with its endless scream, I wouldn't even be asking myself the same jarring question my subconscious spits at me every day: WWDD?

What would Davis do?

The answer?

Get up, Pru.

So, I do.

BD, I awoke before the alarm peeped even once and started up our favorite 80s new wave music, dancing and singing while I got ready for school. Davis had long ago convinced me that 80s alternative absolutely outshines the current bubblegum pop and rap-crap hogging the Top 40. AD? New wave rips my heart out. I've settled for wearing 80s band tees instead. Besides, a predominately black wardrobe makes dressing mindlessly simple. The less I have to think these days, the better.

I grab a vintage The Cure concert t-shirt from a hanger and a crumpled ball of black denim from what is, hopefully, the clean pile off the closet floor. I don't bother with a whiff test. Gross? Maybe. But there are no food stains on either, and I don't get close enough to anyone for it to matter anyway.

I've never been great with makeup but have become the master of applying a smudge of black liner without a mirror.

Tugging my massive wad of brown frizz through a scrunchie gets my hair presentable enough as well. BD, I kept it shoulder-length and manageable. AD, I have zero tolerance for small talk with some gabby stylist about *"what's new and exciting."* My only interests come from the same era as my musical tastes, so there goes the new. And even as a senior, I couldn't care less about graduation and all the related pageantry. So much for exciting. It's fine. I didn't fit in BD either. Back then, it didn't matter—'cause I always had my brother—but now?

Well, I guess it's all irrelevant, 'cause nothing matters anymore.

I tug black-and-white high-top Chucks—my pride and joy—onto my feet. I saved every dime I earned babysitting to afford them. They look exactly like the pair Davis always wore, clear down to the Muppets Bow Biters that I took off his too-big pair. He discovered the set—Animal, of course—at the place where all things magical are found: the thrift store. Now, every time I look down, Davis is with me.

Backpack on, I hesitate at the door, listening. Avoiding my parents is key to starting my day right. Hearing nothing, I pop open the door with a soft *click* and slip into the hallway.

At the end of the hall, Davis's door is open a crack. I can't bear the thought of stepping inside, but I torture myself a bit by pressing my forehead to the wood and peering past the doorframe. Dust particles reflect the sunlight, pirouetting in glittering eddies. The empty room stinks of loss. Sterile. Chemical.

All year, the room lay untouched, the same as Davis left it. I could still go inside. Sprawl across his bed. Finger all his things. Pretend that Davis would rush in at any minute, red-faced and breathless from football practice, and catch me rifling through his stuff.

Last week, out of nowhere, Dad hired movers to clear everything out and deliver the boxes to the thrift store. Then yesterday, a cleaning service scrubbed down the shell that was left. Every trace of Davis, gone.

My eyes burn, and I bite the inside of my cheek. Hard.

No more tears.

Still, I won't forgive Dad for this, and neither will mom. Not that she'll ever tell him. She doesn't tell anyone anything anymore.

Speaking of…

I glance toward her door. There's no light shining underneath. Tiptoeing up to it, I press my ear against the wood and detect a faint shuffling. Something slowly sliding open. A drawer maybe?

My fingers twitch over the knob, my stomach a mess of butterflies flapping so fiercely I want to puke. It takes all the control I have left inside me not to do it. I want to open the door. I want to see my mom. Smiling, beautiful, radiant. Honey-blonde hair the same color as Davis's hanging in perfect ringlets, a flower plucked from some bouquet Dad gifted her tucked behind one ear. Her brightly painted toenails wriggling under frayed denim cuffs from inside her ratty flip-flops—her favorite next to being barefoot. I long to hear *"Good morning, my beautiful Prudie!"*

Mom's the *only* person allowed to call me that. Of course, she's also the only person I could ever forgive for naming me Prudence Sabine in the first place. I would give anything to hear her ridiculous nickname now.

A muttered curse and then quiet sobbing yank me out of my thoughts.

Nope. Prudie Mom is a BD relic. The mom behind this door is all AD.

Zombie Mom.

Zombie Mom abandoned Dad at their accounting firm. Zombie Mom rarely showers, wears only her bathrobe and slippers, and hides in her bedroom all day. She randomly comes out but only to clean her precious china. God forbid anyone touches it or the prom decorations still hanging in that hideous dining room. I never see her. We don't talk.

So, yeah, I realize she is crying, but I don't dare open the door.

A crash in the kitchen startles me, and I bump into the doorframe.

The sniffles stop.

Crap!

I take the stairs two at a time.

But downstairs, it's even worse. I can't ignore the pillow and blankets on the outstretched recliner or the clothes draped across the back of the sofa. Dad's makeshift bedroom.

Maybe part of this is because of Zombie Mom. But it's also because Dad doesn't know what to do AD either.

BD, he was the cool dad. He went to work in faded jeans, untucked shirts, biker boots, and long hair that he wore pulled back into a ponytail. At the end of the day, Mom would remove his hair tie and run her long fingers through his wavy locks. *"My Hairy Larry,"* she'd croon, and he'd blush. He and Mom were disgustingly romantic like that. They were inseparable. We all were. We dared each other to pull Hairy Larry's ponytail and zigzagged around the house and yard to avoid Dad's bone-crushing bear hugs that were his payback. Once captured, we'd have our cheeks smothered with kisses before Dad lowered Mom into a dramatic dip and planted one on her mouth. That was our life. Laughing, joking. Always happy.

AD, Hairy Larry is long gone, his trademark ponytail shorn. He could be the poster boy for Accountants R Us in his business casual belted khakis, tucked button-up, and the noose of a tie taut beneath his Adam's apple. If Mom is a zombie, Dad is a robot. His protocol? *Get up. Avoid wife. Ignore daughter. Work. Pay bills. Stop caring.*

Wash. Rinse. Repeat.

"Hey, Pru, sorry about the noise." Dad gestures toward the sink. "Broke a glass."

He actually holds my gaze, and it reminds me of BD times. Back when Dad stopped anything he was doing when we entered the room. Back when we were the most important thing.

When I smile, his eyes widen and the spell breaks. He looks away and rearranges doughnuts on a plate, stacking them into piles only to separate and spread them out in straight lines across the oval platter again. He doesn't look back up when he speaks. "Day-olds. Sorry," he mutters.

Stupid me. I should have known better. No one looks at me too long anymore for the same reason I avoid mirrors. *"You're the best of all of us, Pru,"* Dad would whisper while cupping my chin in his hand. *"Mom's peepers, Davis's grin, my schnoz, and all in the right order!"* My face—my smile just like Davis's—is a constant reminder of all that's lost.

"Working late. Sorry. You good on dinner?" The plate squeaks against the countertop as he pushes it toward me.

I hate Robo-Dad tone—cold, clipped, factual. And always apologetic. As though it fixes anything.

I'm not hungry, but I grab a stale doughnut and shove it into my mouth, giving the perfect excuse to merely nod as I head for the door. Of course I have dinner under control. This isn't my first night AD surviving alone.

Once outside on the stoop, I sag against the closed door. Blood is rushing in my ears so loud I hear nothing else. A scream builds inside me—in my brain, in my chest, in my throat. These days, I'm always on the verge of screaming at everyone. I'm either angry all the time or numb and feel nothing, like my entire body's embalmed with cotton balls. I guess it's better than perpetually crying. Right after Davis died, everywhere I went, everything I did, I cried. I bawled so much it washed away every other feeling. And now, all I'm left with are the ones that burn.

I close my eyes and count until the threat of spontaneous combustion passes and my pulse slows. What I desperately need is a sugar fix; the doughnut wasn't enough. Thankfully I always stash candy in my backpack.

I fish through the pockets till I find it. A half-eaten bag of jellybeans. I pop a couple into my mouth, sucking off the sugary coating until they shift into gooey-bodied jelly slugs on my tongue. My own body follows, muscles unwinding and melting against the cold wooden door. Davis always said sweets make me sweet. He used to share his Halloween and Valentine's candy with me every year. Davis preferred fruity desserts—apple pie, peach cobbler, banana bread, raspberry sherbet. When I was stuck grounded in my bedroom, he'd slip packets of grape-flavored Nerds under my door.

I crumple the top of the bag and cram it into the front pocket of my jeans for easy access. Lord knows I'll need them again sooner than later. I get moving before Robo-Dad leaves for work. I can't risk bumping into him again and being forced into small talk and strained conversation.

The walk to school takes twenty-five minutes if I take it fast. BD, Davis would drive us. His Monte Carlo would have become mine, but the transmission or something in the engine died right before prom last year. I'd rather not hitch rides with Robo-Dad, so rain or snow or blistering sun, I walk. Podunk is small enough that you only really need a car for the outlying places anyway.

Halfway there, I have goosebumps on my goosebumps. I wish I had grabbed my jean jacket. It's colder out than it looked. Picking up my pace, I turn the corner and practically plow into a girl standing in the middle of the sidewalk waving and calling to her friend crossing the street. She spots me in time to sidestep off the curb right before we collide.

"Oh! Sorry," she says even though I was the one not paying attention to where I was going. Same as Dad, her eyes flit from my face to the ground and back. She opens her mouth as if to say something more but closes it. Her cheeks redden, and she turns to greet her friend. They link arms, and I watch them move up the street. I hang back to give them space but not so much that I can't hear that they are whispering. The one named Poppy slows and darts conspicuous eyes over her shoulder. She tilts her head and gives me the barest of smiles.

For a split second, I consider catching up to walk beside them until Poppy slips her finger beneath her round golden glasses to rub her watery eyes.

Her sad face says it all. We'd have nothing good to say to each other.

Besides, if I try, they will ask how I've been. I won't have an answer they'll like. It's been a year, and nothing's changed. I'm still stuck inside the same lost loop since the day Davis died. I don't even know Poppy and her friend that well, but they know everything about my life's current status. Another small-town Dead Sibling Club bonus for me. The awkward little sister, left brotherless, fitting in absolutely nowhere. The walking memorial of someone better.

Poppy sniffles as the first girl tugs harder on her arm, pulling her along faster. It's all right; I don't need the company.

Focus on the plan, Pru. Graduate. Escape Podunk. Nothing else matters.

Campus sprawls across a hilly plateau surrounded by miles of wilderness on three sides. The wind kicks up, scenting the air with the sweet musk of forest in early springtime.

Grimacing, I press up the hill, passing Poppy and her friend. As much as I don't want to spend more time than I have to inside the scholastic red brick prison, too many memories linger outside near the woods. Hiking. Exploring. Post-football-win bonfire celebrations. Davis and I weren't wastoids glued to the sofa, captive to our phones or computers. We were always going places and doing things. Driving everywhere in the Gherkin. Our beastly pickle-green muscle car gave us wings. With the windows down, the music blasting, and Davis behind the wheel, I never felt happier and more alive—free and safe all at once. We always spent that kind of quality time face-to-face and talking instead of separated by strings of mindless texts. Not like Poppy and her friends she's caught up with. All have their noses plastered against their cell phone screens. I slip through the front doors and rush to art class.

Getting to the classroom early means I am the first in the room and can nab the table closest to the door. It's always a toss-up which seat is best—sitting at the back of a classroom with no eyes upon you the entire period aside from the teachers, or sitting near the exit for a fast escape. Today, I opt for the easy out. The walk to school drained me. The day's barely started, and I am already all peopled out.

A glance at the clock shows I have twelve minutes until the bell rings. Even the teacher is MIA. Settling into my seat, I drag my pack onto the table and dig through it for my art journal and another amazing thrift store find: a tin large enough to hold all my favorite markers with the album art from *Mirror Moves* by the Psychedelic Furs on the lid.

These days, I only feel alive when I'm drawing, and lately all I want to draw is Davis. I started documenting our most recent moments, but it wasn't enough. So, I dusted off our old family photo album last week for inspiration. In one sleepless night, I penciled the outlines from all my favorite pictures into my journal, sketching my way through his life. I haven't added color or detailed embellishments to any of them yet, and I still have the loose photos tucked between the pages of my journal for reference. I flip through them until I find the best one: proof Davis and I were inseparable before I was even born.

Dad's standing behind Mom, his hands high on her hips, and a nine-month-old Davis lies across her rounded belly, arms flung wide. His baby face is scrunched halfway into the folds of her flowy striped dress, but his smile is unmistakably huge. Mom said he was always this way, hugging me and babbling to me, and that I would kick her stomach in response to his voice and laughter. Dad said his first word wasn't *Mama* or *Dada* but *baby*. As in *his* baby. He cried if they teased him about me being theirs. I was his and his alone.

And he was mine.

We're born only a year apart. To the day. Best friends from the beginning. Linked like constellations. As tight as identical twins.

I shuffle through the stack and find another of us in the hospital, my newborn fist wrapped around Davis's baby finger. His eyes are wide, his mouth formed in a tiny little O of surprise as he meets me, memorizes me. From that point on, my hand was firmly in his. Always. My whole life, he guided me.

Grabbing a marker, I let the Davis memories guide my hand across the paper. As soon as ink floods the page, my stomach knots unfurl. It's the perfect escape.

I'm so lost in my work I don't realize Miss Painter has entered the classroom and snuck up behind me. Everyone always hears her coming—the quick *tick-tick-tick* of her high heels clattering across the floor announces her whereabouts like a jangling dog collar—but I'm oblivious till her soft southern drawl croons far too close to my ear.

"Creative use of color and form, Prudence. The image would be stronger if you followed the rule of thirds and drew the children in the center. What do you think?"

Miss Painter, looking fresh out of college, took over a month ago for Mrs. Maven—the sweetest, most talented teacher who always encouraged creativity and helped everyone find their unique artistic voice. If you scrubbed her expertly applied makeup off her face, I bet Miss Painter could pass for a junior high student. She asserts her knowledge and expertise in a class that practically runs itself by constantly commenting on everyone's work. Her MO is to deliver a compliment followed by constructive criticism peppered with artistic element suggestions. It's all she can contribute. We have nothing new to learn or do. The only assignment left is to finish our end-of-year project, which we began well before Mrs. Maven moved out of state to care for her mom when her father passed away. Miss Painter is no Mrs. Maven despite her artsy surname.

My art journal is private. I don't like sharing the images with anyone. I cap my pen and move to close the book, but Miss Painter's tiny hand darts hummingbird fast, pinning the journal in place.

"Hang on." She leans in close enough I can see the small empty holes where piercings would adorn her nose, the center of her cheeks, and the edge of one eyebrow. "Is this you?"

Nodding, I attempt to slide the book out from under her splayed fingers, but she presses down harder in response. The journal doesn't budge.

"And your brother, I'm guessing?"

"Yes." My voice is soft, but my grip is firm around her wrist when I remove her hand from the page. Her eyes flit to mine. "Still wet," I murmur.

"Get out! He looks the same age as my brother. Are you guys close?"

The temperature in the room kicks up ten degrees. I finger the collar of my shirt. "My brother is dead." The words scrape past my tightening jaw, sharper than intended.

Miss Painter *laughs*. A high-pitched, breathy giggle that sets me on edge. Who the hell laughs when told something sad or difficult? I don't know what's worse: her disbelief, or the suffocating sympathy that will follow when she realizes it's the truth.

Glaring, I slam the journal closed. "He's been gone a year."

Miss Painter stumbles back a step and grasps a black stone hanging from a silver chain around her neck. She squeezes it hard, blinking rapidly as though by doing so I will vanish before her eyes. Her pinstripe jacket slides back from her wrist, revealing a small heart-leaf shamrock tattoo. The raspberry-colored ink gets lost within the red flush creeping over every inch of her skin.

"I—" she stammers. "Sorry. I didn't know."

"It's fine," I tell her with a stiff shrug. Everything is far from fine as I stuff the journal back inside my pack.

When the bell rings, relief washes over her face. She pats my shoulder and hurries to her desk. I sense her eyes on me from across the room, prickling between my shoulder blades. I should grab my art project. Instead, I wait until the rest of the class has theirs before retrieving my classwork and supplies from the storage bins lining the back wall. I weave through tables, avoiding Miss Painter's desk. Art class is not my safe haven anymore. At least I don't have geometry on today's block schedule. Even though my schedule switches around a lot, every day still feels the same: like garbage.

English is a sit-in-the-back kind of class. Mr. Nelson usually engages with the students in the first two rows only, as though nearsighted. Keeping my head down when I enter and moving to the far left corner lets anyone who might care know I'm all talked out for the day. I wish I could either sleep all period or draw, but that would definitely nab the teacher's attention, so I settle for staring out the window and daydreaming instead while the class debates the importance of the title and symbols in *Wuthering Heights*.

When the bell finally rings, I need a bathroom break for both my bladder and my sanity. Five precious minutes alone to breathe in silence before I face down the rest of this dreadful day. I wait until the class files out of the room, then pull out my journal and markers to head out the door.

Last year, I would walk the halls with my brother and his friends. Davis always strode with his head held high, smiling, and waving at everyone. AD, I walk alone. I've mastered doodle-navigating my way through the halls, knowing how to focus on lightly coloring while watching my feet in the periphery of my vision. I have the hallways perfectly memorized. I know where all the permanent scuff marks are. Where chunks of linoleum are missing, mini potholes in my route. And most important, how many tiles it takes to get to the exit from any given point in the hall.

Never looking up means no eye contact and no conversation. I focus only on my drawing and the shuffling of knees and feet as they walk on by. Zero interaction, zero peopling. It's perfect. An art. Ha.

I round the corner, shuffle around the small line of bodies at the water fountain, push open the bathroom door with my foot and—

"Oh my God! That scent is on *fire!*"

Great. It's Maddison Wells—*Maddi, spelled M, A, double-Ds,* hair toss, giggle, *and an I*—along with Ashley and Isabella. They're high school royalty. The ones who call the shots. The ones everyone watches.

We used to hang out all the time as kids. Maddi and Ashley, inseparable since kindergarten, used to invite me to every birthday and slumber party throughout elementary school. But in junior high, they both made cheer squad. Things were different. Maddi said everything had changed. I wasn't cool, pretty, or talented enough to hang out with them anymore. At least that's what she'd told me.

Maddison also dated Davis for about a month. He dumped her about six weeks before prom last year. He said she wasn't his type even though she's everyone's type. Davis was the only guy brave enough to say no to her, which of course shifted her bitch-o-meter into overdrive. She's hated me ever since, as though I am to blame for Davis coming to his senses. And Ashley just blindly follows everything Maddi does.

Isabella moved here from Spain in the middle of seventh grade. We used to eat lunch together daily. She'd wave me down, save me a seat, and share her mother's homemade pan tumaca, a rich, crusty tomato bread I fell in love with and came to crave. She'd always ask about my day and tell funny stories of her life in Madrid to make me laugh. We were becoming good friends.

Until the day Maddi cornered us in the lunchroom.

"Ash and I eat lunch over there. You should join us." She made a big production of gesturing to the popular table, where everyone had eyes on Isabella. Then Maddi turned her back on me.

Isabella stood and encouraged me to follow, but Maddi laughed over her shoulder.

"Oh, sorry. We only have room for one."

I expected Isabella to decline Maddi at that point and sit back down, ask me what was with this bitch. But she shrugged and followed Maddi instead.

Everyone always bows down to Queen Maddi.

Too nauseated and humiliated to eat after that, I slunk to the nurse's office and told them I'd vomited in the cafeteria so they'd call my parents. I spent the rest of the day crying in bed until Davis got home. He snuck me a bowl of ice cream and told me to let Isabella go. He said only true friends stick around.

Dammit, Davis. Why couldn't you?

"Oh my God, you're so gonna get lucky tonight! Wear nothing but that perfume and some killer heels. When Stevie comes over for a little Netflix and chill, he'll drag you straight to bed for the good part." Isabella squeals as Ashley thrusts her hips, grinding against Isabella's leg.

Maddison, lips pouting and mascaraed false lashes fanning, poses in front of the mirror while drenching all of herself in perfume. Isabella and Ashley record this momentous occasion by posting selfies online. No one wants to see the high school bathroom all over their feed. Bet they lie about it. Edit the pics to appear they're lounging poolside versus toiletside. They're all so phony, and no one sees it. This year, Maddi's hair is auburn. Everyone forgets she's a towhead with brows so pale she pencils them in. She's as fake as that intense stench she's spraying all over the friggin' bathroom. I'd leave if I didn't have to pee so badly.

Maddison whirls, her trigger finger steadily pumping the bottle of stink bomb and releases a cloud of putrid mist my way.

My nose twitches, and the first sneeze escapes—no control, massive force, with potential for projectile snot on the next. I stop counting after the third.

Squeals of *ew, gross,* and *nasty* erupt, followed by mean laughter.

"Thought I smelled you coming, Pru-*dung*," Maddi taunts before squirting me a second time.

I grope for the wall. That cotton-candy-baby-powder-apple-flower funk will cling to me all day. Hauling ass out of here is my priority, but I dropped my marker lid while sneezing my head off. I don't want my new favorite pen to dry out, so I've got to find a way to retrieve it without actually entering the room any further. I slide my leg closer. If I could only . . .

"Whatcha starin' at, creeper?" Maddison looks from me to the lid and back again. She narrows her eyes and sneers.

My breath held, I attempt nonchalance and fail.

"This stupid thing?" she asks, eyes locked on mine.

Triumph gleams in her gaze as she stalks to where the cap sits and slams her foot down on the plastic. Somehow, she applies enough pressure that the lid flies into the air, hits the wall, and *plunks* into the goop-filled sink plugged with water, soapy foam, and God knows what else.

"Whoopsie."

A different bathroom it is, then. I can hear their laughter well after the door closes behind me.

"Pru! Hey, Pru!" Wearing his signature elf ears and green cape that stinks of wet Cheetos, and blocking the only other bathroom on this floor, Bruce Baumgarten grins and flails his arms in a wild wave. "It's me, Bru-meister!"

Unlike the Maddi-types of the school, Bruce keeps it real. He's totally unafraid to be himself, which is hella cool. But his reference to my old nickname for him still makes me cringe. We were becoming close, but when Davis died, I lost all my relationships that mattered. And now, I don't know how to be anyone's friend anymore.

After my shitty morning, I can't deal with this right now.

I pivot and slam into the hard wall of someone's chest.

Stuff flies everywhere—my tin, my journal, someone else's books and papers. Hands and elbows thrash all over the place as the two of us rush to gather stuff.

"Hey, you missed a few pens. Here you go." A large hand drops them into mine, their warm fingertips grazing my outstretched palm. I look up into the most incredible eyes I have ever seen in my entire life. Familiar eyes. Peacock green merged with electric blue, deep and dark and ringed in graphite with sparkles of gold lining each pupil. I know these eyes shift and change. I know these eyes are sometimes blue, sometimes green, sometimes this amazing blend of both, sparkling like some exotic gemstone as they are now. I know because I filled most of my first art journal failing to capture their intensity.

My heart plummets straight into my gut.

Steve-freaking-Nolan. Davis's best friend since forever. My unofficial second brother, elementary school crush, and the sole reason my entire family's lives are ruined.

The only good luck I've had AD is no more Steve everywhere I look. We don't have shared classes, and I no longer hang out at football practice or go to any games. He hasn't been to the house *once* since Davis died. Not even to apologize to his so-called second parents. All that bullshit over the years about *family* and *acceptance*, about how much he *loved* us, about how much we *changed his entire life*. Hell, the assaholic didn't even bother showing up to the funeral. Until now, I've been able to avoid close contact with him all year.

I snatch the markers, pulling my hand to my chest. His chameleon eyes shift from blue to green, an ocean tide of his moods. My treacherous heart skips a beat while he stares.

I can't do this. I gotta get out of here.

After fumbling with the zipper, I somehow manage to get my journal and markers shoved inside my backpack without dropping them. Blood rushes to my head as I stand, and I fling my pack in too wide an arc. Instead of landing square on my shoulder, it thuds off someone I never saw approaching.

A high-pitched yelp echoes. "Ow! Watch it!" Then the person gasps.

Steve's eyes widen as he stands. "Are you all right?" He holds out his hand to my backpack's victim.

Maddison teeters on her spindly heels, falling against Steve. "She broke my lolly, Stevie!" She pops her pink sucker back in her mouth and flicks the end of the dangling, near-severed stick, her chin red and puffy where the pack smacked her face. Bullseye.

"I'll get you another one, babe."

She presses her body tighter to his, nestling her head beneath his chin, and sticks her sugar-pink tongue out at me.

"She hit me on purpose," Maddi whines. Birds could nest on that pouting lower lip. Steve brushes his fingers gently across her cheek, and she relaxes against him with a soft sigh.

So, Steve Nolan and the "Stevie" Ashley was going on about in the bathroom are one in the same. I had no clue Steve and Maddison liked each other, let alone started dating. I'm surprised. Steve knows our craptastic history—knows every cruel thing Maddison has ever said or done to me. It shouldn't matter, I shouldn't care, but seeing them together? The way he holds and comforts her? A burning scream rises from my chest to my throat, a scream that would remind him exactly who she is. But I swallow it, fingering the jellybean bag in my pocket instead.

Honestly, he's way worse than Maddi. They totally deserve each other.

"What's that thing?" Maddison points her foot toward me.

I glance where the toe of her shoe indicates: the Hamsa I drew on my palm during geometry class on Monday. Hamsa hands are all about protection, and I designed the eye to look like Davis's, daydreaming he could see me as I doodled. Watch over me. Keep me safe, same as always.

I clench my fist shut. Maybe Davis shouldn't be watching *right* now.

"Seriously, Stevie," Maddi says, "she's weird."

"Eh, Pru doesn't care how she comes across," Steve says, as though he knows me anymore. As though he's got the right to comment about me.

She stands straight, crossing her arms over her chest and smirking around that stupid *lolly*. "Too bad Davis got all the impressive genes."

Every muscle tightens. How dare she mention his name. My eyes burn.

Oh God. Don't cry. Please. Not now.

I try to shove my way past them—the bathroom is right *there*—but that jackass Steve mirrors my steps, bumping against me and cutting off my escape.

"What the hell!" My scream is louder than intended.

People gather and whisper.

There's an exit behind me, just past Bruce, who has apparently watched this whole exchange. Lovely.

I bolt. Steve grabs my arm hard.

And I fall on my ass.

The crowd's hushed whispers are not so hushed anymore.

Can I die now?

"Oh my God, I'm so sorry, Pru-Pru."

Before I can get my feet planted, Steve's dragging me upright. His hands are a blistering fire against my skin. I need to get as far away from him as possible. But the more I fight his grasp, the more my tread-worn Chucks slide against the slick floor, so instead of escaping, I'm uselessly hanging with my elbows bent awkwardly around my ears, flopping around like a fisherman's catch for everyone to see.

My feet find the floor, and *finally* Steve lets me go.

"Don't touch me!" I slam my palms against his chest, shaking as I shove him away. "And don't call me Pru-Pru! You are not my brother. You… you are nothing. *Nothing!*" I'm pissed as hell and want him to hurt the way he's hurt me, but that's the best I can come up with? Seriously? And to top it off, I can't stop bawling. Nothing screams *"No, truly, I really fucking hate you!"* like tears.

It's not fair. This sorry excuse of a human is still alive, walking around all smug as if nothing happened and life is perfect, and my brother isn't.

We are *done* here.

I hit the doors running.

It's several minutes before the cold air registers, and I realize I ran farther than probably necessary. I'm also on the verge of peeing my pants. Mini-mart toilet it is.

The guy behind the counter has thick, curly, sheepdog bangs covering his eyes. With his head propped on his hands and dimpled elbows lodged upon the greasy counter, he appears to be sleeping standing up.

I bounce and duck low, peeking to see if I can find eyes somewhere behind his wild fringe. "Bathroom key, please?"

He doesn't move for the longest time. Then, finally, he rises, pointing over his shoulder toward a sign on the wall. "Gotta buy something first." Sheepdog shakes his head, curls bouncing.

I pull three quarters, empty candy wrappers, an eraser, and lint out of one pocket and the jellybean bag from the other. I know I've got thirty bucks in my jacket pocket, which is...

At home. Hanging in the closet.

This is so not my day.

I slap the quarters on the counter. "Whatever this gets me, I'll take it."

Sheepdog flips his bangs again and motions toward the door. "We have a gumball machine, but I don't think that counts as—"

"Dude! There's about to be a cleanup needed in aisle seven if you don't bend this rule that isn't even yours."

He blankly stares and gnaws at his lip. "We don't have seven aisles."

"That's not the—" I'm wondering if I can somehow cop a squat behind the magazine rack when he *finally* extracts the key from under the counter.

"Around back," he says.

I don't thank him, I just run.

It takes three shoves to get the door open, and...

I want my quarters back. It's a landmine of nasty—trash, diapers, puddles of unknown substances neither yellow nor brown but green, and flies everywhere.

With the grace of a rhino, I get to the stall without touching anything but my zipper. Barely. There's no TP, so I hover, thighs burning. I don't dare sit. Unbelievably, I wish I had Maddison's perfume to spray up my nostrils instead of smelling this.

The sink is almost as disgusting as the floor, so I don't even wash my hands. I can't get out of here fast enough. I ninja step to the door, and... the knob won't turn. It's like it's locked from the outside. Pounding and screaming won't do any good. The sheepdog attendant won't come when he's called.

"Fuck you, Steve Nolan!" I wouldn't be in this stink hole in the first place if he'd kept his grabby hands to himself.

My knees buckle, and I want nothing more than to collapse in a heap on the floor and never get up but settle for kicking over the trashcan instead.

It doesn't help.

My jaw throbs; I'm clenching it too tight. My traitorous eyes still sting. I used to think Steve had it rough, but that was before he annihilated my family, my life. His mom was sick for a long time. She died when he was little. His dad couldn't handle living in the city without her, so they moved here to Dinksburgh. He was in my homeroom but had advanced math with Davis. Even though they were a year apart, they became best friends the second they met.

Davis started bringing him home after school. When my parents found out Steve was spending most of his time at home alone because his dad worked so much, they made his visits mandatory—even during tax season, that craptastic time when Mom and Dad dealt with the mess of their clients' financials nearly 24/7. Other friends were forbidden when Davis got himself grounded or brought home subpar grades, but Steve was expected. He practically lived with us.

Now, the thought of him makes me sick.

The door rattles, and I jump.

"Hey! You sure have been in there a long time."

"I can't get the door open."

"Use the key. It locks both ways."

Of course it freaking does.

The door swings wide, and I throw the key in Sheepdog's general direction as I head for the curb. I don't even go back for the gumballs. Thunder rumbles and the first drops of rain tickle my face, but I stay out from under the cover of the nearby trees, breathing in the clean air.

I hear the school bell in the distance and know I should probably go back. But the light drizzle turns into a downpour, rendering me a human sponge. If I show up drenched now, everyone will know I ditched. Luckily, we have an open campus, which means lunchtime comes with options, and my feet already know where I'm heading. So does my stomach.

Giallanza's is the best Italian restaurant in town. That's fact, not bias 'cause I know them personally. They used to watch Davis and me, especially during tax season, and now I babysit for them. It's about a ten-minute walk from our house and from the school, which is likely how I'm still alive. I can't live without their pizza.

Hopefully, my favorite L-shaped booth in the corner is open. I can see everything inside and out from there. If anyone I recognize approaches, I can slip past the counter, through the kitchen, and out the back. I do it all the time. Sometimes, I even eat in the back while Anne-Marie cooks and John mans the front. It's a family business, and I'm practically family.

It's only turning eleven o'clock, but inside it's already packed. The noise drowns out the thunderclaps. The line is long, and I can't see if Anne-Marie or any staff I know are in the kitchen from this angle. I can see my quick-escape seat is taken, however. A smiling mother bounces her gurgling baby, laughing as the infant parrots back her singsong baby talk. The table's covered in toys and pizza—three different types—all ignored. Her other kids have made Giallanza's their personal playground. The boys stand in their seats, sword fighting with plastic knives while her daughter races around the room and stops periodically to spin and spin and spin. It's overwhelming. Still, she gives her family more attention than my own folks have given me all year as she referees the boys' antics and feeds the baby a hunk of cheese.

They aren't budging anytime soon.

"Gemma! Gemma, sit down!"

The mom gets the toddler version of the middle finger—a raspberry blown with enough spit to shine the floor. Respect, Gemma.

I'd love to give my mom the finger myself. I only dared so once when I was thirteen. Davis had to smuggle me desserts for an entire month. That was actually when Steve bought me my first art journal to pass the time.

I grind my teeth in frustration, the memory tainted.

Gemma slaloms between customers until she slams into me, almost toppling us both.

"Woah there!" I turn the *whoa* into a warbling horse whinny. The Giallanza kids love it when I do that. It's magic for Gemma, too; she stops and stares.

"Hi," I whisper, and wink.

She looks me up and down, grabs my hand, and traces sticky fingers all over my Hamsa. "Ooh, ooh, ooh…"

"Gemma, leave the girl alone."

Gemma glances over her shoulder, giggles, then turns back and motions for me to lean close.

I present my ear for her secret.

She rewards me with a froggy, "I like you!"

"*Now*, Gemma!" Mean, serious-mom voice makes us both jump.

Gemma releases me, reaches into her pocket, and hands me a half-eaten chocolate chip cookie. "It's the last one," she whispers before skipping back to her family.

"Hey, Pru! What'll it be?" John Giallanza's cocked eyebrow says he knows I should be in class, but his crooked grin says he'll keep my secret.

I love the Giallanzas. Entire conversations without saying a word, plus pizza.

Except I left my money at home. Aw, hell.

Anne-Marie races from the kitchen in a flurry of flour. "Hiya, Pru! So glad you're here. I've been looking for a free moment to call you. Any chance you're able to watch the kids tonight? I know it's very last minute, but it won't be a late night. Ten at the latest."

"You know I'm there. What time?"

She moves toward the far end of the counter as she continues talking. "Oh, let's say six?"

"Sounds great."

Anne-Marie beams. "Lunch is on me today. Whatcha having? The sausage Alfredo is especially good today if I say so myself." She spins, grabs a cup, and fills it with my favorite: cherry cola.

She sets it in front of me and really looks at me now. I don't know what she sees, but those little worry lines of hers crease her forehead as she pats my hand.

"You know you're not alone, right?" She doesn't press, but her frown doesn't fully fade either. "If you ever need to talk…"

"Yeah. Thanks. I know." I barely get the words out past the lump in my throat.

She squeezes my hand. "Good." The pause between us feels too heavy, my smile too forced, but thankfully she changes the subject back to the safety of food. "So? Alfredo? Yes? No?"

"A calzone would be lifesaving."

"Pfft! You're the lifesaver, Pru," she says, squeezing my hand again. I'm hyperaware of her touch, and my palm sweats. Her attention is too much. "Lemme grab that for you." She races off, returning some minutes later with a steaming golden loaf of gooey perfection. "Can't thank you enough. See you tonight!"

Before I can thank her in turn for the free lunch, she's back in the kitchen. At the counter, the line has already doubled, and my booth is *still* occupied. Definitely not sticking around.

I wave at Gemma as I'm leaving, and she glances at my hand. I realize I am still holding her cookie, her gift, her last one, now soft and melty in my palm. I don't want it, but she looks way hopeful, so I shove it in my mouth anyway. Her smile is worth it.

Until booth-stealing-mom smacks the table, grabbing Gemma's attention.

S'OK. It gets me out the door fast.

The cookie lodges in my throat, all the expected sweetness turning bitter with the reminder of one of my earliest memories of me, Davis, and the last cookie.

The sky was cloudy, the same as today. Not a bit of blue anywhere. But the sun shone casting everything aglow in an eerie fog. Mom and Dad were outside, barefoot and dancing in the wet green grass, and the whole house smelled of chocolate.

Mom told us we couldn't eat any of the cookies we'd helped bake till after dinner, but as Davis stood watch at the sliding glass door, I snuck into the kitchen for one.

The chair wobbled as I stretched for the yellow ceramic bird that held *my* cookies in *its* tummy. I remember the second I started falling, that gasping sensation when you feel nothing but air beneath your feet.

And then there Davis was, stopping gravity.

He was a silent sentinel as I pulled the jar into my lap and shoveled cookies in my face. He never asked me to share. He never yelled back when one fell to the floor and I screeched at him for daring to touch it.

And when Mom caught us red-handed, he told her it was all his idea.

When Dad lectured him about what it meant to be a big brother—that he needed to protect me instead of enlist me in his dirty work—Davis stood there nodding gently, his hands behind his back, his round face so calm and serious.

He never corrected Dad.

Later, Davis met me in the hallway. Cradled in his outstretched palm was the cookie he had scrounged from the floor. A few chunks were missing, and the chocolate chips bore indentations from him clutching its softness too tightly. "It's the last one, Pru-Pru, I saved it for you." He was teary-eyed and smiling all at the same time. Wiggling with excitement, so proud he'd kept it hidden, elated to gift me his prize in this stolen moment.

And what did I do? I grabbed it and ate it, never thinking to share.

"Was it good?" His voice was so soft, his expression so expectant, his smile so sweet.

The cookie felt dry in my throat and stuck. He would never know how great they were for forever, because Mom had said he would have no cookies.

He held my hand as we walked down the stairs and whispered, "It's OK. Please, don't cry. Sweets are supposed to make you sweet, not sad."

At the table, Mom and Dad grilled us. Did we learn from our mistake? Did we promise to be better? Could they trust us to behave next time?

Yes, yes, and yes, Davis responded for both of us, promising to be a better big brother as he held my hand under the table. Every squeeze was a little heart hug as our palms, tacky with sugary sweat, stuck together beneath the plastic tablecloth.

In that second, even as young as I was then, I knew unconditional love.

It was Davis.

The rain pelts my face, and I shake off the memory. I had no plans of going home early, but I find I'm standing in the alley behind my house, facing the detached garage. I haven't been in it all year.

Neither has anyone else apparently. The garage smells like wet socks, but I flick back a gritty tarp, and right in front of me is the very last of Davis—his 1971 Monte Carlo.

BD, Sleazle Steve helped Davis with maintenance. He'd worked in his dad's auto shop since he had been old enough to hold a wrench and taught Davis everything he knew. AD, the Gherkin lies prisoner here after it died before prom. The engine, transmission... something. Untouched all this time, she's still shiny. Her hood feels ice cold. Lifeless. I can't stand touching her in one spot for too long.

As I tug the huge canvas to a corner of the garage, I remember when Davis turned sixteen and got his license. It was the same day I passed my permit test. Nana and Papa Lewis had gotten a new car and gifted us the Gherkin. It was a boat—huge and hard to drive with no power steering. Davis loved driving her. I, however, did not, so the pickle-mobile became his. And he knew how to let her make summers fun. We spent endless hours scrubbing her till she squeaked, squirting each other with hoses turned on full blast, soap bubbles in our hair. We'd never gotten every scratch—most inflicted by me—buffed out, but she's perfect even with her battle scars—and in many ways because of them. The scratches on the passenger side rear door are from a shopping cart parking lot race gone wild. The dented back bumper? Gherkin, one; Spellmeyer mailbox, zero. The little doodle I created of the real "Love Shack"—a log cabin deep in the woods—lives inside the trunk with *15 Miles* calligraphed beneath it. The artwork is surrounded by old peeling patches of black-and-white houndstooth matting and preserved forever under a shit ton of clear coat.

And the inside...

Oh my God, she smells like Davis. He only wore cologne on special occasions—celebrating a football win, our shared birthday dinner, pre-holiday ice skating, the rare date—but it is a scent so specifically him—clear morning air *just* warmed by the sun and peppermint pie. Then something else. Not quite the forest. Not quite the beach. But completely outdoorsy and totally Davis.

The bottle is exactly where he always kept it: in the glove box wedged between the maintenance and owner's manuals alongside two baseball caps tucked together, a mini-Nerf football, and a key ring I don't recognize. Metal letters—a D and an S—in cursive script dangle from a heavy black iron keyring. D for Davis, S for Spellmeyer, I assume. They look brand new.

A shuddering inhale turns into a hard yawn. I'm also so freakin' tired. I just wanna sleep forever. Pretend this day never happened. And sleeping here, surrounded by Davis, sounds perfect. I stuff everything back into the glove compartment and climb over the front seat.

My shoe catches on the headrest, and I miss the back bench completely, face-planting into what should be the floor mat. Instead of stiff plastic, I feel soft, nubby wool.

Finding the back seat, I pull the soft, crumpled mass into the dim light of my phone. It's Davis's letterman jacket. I'd forgotten all about it. I thought for sure Dad got rid of it along with the rest of Davis's stuff. Seeing it again… it's horrible. And wonderful. It's like being wrapped in a Davis bear hug, worn soft and smelling exactly like him.

It's also a better blanket than my backpack is a pillow.

2

And She Was ~ Talking Heads

Snow was falling. Gold and silver flakes cascaded around her, tinkling like bells. A bird glided overhead, shadowy wings spreading over the asphalt below where Pru stood barefoot in the middle of the street. Row after row of city brownstones lined the sidewalks as far as she could see. Pru squinted, peering through the metallic flakes that reflected shimmery light brighter than the sun.

The air hummed and vibrated as the glittery motes clung to her skin. Catching one on the tip of her finger, Pru gasped as an electric zing shot up her arm. The snowflake didn't melt. Instead, it rolled down her finger, settled into the center of her palm, and rotated in lazy circles as it swelled from pea-sized to marble.

Within the translucent sphere spun a miniature universe. Ragged mountains rose from indigo lakes, shifting and sinking and rising again. Jagged stone metamorphosed into leaf-budding trees, into thick forests that burst into showers of leaves before sinking into earth, re-emerging as azure waters, hardening back into mountains, repeating the entire process again and again. Pru tried pinching the mote between her fingers, tried picking it up and cradling it close, but it rose off her palm, pinwheeling into the sky where it joined others in a thick oscillating whorl. They swirled in thick waves, encircled her waist, pressed upon her back, urged her forward.

Pru moved down the street, and the glimmering snow motes guided her steps, stopping before a purple-doored townhome with a cracked, uneven stoop atop two cracked, uneven steps. All the other buildings stood empty, dark, and still, but this one was alive and breathing. The front door undulated while "Lovesong" by The Cure poured from windows with billowing lace curtains. Inside, a flailing fish-out-of-water silhouette floundered gloriously offbeat to the thumping bass.

The door and dancer moved as one, a beckoning siren song that eclipsed everything else. Pru felt a tug low in the pit of her stomach, heard words slip toward her on a peppermint-scented wind.

Come home.

Pru cut through the yard. Glittering eddies escorted her up the porch. Breathless with wonder, she trembled before the dancing door and turned the knob.

The world exploded in blinding light as she toppled through space.

"I've been calling and calling, and you're finally home!"

The disembodied voice was everywhere at once. It echoed off the walls. It reverberated inside her head. It took root in her stomach and sped through her veins. Hands—warm, strong, sure—slipped beneath her armpits, righting her with ease. The scent of woods and mint and morning dew filled her nostrils as she melted into the tightest of hugs. That familiar, ethereal voice chirruped near her ear this time. "God, how I've missed you, Pru. I've missed you so much."

Pru, chest tight with anxiety, clasped a hand to her numb and tingling lips, still zinging from her zap through the door. She barely dared to hope.

"Davis?" she whispered. Her voice sounded hollow, tinny, and distant in her own ears.

"Who else?" the rumbling voice laughed.

Pru turned and squinted, trying to better make out the lanky form within the glittery haze. She never saw him move, but he was farther away than a moment ago.

The figure clapped. Two sharp staccato slaps that echoed far louder than they should have. The glitter motes vanished, and there stood her brother as though he'd never left. Teary-eyed, solid.

Real.

Pru gasped and stuttered as Davis materialized beside her again without taking a step.

"Can you believe it, Pru? Look—our very own apartment!"

She grabbed his hand, afraid he'd vanish, and gave it a soft squeeze. When he didn't disintegrate, she tested his permanency with a harder pinch. A zing raced up her spine, and her stomach fluttered. The sensation of his very real, very warm skin against hers was sheer joy. Grinning, she pinched him again.

"Ow! It's not the *Love is Blind* ranch, but no shack-shaming." He pinched her back, laughing when she squealed.

"I just can't believe—is this—are you—"

"Yes, yes, and yes. Ready for the tour?" He cleared his throat and lowered his voice dramatically. "Here we stand in the *bodacious* grand foyer." Davis nudged Pru with his shoulder. Pru's heartbeat escalated. How had she forgotten their old teasing little shoves? Feeling the warming comfort of his touch—that specific point of contact where his shoulder bounced off hers—brought it all roaring back.

He was really here. Or she was really *somewhere* with him.

Pru squinted. The air around the front door shimmered, a heat mirage blurring and obstructing the exit. "What's with all the dust?"

Davis's eye twitched. "Construction dreck. I'm working on it." He pivoted Pru to the left. "Here lies the grand view." He smiled as he pointed toward the same window she had watched him dancing in front of from the street. "Behind us, there's two bedrooms. I tried for three but couldn't manage it."

It would have been perfect. Three bedrooms: her, Davis, and Mom and Dad.

"*But* the living room is large enough for a foldout sofa. We have plenty of room to work with. I'm just excited we finally have our own place, like we always planned."

He tugged her ponytail to twist her head to the right. "Chef-style kitchen and eatery. And, of course, we stand at this moment in the formal sitting room." A final twirl brought them full circle, and with a flourishing bow, he nodded toward a yellowed wall. "I haven't decorated yet, but with your help, everything will be perfect."

Half the wall was covered in pixilated photographs. Three large iron scrollwork letters with Davis's initials, DPS for Davis Patrick Spellmeyer, hung above them. Mesmerized, Pru stared as the letters glowed and the photo images shifted within the frames, a kaleidoscope—coming together, breaking apart, never fully forming, always totally blurred. She couldn't see a single thing clearly.

"You gotta stay for dinner." Davis tugged Pru's hand, dragging her from the wall to the kitchen. "It's your favorite— dessert for dinner and dinner for dessert."

He pulled her hand to his chest, giving it a squeeze, his eyes watery as he studied her. "You're here. You're really here." His dimple deepened as he smiled, then he released her hand to clap.

The kitchen smelled like a bakery. Steam billowed from the cracked-open oven door. The counters overflowed with piles of treats. Each time he clapped, a new plateful appeared.

"Eat up. This is all for you. A thank you for coming… and a bribe to stay." He winked, nudging her ribs with his elbow. "Go on. Sweets make you sweet."

Pru scooped a double chocolate cupcake from a bronze plate. Thick, fudgy icing coated her fingers as she drew the moist treat to her lips, closed her eyes, and bit.

Her eyes popped open. "Woah. That's not chocolate!" She choked down what tasted like a stale powdered doughnut and set the remainder on the counter.

"I'm still getting the hang of this. Here, try a brownie." Smiling, he handed her a peanut-butter swirled chocolate hunk still warm from a pan.

It smelled like a brownie. It looked like a brownie. Pru licked it before biting down and the confection crumbled, revealing a pink, jawbreaker lollypop with a nearly severed stick.

Pru dragged the sucker down her tongue. It fizzed like soda and tasted of cherry ice cream. She laughed. "I think your oven is busted."

"There's nothing wrong with the apartment," Davis grumped, and the overhead lights flickered.

Dropping the candy on the counter with a clink, Pru grabbed a cookie. This time, the expected chocolate chips and macadamia nuts filled her mouth. "Mmmm. Much better," she mumbled, wiping crumbs from her chin. "I could eat these all day."

Davis pumped his fist into the air. "Belly up to the bar and grab a seat. Ding, ding, ding—"

"—We have a winner!" they crowed in unison.

Pru's heart swelled. Davis was with her. They were together, in sync and connected. They swung their bent arms up and down, stiff and robotic. "Oh. Oh, my goodness. Oh!" they parroted, moving and talking like C-3PO.

Bursting into fits of giggles, Davis and Pru high-fived one another. Their palms connected.

CLAP!

A barstool materialized beneath Pru, sliding against the backs of her thighs, toppling her backward against the wooden ladderback. With an engine's rumble, the barstool skyrocketed into the air. Pru pressed herself tight against the splintering wood, feeling its bite, sharp and thorny, in her skin.

"Don't worry, I've gotcha, Pru-Pru!"

And he clapped. Same as he had done a million times on the football field. Breaking the huddle. Leading the team. Taking control. Two sharp staccato slaps and a *"Let's go."*

Pru closed her eyes. Breathed in the memory. His confidence was a comfort as she soared through the ceiling, beyond the Hamsa hand swirling in the sky, deep inside a void of inky static that crackled and buzzed.

Below her, Davis's voice sounded a million miles away: *"Hold on!"*

The chair vibrated and swayed, stretching to impossibly large proportions, taking her impossibly high. It creaked and groaned as it teetered, a too-heavy head on a thin and bony neck. Pru squeezed her eyes shut, yelping as the seat lurched.

"Davis, hurry. Get me down from here."

The more he clapped, the more the chair moved—soaring three feet higher before plummeting two feet down, lurching sideways before spinning like a top. The longer it danced high in the air, the more agitated and vocal Pru became.

"What's wrong? Why isn't this working? I'm scared!" quickly escalated to *"What the hell, Davis? Enough! I can't do this anymore. YOUR APARTMENT IS SO FUCKED UP!"*

She screamed those final words, and the apartment shook, the chair quaked, and Davis convulsed. His jaw twitched, his eyes rapidly blinking. He clenched and unclenched his fists, and a tremor rolled up his spine, bowing and jerking his back in sickening contortions. The night condensed around Pru. Shadows gathered, breathing, creeping closer, obscuring her view of Davis and the apartment beneath. In long, liquid strands the darkness dropped, absorbing into the apartment's foundation as though it were a sponge.

"You don't remember what it's like. You've never lived suffocated by expectations. I just want an average place where I can be my average self. Don't you get it? You always did before. Memories are everything, so why did you forget all the important stuff?"

The chair stilled, and the apartment calmed. Davis took a deep breath and clapped.

From high above, Pru heard a *click* and saw a simultaneous pulse of light, lightning quick like a camera flash. The entire dreamland apartment winked away and then back, the air rippling and wavering. Milky fog swirled around the floor, weaving through Davis's legs. A translucent veil snapped into place over the living room, a flickering, interactive overlay.

From within the fog, holographic figures emerged. Pru squinted to better discern their iridescent forms.

When Pru heard the laughter, her chest tightened. She, Davis, and Steve huddled in a hammock watching the stars. She loved simple moments with her brother the best. Lazy summer days, hot summer nights, the joy of simply existing together.

The apartment clicked and flashed again, followed by a whirring *thbbtz,* like a Polaroid processing film. Davis clutched his hands to his heart, and his empty longing rattled hollow in her own chest.

The hammock vanished. The Spellmeyer den rose to take its place. A holographic Pru, Davis, and Steve danced and sang into hairbrushes, going all Elvis, swinging their hips. Davis reached out to touch the glittery apparitions. They vanished as he did so.

Click. Flash. Thbbtz.

Pru, Davis, and Steve crammed together on the sofa watching cringeworthy 80s movies. Davis reached into the memory and changed the channel on the TV.

Click. Flash. Thbbtz.

Pru, Davis, and Steve waded in the crick, pants rolled above their dimpled, sun-pinked knees. Crawdads nipped their toes. Davis reached inside the memory and splashed the holographic trio.

Click. Flash. Thbbtz.

Faster and faster the memories spun. Pru closed her eyes, but snapshots of Davis's life still flashed through her mind and plucked at her heart.

"See?" Davis yelled. "The apartment is fine. Everything's working out perfectly. I got this."

Davis clapped. The fog cleared. The memory haze lifted. And her chair broke.

Pru's scream was lost in the thundering crack of splintering wood as the ladderback split from the chair's frame, pitching her backward through empty space.

"Trust me, I gotcha Pru-Pru!"

At the sound of his voice, her trajectory slowed. Featherlike, she drifted into Davis's outstretched arms and tried to remember how to breathe. Looking up, she noticed the towering barstool was gone and the roof had reformed. Where the wall met the ceiling, a tarry black seam glued the apartment together. Pru thought she saw it move. Small, blackened insects in a scurrying swarm sank beneath the plaster and flowed toward the hall, vanishing when she blinked. Pru rubbed her eyes, unsure whether she had imagined it.

Davis clapped a hand to her shoulder. "Look," he whispered in her ear, breath smelling faintly of candied peaches and bread. "This is the best part." He pointed to the wall of frames, each one filled and moving. Whispers emanated from the photographs—words and laughter from memories carefully pinned beneath glass.

Pru smiled and reached up to ruffle Davis's hair.

He beamed, ruddy cheeks glowing, dimples popping, eyes dancing. "None of this would matter without you. I am so glad you are finally here." He pulled her to his chest, his heartbeat thudding solid and true beneath her ear. Pru pressed her face into his t-shirt, inhaling deep as he hugged her tight.

"I don't understand what any of this is—how we're together, how this all works—but if it's real? You've gotta work out some of the kinks."

Davis's smile dropped. His jaw twitched. The overhead lights flickered and dimmed. The hair on the back of Pru's neck rose as the temperature plummeted. Shadowy tendrils slunk from the hall, hugging the corner as they slithered toward the photographs with a scratching hiss.

3

Real Wild Child (Wild One) ~ Iggy Pop

I jerk awake in the seat. My head and heart feel about to explode into messy piles of glittering dust. Even though I have hardly dreamed at all this past year, I know I've never had a dream like this. So vivid. So real. So unbelievable.

I scramble to find my journal in my backpack. I need to record everything. The little dimple near Davis's chin when he smiles. His crane-on-crack dance moves. Tiny details I can't believe I forgot.

The pen shakes in my grip, my hand still asleep from propping my head up. I wish I could get the sound of his voice onto paper too. His off-key singing, the husky rasp of his laugh.

My phone chirps, and I almost smudge the whole page.

It's a notification I should have long ago set to never receive. Seeing that Sleazle Steve and Monster Maddison are *"together forever"* per her latest social media update makes me want to puke.

"Get over yourselves," I mutter. Nothing is forever. Everything dies.

I'm closing out the app when I notice it—the bright colors of Steve's t-shirt framed by his jacket. I don't mean to, but I zoom in on the image.

I can't believe he still has his, let alone wears it. Mine is in a crumpled ball in the back of the closet. Davis's got shipped off to the thrift store when Robo-Dad gutted his room. But there it is. Plain as day.

We found the old beige fabric in a steamer trunk at Steve's place. I don't remember what we were looking for when we opened the lid, but I do remember the way Steve's lip quivered as he ran his fingers over the cloth. How he cradled the cotton gently in his hands as though it would dissolve. And how he trusted me—*me*—to transform it all with fabric paint. *"I know you never knew her, but she would have been your second mom."* Just as we were always Steve's second family after she died.

His words from that day rattle around in my head. I scrunch my eyes shut, but I still see him sewing, cutting, reforming the scraps. Still feel his arms wrapped around me in the tightest of hugs, squeezing so hard I thought I would burst. *"I'll always have the two most important girls worn near my heart."*

"Ugh!"

I find and pour the last of my jellybeans into my mouth and toss the empty bag up into the passenger seat. Now, I'm running late for the Giallanza's. Thanks again, Sleazle.

I climb out of the back of the Gherkin, leaving the tarp in a crumpled lump on the garage floor but double-checking the car's doors, making sure everything's locked up tight. As if by doing so, I can keep Davis safe, secure. Alive in those seats.

It's quiet and there's no sign of Robo-Dad's car—working late as usual, no doubt—but I notice the lights on in Zombie Mom's room as I head inside.

I grab my jacket and umbrella. Even though I know they don't care and probably won't read it, I leave a message on the family chalkboard.

BABYSITTING @ GIALLANZAS
HOME 11-ISH
♥ PRU

Then I all but spring outside before I change my mind and wipe it off.

I'm ringing the Giallanzas' doorbell when I realize I forgot to swap my school backpack for my babysitting tote. The kids love that thing, and I added new treasures last week—a Stretch Armstrong, two matchbox cars, a rainbow-maned pony, all uncovered within the precious oldies but goodies section of the thrift store. Plus, it has a card deck of their favorite animals that I drew. They will be so disappointed.

There's a screech and two thuds against the door.

"Lemme open the door. Move it, Tony!"

"You move it, Nikki. *Move!*"

"You're too little to open the door for strangers, Tony!"

"Neither one of you is allowed to open the door without an adult. Now scoot. Both of you." John Giallanza opens the door with an apologetic smile. "Hi, Pru. Not too late to back out…" But he shuts the door behind me. "Anne-Marie would kill me if I let you go though." He chuckles and gestures for my bag. "Come on inside. She's almost ready. Nicolette, Antony: *settle!*"

They do.

Note to self: learn how to speak in booming dad voice. It works.

Or not.

Tony kicks Nikki, who pinches him back.

The race is on. I recognize their bouncing-off-the-walls mania. They are riding a freaking sugar high. Which means getting them into bed early enough so I can finish journaling before Anne-Marie and John return will be nearly impossible.

Mr. G tosses my backpack on the top shelf of the hall closet, out of sight and out of reach. "Behave, both of you, or no special bag fun. Dinner, bath, bed. That'll be it."

I become a human jungle gym as they start pulling on my arms, fingers, shirt, legs. I choose not to mention that the bag he's hidden is not the special tote. I also choose not to listen to the part of my mind insisting Davis never would have forgotten the fun bag.

"Did you hear your dad, guys? I brought something special to do *if* you're both good. We can open it after dinner. OK?" Maybe my markers will be exciting enough to calm them down and keep them happy.

Nikki nods and grabs Tony's hand, dragging him to the toy-covered living room to the tune of his grumbling.

"There you are! So glad you could make it." Anne-Marie expertly air kisses my cheeks without transferring a single smear of gloss to my face. She smells of lilacs and summer. Soft and sweet. It suits her perfectly. "I set out a box of mac and cheese. I know I usually have leftovers on hand, but you're good with light cooking, yes? Some kind of a fruit or a vegetable wouldn't hurt either."

Davis and I learned kitchen basics during our tax-orphan days. Boil water on stove? Check. Follow instructions on side of box? Check. Cut up apple and put out baby carrots? Check and check. I nod and smile.

"Oh! Almost forgot. Do not let them talk you into skipping bath time. In fact, if you could bathe them right after dinner, instead of directly before bed, their hair will have time to dry. We have family portraits tomorrow, and I won't have time to do more than rush them straight to the studio. If you could get all the tangles out of Nikki's hair, that'd be lifesaving."

"That's what I'm here for. The life saving."

"Thanks so much, Pru." She grins and wiggles her fingers, gesturing her babies closer. Mr. G tosses Nikki into the air and catches her while Anne-Marie squats to give Tony some serious Eskimo kisses, his pudgy hands squishing her cheeks as he scrubs his nose against hers.

My throat tightens and I look away.

"Call if you need anything," Mr. G says, opening the door as he peels a squealing Tony off his leg.

"Will do. Thanks."

I lock the door behind them, and the kids race toward the kitchen.

Tony climbs into his seat at the table while Nikki pulls out forks and plates. In seconds, they are banging utensils on the table and singing "Tony Baloney wants macaroni" over and over at the top of their lungs. Fitting, actually, since Tony almost exclusively eats baloney sandwiches or mac 'n' cheese.

"Can I have my apple now?" Nikki asks.

Soon as the plate of fruit touches the table, Tony scrunches his face and gags. Repeatedly. Louder and louder, bait for a reaction from me.

"Tony'll eat 'em with cheese sauce," Nikki announces around an apple wedge. She leans over and gently pats his arm. The gesture is so tender, so Davis-like, I can't breathe.

And then, Tony stops squirming and grabs Nikki's hand with the biggest smile.

My throat is too tight to breathe.

Oh no. Please no. Not now.

"Really?" My voice is far too loud. I'm compensating. I don't care. "I thought apples turned Tony into... *the barf beast!* RAWWWRRR!" I growl and claw the air. Anything to stop the waterworks in front of the kids.

Tony squeals and throws himself into his sister's arms, dragging her to the floor. Nikki shrieks and grabs onto his neck. Tony burrows his head against her skin and blows a loud raspberry.

I stumble to the fridge to grab that magical cheese sauce.

"Cheeeeeeseeee!" Tony buzzes, inchworming his way toward Nikki.

Nikki screeches and rolls away, practically bowling me over but slamming into the wall instead. A book flies off a shelf above, missing Tony's noggin by inches.

"OK, enough. At the table to eat. Cheese Louise!"

Nikki laughs so hard she snorts. Tony kneels in his chair, dipping apples while singing praises to cheddar between each bite. And I bend to pick up the fallen book off the floor. But when I reach to place it back on the shelf, a photo falls out. I scoop it up and stumble into the wall.

The photo is of me, Davis, and Steve. I cover Steve's face with my thumb so it's only my brother and me. We're in aprons in Anne-Marie's kitchen, covered head to toe in flour. Davis's head is flung back, his cheeks red with laughter as I am mid-flick to send more dusty powder in his direction, my fingers coated to the knuckle, the white particles suspended in midair, frozen between us.

There's a crash and a unified "Uh-oh!"

Cheese and glass are everywhere.

And, of course, both kids are barefoot.

Great.

"Hold tight. I'll carry you guys to the living room." I ferry them both to the couch and grab the remote. "Nikki, watch your brother so I can clean up, OK? Then I'll finish making dinner. Don't go back in there till I call you. I don't want you guys to cut your feet." I switch the TV to cartoons. They squeal at the special television treat and hug my neck tight, squishing their faces into me and, in Tony's case, smearing cheese sauce on my shirt. Then Tony curls on his side, thumb in his mouth, and drops his head into Nikki's lap. She pets him like a pup as they lock onto the screen. Their eyes glaze over.

I'm shaking when I return to the kitchen. The photo's still on the floor where I dropped it. But I set the pot of water on the stove and wait for it to boil instead of picking it up, willing the bubbles to flood over the house and carry me away as I drop the pasta in.

This mess will take forever to clean. Glass glitters from every corner of the floor. How cheese splattered on the walls, cupboard doors, and fridge from across the room, I'll never know. But it's the hand-painted swirls hardening on the table that totally take the cake. Cheese. Yay.

The bottle of cleaner beneath the sink is nearly empty. I'm pretty sure Anne-Marie keeps extras in the hall closet. "Nearly there, kiddos," I lie as I swing through the living room.

Except, while the TV's blaring, Nikki and Tony aren't where I left them.

I lower the volume and hear shrieks and laughter coming down the hall at the same time I notice the front closet door is wide open, a chair sitting crooked inside it.

Oh no.

My pack is completely unzipped, lying upended in the middle of the foyer floor. Textbooks are scattered everywhere, as is my journal. I pick it up and set it out of reach. I look for my marker tin to do the same, but it is missing.

"No-no-no-no-no!"

It isn't just a little color. Nope. The rainbow runs down the walls of the entire hallway—Nikki's crimson a good foot above Tony's azure—past their own bedroom, past the bathroom, and into one of the few off-limits areas of the whole house.

The primary bedroom.

Bile backs up into my throat. I nudge the door open.

It's a horror show: my marker tin empty on the floor, lidless pens scattered around the room, the walls and bedspread covered in art.

It also smells as if a field of lilacs sprouted somewhere in the room.

I spot Anne-Marie's perfume bottle, tipped upside down on the floor, the last drops soaking into the carpet.

I was gone five seconds!

"Kids?" My big voice sounds so weak compared to Mr. G's. No way can I fix this shitstorm. Anne-Marie and John are gonna be so pissed.

I hear laughing and splashing. Water running. I'm terrified to open the bathroom door.

Davis would know exactly how to get the kids calm and fix everything, but I've got no clue where to start. I'm on my own, abandoned. A hard lump threatens to close my throat.

Come on, Pru. Suck it up and open the stupid door.

I turn the knob and push.

Every container on the counter has been freed of its contents—shaving cream, toothpaste, mouthwash, another bottle of perfume. A river of muck flows from the sink onto the floor, where it connects with another body of water bubbling out of the toilet, in which they apparently tried to flush the perfume stopper.

"Woah." This is beyond bad. "You guys…"

Water flows dangerously close to the lip of the bathtub, where they crouch naked, soaked, and covered in permanent marker. Tony's scribbles adorn his legs and Nikki's hands and feet. Nikki has branded her name in all caps, in every color I own, across her brother's chest, arms, and neck. Smaller Xs and Os cover his cheeks.

"Pru!" Tony beams, holding out his arms with pride. "Look!"

Nikki knows they're in deep doo. She shuts off the bathtub faucet and stares at the floor.

A piercing whistle make us all jump.

Crying, the kids clamp their hands over their ears while I search for the source of the murderous sound.

Then it hits me…

"Stay *here*. Clean this mess. Now!"

My temples throb in time with the caterwauling of the smoke detector as I run for the kitchen.

Foam from the pasta pot slides over the stovetop and hits the floor with a *plop*. Noodles sizzle as they fry in the open gas flame. There's enough steam to shower in. I turn everything off.

I have to stand on a chair to reach the smoke alarm but manage to get it turned off in time to hear the sniffles behind me.

"I'm hungry," Tony wails, louder than the alarm, of course. I'll be deaf for days.

"Me too," Nikki whimpers. "Is dinner burnt?"

Why would they have stayed put? No, that would have been too easy. Now, a perfume, toothpaste, and shaving cream trail streaks the carpet all the way through the hall.

Everything—my shoulders, my neck, my jaw—instantly tightens. It's my body's AD way of hanging onto something—anything—while the world careens out of control.

"Why can't you listen and be good for once?" My face burns hot, as intense as the growling, biting words. Davis would never lose it like this, but I can't seem to stop. I jump off the chair, landing in front of them, and trigger another chorus of wails.

Tony stumbles backward, then falls.

"Clean up your mess!" I toss the towels I used on the foamy mac-tastrophe, and one hits Nikki in the face with a wet *smack*.

She too screams louder than the fire alarm.

Crap.

I'm managing *way* worse than Gemma's mom from the restaurant. I feel nauseated. I didn't mean to make them cry. "Sorry!" I say. "I'm so—"

The front door slams open, and for the second time, we all jump.

"Is everything OK?" Anne-Marie is flushed and wild-eyed. "Oh, Nikki! Tony!" She drops to her knees, dragging her dress through cheesy, foamy bathroom goop, and hugs them tight, seeming not to care how filthy they are.

Yet.

"I don't see smoke. See? I told you we should have called first." Mr. G laughs, poking at the smart home alert on his phone. Pocketing his cell, he finally looks around. "What in the... What happened?" He resembles a cartoon character. The kind whose eyes pop out of their head, their jaw bouncing up and down on the ground.

Anne-Marie looks at the kids, then looks at me.

I want to vanish, blend into the wall, but no.

She turns back to her kids and asks, "What did you two do?"

"We wanted to be cool, like Pru," Nikki whispers.

"What?"

"Cool like Pru." Tony sniffles, hiccups, then runs to me, grabs my hand, and trails his fingers over my art-doodled palm.

"I see," says Anne-Marie, giving the scene a slow, hard look.

I squirm under her stare more than the kids do. A stellar role model I am. *Way to go, Pru.*

"Tony started it!" Nikki yells, stomping her foot. "He colored me first."

"Didn't!" Tony screams, his fat fingers clamping tight around mine, his dank wet-dog mop of hair flapping back and forth.

Nikki stomps closer, screaming as loud as she can. Tony matches her every *did* with an ear-splitting *did not*.

Mr. G lowers the boom. "*Enough!*"

Everything stops. Everyone stops moving. Stops breathing.

"I don't care *who* started *what*, this ends *now!*"

Three more steps, and I can reach the door, slip out of here…

"I told both of you to stay out of Pru's things."

I freeze as Mr. G's gaze lands on me. Nope. No escape for me.

"Did you steal her markers?" he asks them.

I can tell the kids want to be anywhere else but here, same as me.

"*Answer me!*"

My verbal diarrhea strikes before the kids can say anything. "I'm so, so sorry. A cheese jar broke. I turned on the TV. There were cartoons, but the kitchen was a mess, and I didn't hear them get the chair for the closet, so it's all my fault. I should have been watching, and I wasn't. I'm sorry."

Mr. G's hand hasn't left his forehead since they walked in. I am pretty sure it's the only thing holding in his brain. Then he strides out of the kitchen, following the trail of destruction to his bedroom.

"It gets worse," I mumble.

"Sweet Christ on a—"

"Language!" Anne-Marie says as I follow her down the hall.

From the bedroom doorway, I glance at Mr. G as he emerges from the bathroom. He's pale and looks older than when he left the kitchen. He opens his mouth, closes it, and then opens it again. Instead of saying anything, he shakes his head, moves toward the closet, pulls out a bunch of cleaning supplies, and marches toward the kitchen. Somehow, his silence is louder than any angry outburst.

Anne-Marie doesn't say anything, but I know she's taking in all the damage.

"Anne-Marie, if I can't get the ink off the walls, I've got paint in the attic at home. It probably won't match, but I can… uh… I'll cover the cost of matching paint. Yeah, don't pay me. I'll pay you. I'll come paint your hall this weekend and—"

She laughs. "Don't be silly."

Anne-Marie still hasn't seen the bathroom though. She doesn't realize it's worse. Way worse.

The boulder wedged in the back of my throat grows another inch as I watch her push the door open. She gasps and grabs my hand, squeezing tight as she takes it all in. The soaked carpet, the sticky white footprints, the walls, the toilet river and sink lake.

And the smell.

The room spins faster and faster in her silence.

"OK then!" Her decisive voice startles me. "I'll be paying you double for your suffering tonight and whatever it costs to replace your pens. I am so sorry, Pru."

Uh… what? "But… how… I…" I look around the room again and shake my head. "I absolutely failed to watch them."

She laughs, soft as bells, and tucks my hair behind my ear.

I want to lean into her hand almost as much as I want to run for the door. Instead, I reach for the pen at my feet, using the time it takes to recap it to try to pull myself together. It doesn't quite do the job, but it keeps me from seeing the pity and sadness in her eyes. Keeps her touch a safe distance away.

"Oh, Pru, I'm surprised they haven't done this sooner to be honest. You need to be four people to keep them out of trouble." She sits on the foot of the bed, her shoulders sagging as much as the mattress. "But now the question is, how are we going to keep you when we add the third to the mix?" She rubs her stomach.

I glance at her hands cupping her belly and take in the baggy dress I thought was simply bohemian chic. "You're pregnant?"

"Yeah." The word sounds so sad. She scrunches her toes repeatedly in the shag carpet while staring at the ground.

I pick at my jeans. I wait for her to say more. For a few moments, her eyes are all over the place, flying from her feet to the walls to the bathroom, before landing back on me.

49

I ease into the spot beside her.

"That's the reason for the family portrait tomorrow. I want this moment with all five of us forever. I'm not that far along yet, only fifteen weeks. But… this is when we lost our other daughter. Abrielle Marie."

I didn't know. I don't know what to say. "Did she—what happened?"

"I miscarried. Right before you lost your brother, in fact." Anne-Marie's hand is shaking when she touches my knee. "I'm so sorry I wasn't there for you. I know how much you love Davis."

My body overrides my brain. I grab her hand and drop my head to her shoulder. She doesn't jump at my touch the way I did hers.

"We want to name him Giovanni Davis. With your permission, of course."

I look at her. My throat is tight and my voice cracks when I speak, but she has to know. "It's perfect."

"John and I always loved looking after you two when you were little, and now, here you are watching our brood." Her soft laughter returns as she points at the devastation. "I think you got the short end of the stick on that one."

"Nah, I love them." And I do. Deeply, I realize, which rattles me.

Love means loss.

She grabs my arm. "Let's see the art that inspired my monkeys." Her fingers tickle as she traces the design on my palm. "Lots of detail and color. I see why they love it."

She smiles and I blush.

"Thanks?" I hate that it comes out a question.

She bumps my shoulder with hers. "It's good. I'd love to see more of your art if you're up for it sometime. Maybe on paper?"

"I've been drawing my brother." Heat floods my face. I intended on never telling a soul about that strange Davis dream, but she shared an incredibly raw secret with me. If this isn't the time to tell someone, I don't know what is. "I had a dream so vivid and real I thought he was alive again…"

"I get that. I dream of Abri too. Some nights, I'm so sure I can hear her crying, hungry, needing to be held. In my dreams, she's learning to walk. She would be now if…"

A huge tear rolls down her cheek.

I can't breathe.

I had my whole life with Davis. The Giallanzas were robbed of all their time with Abrielle Marie. It sucks. Life doesn't last for anybody. I slowly release the trapped air in my lungs and focus on counting as I draw the next breath in through my nose, slow and deep. It's a trick Davis taught me to keep from crying. I know if I start, I won't stop. AD, tears are a fuse to the explosive sadness alive within my chest. But I can't keep losing control all the time. Especially not now when Anne-Marie needs me strong and supportive. I couldn't bear it if she noticed that any power or helpfulness I ever possessed vanished alongside Davis.

"You know"—Anne-Marie straightens and wipes her face—"John's nonna had the sight. She told me, none too kindly, that holding on to Abri's memory was only hurting my baby girl. She dragged us to mass every night for a month to light candles. Said it would guide Abri home."

"Mr. G goes to church?"

"A traditional Italian boy? His family would have it no other way. We all went to mass, or Nonna would have put the malocchio on us." She chuckles. "Her views always swayed toward the mystical. I never believed any of it. That is, not until she died and began invading my dreams. We lost her last month, you know."

I nod. Of course I know. Small-town business is every-one's business, no matter how distracted I have been. I should apologize and offer sympathy, like normal folks, but no. My curiosity wins out. "What's Nonna like? In your dreams."

Anne-Marie bursts out laughing. "Pretty much the same as when she was alive: like walking through a field of yellow jackets. She never minces words, has plenty of opinions to go around. But she loves her family above all else."

She giggles more, and I can't stop my smile as I listen to her. She gives me hope. I want Davis to invade all my dreams. Maybe then when I talk about him, I will feel as light and happy as she looks, not heavy and lost.

"She brings Abri to me."

My thoughts spin, outracing my pounding heart. I want this to be true so much, the tight knot that rarely leaves my stomach returns. "Do you think it's real? That you're really see-ing her?" I groan. "That sounds nuts."

She doesn't giggle though. Only shrugs. "Sometimes, it's just a dream, but sometimes, it's definitely more."

I watch Anne-Marie's thumb as she strokes my hand.

"Nonna once said loved ones came to her in dreams and told her the family's future." Anne-Marie smiles. "She threat-ened all six of her boys with being seen by the ancestors. I always thought she used that threat as a way to enforce her mercenary rules, but now I'm not sure. She had this particu-lar way of explaining things. The stories the spirits supposedly shared with her? There's no other way she could know those things unless told by someone watching from above.

"I believe I'm genuinely seeing Nonna Giallanza and my precious Abrielle, so when you tell me you're dreaming of Davis? Maybe it is just a dream, but maybe?" She squeezes my hand. "Maybe it's more." She winks and pulls me into a hug.

AD, I am not a hugger. But as her hands stroke my back, arms wrapping me tight and warm and secure against her, every one of my muscles melts. I'm calm for the first time all night. Maybe even all year.

"Kitchen's clear," Mr. G announces, entering and heading straight for the bathroom, clutching cloths and bottles of cleaner. He groans as he shuts the door behind him.

I ease out of Anne-Marie's grip, still surprised by how good it felt to be held. "Do you have baby oil and cotton balls? I can get most of the tattoos off the kids."

She nods and rises to collect supplies while I round up the children. It takes the entire jumbo pack of cotton balls and all the oil left in the bottle, but only a lingering hint of the darker shades remains by the time we're done.

Neither one budges during the entire process. Their eyes are huge and their chins wobble, especially Nikki's, but there is not a single whimper, whine, or complaint.

I don't blame them either. Since the whole booming-dad-voice-thing, it's the calmest I've seen them. If I hadn't known Mr. G my whole life, he would scare me too. Dark alley, run-the-other-way scary. He's big, tall, and thick, and his furry unibrow gives him a forever frown even when he's grinning. But he's also such a good dad, so gentle with Anne-Marie. He is thoughtful and kind to everyone. A giant teddy bear. I'm sorry he lost his mom.

Once in their jammies, the kids march in silence to the bathroom, and I watch their mirrored reflections as they brush their teeth. I don't have to ask them twice as I usually do. Standing on colorful stools that match their outfits—Tony in red elephants and Nikki in yellow butterflies—they dutifully brush and spit. No bickering, no teasing.

Their truncated images stare back at me, their reflections not who they are. I see Nikki with the same long willowy body as her mom, Tony broader with bushy brows resembling his dad. The more I stare, the more their visages shift. Replicas of the teenagers they could become roll through my head. Tony playing football—a linebacker, thick and beefy and holding his own. Nikki, finally grown into her coltish legs, excelling as a runner, a dancer. Tons of friends surrounding them both, happy, laughing. Tony and Nikki, the center of the world with little Giovanni Davis forever tagging along behind.

Except I can't make out little Giovanni D's face. It blurs as he follows Nikki and Tony across the yard to the car they climb inside. Nikki's driving way too fast and Tony's talking way too loud, his voice booming, same as his father's, his laugh instead of the road holding Nikki's attention. A faceless Giovanni in the backseat begs Nikki to stop the car.

They are flung through darkness. They are airborne. They are mangled in the wreckage. Glass and bone and blood strew the street.

Giovanni's face is Davis's.

"Pru? Will you tuck us in?" Nikki tugs my shirt, breaking my nightmarish reverie.

"S-sure." I catch my breath—and a swaying Tony from the stool. He yawns, snuggling close and growing limp as I scoop him into my arms.

The kids are asleep as soon as the lights flick out. Moments later, Anne-Marie slips me a fifty. The bill weighs my pocket with guilt as Mr. G drives me home.

At home, the windows are dark and Dad's car isn't in the carport. A double win. I head to my room, wincing as the stairs creak. My instincts expect Mom to ambush me in the hall until my thoughts catch up. BD, she would wait up till everyone was home. AD…

Well, she doesn't.

It's barely ten, but her royal zombie-ness probably hasn't even woken up once today. I risk a quick shower and then grab clothes and school stuff for tomorrow, plus my pillow and a thin blanket from beneath the comforter. I pull the quilt up over my bare sheets. Robo-Dad likely won't come upstairs for anything—especially not to enter my room—but I don't want any evidence announcing that I'm not in bed.

I'm smiling as I transfer handfuls of candy from the stash inside my desk to my backpack. This is the most hope, the most joy I've had all year.

Davis, here I come.

I slip into the hall and move as fast and silently as I can to his Monte Carlo. It's been a lifetime since my nap, but the garage and the Gherkin are precisely how I left them. Untouched. Waiting. Completely mine.

I climb in, immediately comfortable. After my talk with Anne-Marie, I'm dying to test out the dream thing—to see if he comes back to me in sleep and ask him something only he could know that I do not. AD, most of my dreams, if I even dream at all, are vague and disjointed, my nights a blank and empty nothingness. That Davis dream earlier was more vivid than my current waking days. Full of color, sensations, light, and, well, Davis. It's scary to hope, but I have to try.

The Monte Carlo's interior lights time out right as Dad's headlights shine through the bay door windows, flooding the garage. I'm pretty sure he didn't notice me hiding out in here, but I slouch low in the backseat and slowly count to one hundred till I figure I'm safe.

I trade out my pillow for Davis's jacket and pull my blanket over my head, trapping the scent around me. This must be what addicts experience.

Everything hurts, but it's impossible to stop.

4

Lullaby ~ The Cure

The carpet squished beneath her feet as she crossed the room, the pile so high it swallowed her feet. The dry, grassy fibers scratched her calves. Each step released a waterlogged spray smelling of old, decayed lilacs that competed with the freshness of the lemony bleach-scrubbed kitchen. Pru smiled as she trailed her fingers across the familiar 70s avocado-green appliances. *His own kitchen*, she thought, shaking her head in amazement.

Everything looked exactly the same as before. The gigantic barstools towering over the counter. The sparse living room. The picture frames and metal letters hanging on the wall. The big bay window framed by flimsy lace curtains overlooking the street.

But something was off. The vibrant humming energy that surrounded her the last time was missing. No glitter motes, no music. Even with every light turned on and the curtains open wide, shadows lurked in the corners, dark and oppressive.

The air was heavy, leaden. Suffocating with its silence.

"Davis?" Her voice echoed back unexpectedly, hollow, tinny, the sound confined to the kitchen. She vaguely remembered…she came with a purpose…questions to ask her brother. Proof that he and this place are real and not her imagination. Shadows crept from beneath the cupboards and slid up the wall. Pru yelped, the hair on the back of her neck leaping upright. "Davis! Where are you?" she screamed, but her words came out a scratchy whisper.

A wind kicked up as though in response, a shrill, agonized howl rising from the back of the apartment. Strong gusts pressed upon her chest, slamming her against the refrigerator. The kitchen walls shook, a vibration that spread to the living room, to the entire apartment. Everything quivered and jerked. The metal letters crashed to the ground. Then the light bulbs burst, plunging Pru into inky night. She flipped the wall light switch, but nothing happened.

Using the walls as her guide, she worked her way through the darkness, wading back through the meadow of carpet now grown past her waist. Verdant strands wound around her middle, tripped up her feet, and chaffed her skin. She willed her rubbery legs to move faster, fighting her way toward the hall, toward the sounds of a storm raging somewhere inside the home.

Thunder roared and a flash of lighting illuminated the space. Half the hallway was warm summer sun, half overcast frigid winter sky. She needed to reach the door with the sunlight beckoning, shining out from the crack beneath it.

The wind yanked her body through the rattling, yawning maw of the other.

It was Davis's bedroom, and it was chaos.

Pru pushed her blowing hair from her eyes. Turbulent sky loomed where the roof should have been. The walls faded in and out of existence, an insubstantial mirage. The wind cried with a sound so pained the torment pulsed within her chest. And in the center of the room, on a bed spinning and spinning and spinning in tight circles, lay Davis.

Davis's body thrashed on the mattress. His eyes rolled into the back of his head, exposing the milky whites, glossy and unseeing. He moaned, but the sound vanished, eaten by the hungry wind.

"Davis!" Pru screamed as the wind slammed her into the bed frame. "*Wake up!*" Throwing herself across the covers, she grabbed a fistful of stained, ratty quilt in one hand and Davis's flailing arm in the other.

ZAP!

It burned. It burned so bad. The electric shock raced from her hand toward her head, searing where it rode her skin. Bile gushed up her throat. The bed spun faster, taking her with it. Her vision blurred.

She dropped his arm, and the fiery jolts and the fear squeezing her heart ceased. "Davis, what's wrong? Please, answer me!" But while the bed scraped across the floor, spinning her almost senseless, sending her limbs akimbo so that she gripped the bedsheets tighter and tighter, Davis lay ridged, mouth frozen in a soundless scream, eyes cold, lifeless, and fixated on the ceiling, unresponsive.

Sobbing, Pru pressed her hand to his cheek, called his name again, pleaded as she touched his forehead, his chin, his neck, fingertips going to pins and needles at every contact. "Wake up! Talk to me!" she demanded.

Her palm ached as the electric pressure built between them again, but she pressed against the pain and saw Davis's lips and chin quiver. She leaned closer, and his putrid breath stung her nose. Two voices rose up inside her head: Davis's and another. Both angry, scared, and urgent. Resonant but unintelligible.

Maybe *stop*, or *slow*, or *don't?* Pru wasn't certain.

The bed spun faster. She sucked her throbbing fingertips. She couldn't tell where she ended and Davis began. But every time she touched him, she was aware of something more.

Something new and different seeping through from Davis to her consciousness.

The tangibility of something clutched tightly in hand.

The sensation of careening through space.

A flash of yellow. Then white. Inky blackness punctuated with shimmers of green.

The scent of pine so thick it choked.

Her body rolled and pitched forward, a limp marionette on broken strings.

KSSSSH!

The pelting sting of one hundred serrated raindrops nipped and gashed at her exposed flesh. Her cheek burst with searing pain. And then...

Davis was upright and screaming.

The storm ended. The bed juddered and stalled against the wall.

Pru's head continued to spin, still caught in a frightening vertigo. "D-D-Davis?"

Horrified, she stared as he rocked, the mattress quaking with his convulsive sobs, his hair knotted into mangled clumps beneath his white-knuckled grip.

Pru's hands shook as she reached out to rub his back. She expected her palm to erupt in flames on contact, but all that met her was an increasingly sharp throb behind her left eye and a deep, dark void of staticky nothingness.

Davis straightened beneath her touch, sniffling and scrubbing his eyes with the back of his hand, same as when they were younger. "Pru-Pru?" He choked on her name like it hurt, his voice thick and slurred.

"You OK?" She rested her hand on his forearm. A slithering warmth hummed beneath his skin. The air crackled, and "Can't Stand Losing You" by the Police drifted in from the living room.

"Yup." He shook his hand free from hers and wiped his palm on the mattress. "Never better."

She reached for him again, but he pulled away and scootched toward the splintered headboard. Pru reached out to stop him from leaning against the broken wood.

He totally wasn't OK. Nothing about him or this place was OK.

"What's going on, Davis? What's happening?"

Davis stared at the wall and picked at a hole in his sock. The music volume rose, tempo speeding faster than the song's typical beat.

"Hey!" she yelled, bobbing her head under his, vying for his attention. "Please tell me what's wrong with this place."

His head snapped up and his eye twitched as he stared at her. "Nothing, Pru-Pru. Nothing at all."

The temperature dropped.

A skittering scratched across the ceiling.

Smoky shadows, wispy and diaphanous, flowed in from the hall and the corners of the bedroom, merging into one congealed, clotted lump over Davis. The hulking blackness, like a spider formed of shadows, hissed as it lowered itself slowly down an inky web toward them.

"I've got it all under control," Davis slurred. "Everything's grrr-eat!" His eyes burned red. He laughed.

And then he pushed Pru off the bed.

5

Regret ~ New Order

I scramble into a tight ball on the seat, scanning the car for killer arachnids. My skin crawls, itchy and tight, while I struggle to catch my breath, and then I realize it's my muted phone alarm's vibrations tickling my leg.

Great. I slept through the first half of art class.

Maybe it's a good thing? I don't want a repeat of yesterday with Miss Painter. All my grades are passing, so who cares if I ditch sometimes? Besides, it's just art. Davis spent his entire life cramming for exams, doing extra credit, perfecting his homework, and for what? He died before he even graduated. All that wasted time...

I'd spend all my time sleeping if I could.

My stomach growls.

Maybe I can slip inside, grab breakfast, and sneak back to the Gherkin for another nap before anyone notices.

After folding Davis's letterman jacket into a neat square on top of my pillow, I cover it with the blanket and slip out of the car. Movement past the garage door window sets my heart racing again—Robo-Dad is halfway across the backyard, making a beeline for the garage. I should hide, but I watch him through the dirty window instead. I dip my fingers into my pocket, but all my candy is inside my backpack.

Less than ten feet from the door, his phone rings and he stops to answer it. I can't make out his words over the blood thundering in my ears, but he nods twice and then pivots, returning to the house. I breathe a sigh of both relief and regret. I'm not sure what he was coming into the garage for, but just in case, I stuff my bedding and Davis's jacket beneath the back seat and grab my backpack. I sift through my candy cache for the most sugary treat possible and find a package of Smarties. I pop the entire roll into my mouth, then shove a few red licorice whips into my front pocket for later.

Half of me wants to stay inside the Monte Carlo and sleep the day away. Half of me is afraid I'll have another nightmare. Everything felt real, resonating deep within my core as truth, even though I failed to ask Davis any telling questions. Could Anne-Marie be right? Is Davis visiting me in my dreams? Regardless, I don't want to risk bumping into Robo-Dad when I should be in class, so I escape while I can.

In the front lawn, chewing the pastel discs into a fine powder of delectable, tasty, calm, I pause. Maybe Dad has noticed I didn't sleep inside. Maybe he's wondering where I am. Through the window I spot him, mulling around the kitchen. Unhurried, unconcerned.

Swallowing the sweetness, I hike my pack firmly onto my shoulders and leave for school.

I am near the base of the ridge below the red brick prison when the passing period bell rings. Perfect. Now, I get to walk into class late—everyone staring, whispering, and laughing while the teacher lambastes me. My head throbs.

It's a hustle up the hill, and then I slip through the front doors in time to hear the speaker system crackle overhead.

"All seniors, please meet in the gymnasium for an important graduation meeting. All seniors, please gather in the gym."

A distraction. I consider backing out the door to take advantage but spy Mr. Roderick, my geometry teacher, watching me. I give him a shaky wave and follow the sheep down the hall and into the gym. Assemblies are almost as good as ditching anyway.

The top three rows of bleachers are the emptiest. Focused on reaching the seat directly beneath the roaring tiger mural on the back wall, I don't notice Maddi until I feel her hands on my arm, pushing me sideways.

"Have a seat, Spellmeyer." She smirks as I stumble and fall into Bruce Baumgarten's lap.

People are laughing and my cheeks burn, but Bruce smiles, all relaxed and calm as though this is nothing bothersome. "Don't give her the satisfaction," he whispers near my ear before waving at Maddi and yelling, "You remind me why friends are so important. Thanks, Maddison. Hope your day is as pleasant as you are."

A warmth spreads through me. Davis used to speak up for me like this. I drape an appreciative arm across Bruce's shoulders, staying in his lap while Maddi gawks. Her mouth gapes open like she wants to say something, but her brains have left the building. With a huff, she turns, moves down the row, and sits.

"Where you going, Maddi? Best seat in the house is right here." Logan and Marshall, two of Bruce's theatre friends, cram into the empty spot beside him and I slide off his lap to the other.

"Something wicked your way comes," Logan yells down the row, waggling his eyebrows at Maddi's back.

Bruce laughs. "Payeth no heed to the cackling canker blossoms."

"Kernelless fusty nuts!" Marshall sends back, and the three high-five one another.

I slide down the bench inconspicuously to give them space. BD, I would have joined them in slinging Shakesperean insults, but it's hard summoning the energy to create new beginnings when everything ends. Besides, Marshall and Logan are Bruce's friends, not mine.

The sea of seniors fills in the gaps and spaces all around me. I have known these people my entire life, yet I can't connect with a single one. It was so easy having Davis as my person. He wasn't going anywhere. He certainly wasn't about to join some new school club and ditch me. Not when I'd be at the dinner table an hour later.

I can't help but wonder if I'll ever find someone who understands me like he did.

"Steve! Steve!" Maddison's shrieking is loud enough to make me jump. "Over here!"

I look, and there's Steve, standing at the foot of the bleachers, smiling to see Maddi, God knows why. He's changed in more ways than one. His hair is longer than I've ever seen it. BD, he sported a buzz cut. But now, beach-messy golden waves start at his crown, kinking more and more as they flow to his forehead, where they end in tight ringlets that frame his face. He brushes his curls out of his eyes, but they spring right back. I never knew his hair curled like that. I wonder if he grew it out for Maddi. My chest tightens, and I push the thought away.

Face alight, he takes the aisle stairs two at a time toward Maddi, the crowd parting to allow the honored couple their reunion. Soon he's wrapping her in his varsity jacket and slipping his hand into hers. She whispers something in his ear, and he throws his head back when he laughs, the sound rising above the chattering hum. It hurts, remembering how Steve always laughs loud and with his entire body, practically vibrating with happiness. His eyes catch mine over Maddi's shoulder as he tips his head forward again. Our gazes lock and my heart stutters as he raises his hand to wave but stops halfway, frowning, and lowers it to his lap. Cold ice spreads in my chest where a Steve-shaped iceberg has been forming since Davis died. The frozen lump is so large now, I couldn't move past it even if I wanted to.

Maddi turns to see who Steve is staring at. Noticing it's me, she pulls the Sleazle's jacket tighter around her shoulders and leans into him. He kisses the top of her head.

I don't understand what he sees in her. Her beauty fades when she frowns, deep lines framing her lips and drooping toward her chin. She's so mean and angry all the time, I bet they will form into permanent wrinkles before she's thirty. I would have thought he would find her bitchiness revolting like Davis always did. Steve used to stand up for people against assholes like Maddi. Maybe he stopped caring about all that the day he wrecked my life. Maybe he never cared, and I simply couldn't see it. Whatever the case, I certainly don't know who he is now.

I pull one of the licorice whips from my pocket and tear off the plastic wrapper with my teeth. Anything to cover up the bad taste in my mouth.

Principal Fineman taps on the microphone, signaling silence and the start of announcements.

"Congratulations, seniors. Your time is near. You have arrived!" Principal Fineman pumps his fist into the air, and the crowd roars, clapping and stomping. I shut my eyes as the metal seats quake and thrum. The rumblings rattle clear to my stomach. But nothing fills the growing black hole inside me. Same as every other AD day, I am out of place. All alone in a mass of people.

I am on my third licorice whip, listening to the principal drone on and on about graduation, credits, and ordering caps and gowns, when something he says about remote learners hits me...

What if I could get my diploma in the mail and skip all this pomp and circum-crap? I could do remote study, finish out the year on my laptop, email in homework and tests, without ever having to set foot in this dismal place again. Better yet, I could do it all from the garage, as close to Davis as is possible for me to get. *Graduation from the Gherkin!* It's perfect.

I need Principal Talks-a-Lot to finish his bland eulogy of grad drivel so I can see Counselor Pederman. Immediately.

I accidentally knee the guy in front of me in my excitement, and he shoots me a dirty look. It happens three more times till things finally wrap up.

I bound out of my seat and straight for the counselor's office.

"Well, well, Miss Spellmeyer, how nice to see you. What class might you be skipping today to grace me with your presence, hmm?" Mrs. Pederman smiles but not sincerely. Her mouth's all happy unicorn, but her eyes are of a hungry lioness.

I focus on her red lipstick—the same shade as her hair, nails, and sweater—as well as the creepy dust-catching figurines littering her desk and shelves.

"Just geometry."

"Just geometry." She draws both words out—*juuust geooometryyy*—and her blood-colored talons peck the keyboard.

"Um, Mrs. Pederman? I, uh, was wondering if we could talk about graduation. Namely, how I can—"

"Graduation should be the least of your worries, Prudence. You have to get through geometry first, yes?"

"Exactly. And I could better get through geometry on my own. I could get through all my classes on my own. Online. Virtually. You know, from home?"

There's a sudden snort.

She slams her freckled hand over her mouth as though she could shove the laughter back inside, but it's too late.

Yeah, that snort def came from her.

"Oh, Prudence. You cannot possibly pass geometry on your own, dear girl. Even if we had such a program in place, you still need a tutor."

"I'm sorry, a—a *what*?"

"You heard me. A tutor." Her nails pitter across the keyboard. "You do realize you've missed precisely"—*tappity-tap-tap*—"twenty-three days, which is more than double your allowed absences, and your grade currently stands at"—*tap-tappity-tap*—"a whopping forty-seven percent." *Tappity-tap, smash, boom.*

I sneak a quick glance at the clock and then at the door.

"I quite agree, Miss Spellmeyer. Class is *exactly* where you should be sitting right now. Your time is much better spent there than here. With me."

OK, maybe not so sneaky. This is so not going as planned.

"You are aware geometry is a graduation requirement, yes?"

There she goes with the whole not-actually-asking-me *yes* crap again. As though I've got all the answers and know how to do her job for her and never should have been in here. *Davis* surely wouldn't have been in here. Davis excelled at math…

"Prudence, this is serious." She appraises me over the top of her cat-eye glasses. The lenses are fake. They have to be. She never actually looks through them, not ever.

I want to tell her I'm serious about switching to remote learning, but I think I've lost my upper hand, the opportunity to prove myself. As if I even had her support in the first place.

"Look at me, Prudence. You will not graduate if you do not pass this class."

That gets my attention. I sit up straighter, swallowing down any further protests.

She removes her glasses and folds them closed, holding them in both hands and taking a deep, wavering breath. "I'm so sorry. I know this year has been hard on you and your family, but this is a prerequisite every student must meet. You cannot receive your diploma, by ceremony or otherwise, without your geometry credits."

I hate how her voice goes all soft and gooey and sympathetic. How suddenly it's hard to breathe around the rock in my throat. I need more candy, but I devoured the last of the licorice at the assembly and I don't think Mrs. Pederman would approve of me digging more out of my pack.

Time seems to stop before the *tappity-tap* of her claws starts again.

"The good news is that this is salvageable. Your average is, surprisingly, high enough that you can still pass the course. If you earn an A on the final." She scribbles something on a red notepad, tears off the page, and slides it across the desk. "Here's the name and contact information of a student who can help you achieve that goal. Text him to set up a study plan, and I'll personally be in touch to ensure he commits."

So it's tutoring or repeating my whole senior year. I stare at the black ink of death scrawled on the page. Her loopy letters are thin but clear.

Steve-freaking-Nolan.

Oh, fuck everything that lives and breathes.

After school, I walk down the hill and head for Rocket Park, named for the three-tiered vertical rocket ship in the middle of the playground. I avoid the pools of water collecting on the sidewalk. Davis loved the rain. We would peel off our shoes and socks, roll up our pants, and race through the street, heedless of the puddles. He marveled at the snails and pill-bugs that came out of hiding to crawl along the damp pavement, the hordes of red-breasted robins landing in the yard to feast on worms. He'd drive us through the forest to watch cloaks of fog spread along the ground and weave through the trees. *"Rainy*

days are magic," he'd say like a mantra, breaths syncing to the rhythm of the drops drumming against the hood and windows of the Monte Carlo.

The park bench overlooks everything: the playground swings, the rocket, the spacious dandelion-dappled fields of grass in need of mowing.

I pull my journal out of my backpack and open it to my latest sketch of Davis, running a finger over his face. My drawing isn't perfect. The ink lies flat and still on the parchment. It doesn't sound, smell, or move like Davis. I can't even render his lashes or dimples quite right. Even the illustrations I've created by copying old photographs look surreal. Like every precious moment we ever shared was only a dream.

Tilting my head back, I roll my tense and knotted neck along my shoulders and close my eyes. I can still see all the details of Davis's dreamland apartment as though laid out before me. Anne-Marie's voice rings in my head: *Sometimes it's just a dream, but sometimes, it's more.* Could it be real? I plan to find out. Test the limits of the apartment, the dream. Try to stay asleep longer. Quiz Davis about why he's suddenly showing up when I sleep. Maybe I can ask him for help with math instead of Steve fucking Nolan, who I will *absolutely not* be texting. All I need is Davis and a week of uninterrupted sleep in the Gherkin.

"Make a wish!"

Blinded by the stupid sun, I have to squint hard to spot the family in the largest dandelion patch. The dad drags the mom upright to slow dance. He slips a woven yellow chain of dandelions around her wrist. Clutching her hand to his chest, they sway. It reminds me of prom. I would have loved a dandelion corsage versus roses or carnations like other girls. *My date,* however, showed up empty-handed, offering nothing but gross sexual innuendos. Worst day of my life.

The children squeal. Oblivious to anything else in the park, the brother blows seeds off flowers offered up by his grinning sister.

They are all clueless that this could be their last happy memory.

Dad's laughter, gone.

Mom's smiles, gone.

Family post-tax-season picnics, gone.

I swat at the seeds floating my way. Several stick to my hand. They feel decayed against my palm. I wonder what they wished for.

Davis? He always wished big. To sprout bat wings so we could fly to the moon, take a bite, and see if it was actually made of cheese. For the tree outside my bedroom to turn into a dragon and chase away my nightmares. For my favorite books to always be at the library so I was never bored. For us to get the Mary Poppins giggles so we could float to the ceiling and walk across the walls like spiders. He never wished only for himself. He included me in every single one.

And me? I cared about the stupidest stuff. New crayons, chocolate for dinner, cookies for breakfast.

All those wishes, wasted.

I have one wish left in me and blow the squashed propeller seeds clinging to my palm.

They drop, heavy and lifeless.

There's no sign of the Robo-D-mobile in the drive nor of undead activity from Zombie Mom in the house when I slip through the front door. Why would today be any different? Since prom, the only reason she leaves her crypt is to visit the dead zone we used to call a dining room.

I step inside the room against my better judgment.

"There was an accident."

The memory assails me. But maybe it will help me dream of Davis again. If it does, I need to be in here.

Today, the room reeks of burnt dust. Everything is ratty and falling apart except the china. Every glass, fork, and plate sparkles, six perfectly poised place settings. Maintaining the illusion of a perfect dining room is more important to Mom than living in reality with me and Dad. I flick a dusty prom streamer drooping low over the dishes, the falling grit turning the plates' gleaming white centers a dull grey. Dust floats on the air like the dandelion seeds above the family in the park. Rubbing my bare wrist, I don't want to remember, but bad memories stalk me.

I hadn't wanted to go to prom with Ricky Morgan. I hadn't wanted to go to prom period. Davis talked me into it.

Didn't matter that he and Steve weren't going; Davis didn't like formal dances and Steve waited too long to ask anyone. By the time he did, everyone already had dates.

"You gotta live, Pru," Davis said.

"Ricky's not a bad guy," he said.

"You'll regret it if you don't go," he said.

I'll regret going to prom for eternity.

I purposely waited till the week before prom to tell Ricky I'd go with him. When Davis found out I planned to attend in jeans and kicks, he freaked, demanding we find something so flawlessly prom-tastic, I'd wanna party like it was 1999.

Our local mall was useless with nothing left on the racks but frilly pastel gowns, yet Davis and Steve wouldn't let me back out. Pay dirt came from the thrift store. Of course. Steve and Davis spotted it at the same time. I gagged when Steve held it up against Davis's frame to show it off. Everything about it, except the color, was hideous.

"It's got great potential," Davis said.

"We can fix it," Steve said, squeezing my hand. "It's perfect! *You'll* be perfect."

I sighed. There wasn't time to find anything better, so… whatever.

But Steve, of all people, surprised me with his mad sewing skills. His mom apparently taught him that sewing was no different than piecing together a car engine. He took miles of shapeless black velvet, mountains of scratchy purple tulle, and enough plum satin to choke the entire junior class and transformed it all. The velvet corset was snug but soft. The black heart neckline accentuated my collarbones in ways I'd never seen them pop. And even with bajillions of little satin bows lacing up the back, it wasn't girly. It wasn't hideous.

Steve was right. It was perfect.

The three of us danced for hours that night, testing the dress as we blasted all our faves from The Cure, B-52s, Duran Duran, and Siouxsie and the Banshees. There wasn't a single wardrobe malfunction. The short layers of tulle skirting floated around my knees soft as butterfly wings. And the best part? No heels required. Even the guys agreed the dress looked great—"very Cyndi Lauper"—with my high-tops.

The day of the prom, Davis was superglued to my side. I'm fairly sure he knew I'd skip town if given the chance. 'Course, all that hovering is totally why I fried my hair with the curler-straightener thing and almost stabbed my eyes out with the mascara wand. I was rocking Robert Smith's tangled mop and the caked-on Boy George look by the time he finally called for Mom.

I knew she and Dad were busy getting our big dinner ready. Most kids go out to eat before the dance. But every year BD, we celebrated the end of tax season with a big Spellmeyer family dinner. Prom night aside, Mom and Dad had planned a fancy banquet for afterward. The only difference was the guest list would include Ricky.

But, busy as she was with preparations, Mom dropped everything to intervene. She shook her head and shooed Davis out of the bathroom door. And she didn't laugh once, not even a smirk, as she took in the full glory of my makeover attempt. Instead, I still remember the soft brush of her hand as she cleared my frizzed hair off my face, the warmth of her eyes when she stared deep into mine.

"Such a beauty. I wouldn't miss this moment for the world, Prudie girl."

By the time she finished, I didn't recognize the girl staring back at me with poppin' cheekbones and smoky cat eyes. The two kinky curls she pulled out of my topknot tickled my neck when I turned to see Davis in the doorway.

"There you are." He smiled as if he'd known I could turn from hag to swag, as though we'd finally uncovered the true Pru. Except then he said, "Though, I know you could have pulled off jeans too."

He never did make me feel like I needed to be anyone but myself.

It was time to go. Of course, the week before, the Gherkin had died, taking with it all hope of being able to meet Ricky at the dance and a possible early escape. I should have taken it as a sign to feign the flu last minute and stay home. But no, I ignored my gut instincts.

Ricky showed up at the door, his red hair that normally grew in every direction slicked back into a shiny helmet with some sort of goop that reeked of orange creamsicles. He whispered near my ear, "Hey there, babycakes. Get ready for a jamming time with the Rickster," before smiling up at my parents with wide, moon pie eyes the color of watered-down cola. It was so charming and polite I thought I'd imagined his words. Maybe he was an odd flirt, I told myself. Maybe he was awkward at breaking the ice. Maybe he was as nervous as I was.

Regardless, I blew off my intuition when I shouldn't have. All because I trusted Davis and Steve's judgment.

The ride to prom was all *the Rickster* this and *babycakes* that. And football. And how lucky I was to have a chance at scoring with someone in his league. And more football. And even more about how great he was. The cloying tang of his hair gel clogged my nose. I could taste it on the back of my tongue. The quick drive felt like hours of pure hell.

Inside was no better. Ricky was an all-eyes-on-me kind of dancer. Shocker. He dragged me to the center of the floor where a circle of screaming dumbass Rickster freaks cheered for his every move. Years of tackle-dodging football stamina kicked my uncoordinated punk ass for an entire song.

"Can't breathe!" I screamed over the thumping bass.

Lacing his fingers through mine, he pulled me toward the refreshment table, fist-bumping *every, single, person* along the way. One of his minions missed his fist and shouldered into me instead, knocking me backward into a solid wall of Rickster.

Next thing I knew, I was pinned in the corner with his tongue shoved down my throat and his hand up my skirt. The more I struggled, the harder he pressed into me.

I smelled the salt of his sweat as he grinded against me, but I no longer felt his touch. I'd gone numb. Frozen, heavy, trapped. My brain screamed to move, run, push him off me. I wanted to scream *STOP*, but it came out a stuttering, incoherent gurgle he either ignored or didn't hear. The cold bricks scratched my back. The corset slipped.

"Hey, kids, break it up!" said a deep raspy voice from the other side of a bright pen light.

Rickster the Dickster dropped me, and my top followed, drooping to my waist.

There I was, living the naked-in-public nightmare.

The Dickster licked his lips and kept his eyes plastered on my chest. The teacher cleared their throat and directed the light to the floor. But it was too late. I could hear the whistles and giggles from everyone close enough to notice.

I yanked the corset up and ran out of the gym. I ran till tall pines blocked out the moon and my legs were rubber. I ran till the forest became unfamiliar and the trail vanished into undergrowth as thick as my brain felt. I ran till I puked.

Only then did I call Davis.

"He *what?*" Davis's voice sounded a million miles away, buried beneath thumping music in the background. "W—— are you now?"

"The woods by school. Davis, please come get me. I'm—"

"Pru? I—"

Then nothing. Battery dead. Call dropped.

It felt as though it took days to walk home. I kept expecting to see Steve's rust-bucket truck around every corner, but he and Davis never showed up.

No one did.

I was beyond pissed off by the time the house came into view, the lights shining through every window like some freaking festive greeting card.

I remember the family photos shaking on the wall when I slammed the front door, the sound of it echoing through the house. There was no music, no dishes clanking, no laughter, not a single voice. I wanted nothing more than to trash my ruined dress, wash the Dickster's handprints off me, and sleep for a bazillion years. But I forced my way toward the dining room. The silence squeezed my head so tight my ears pulsed.

The room was magical. Metallic streamers dripped down the walls in a waterfall of colorful braids, glittery dancers in the flickering candlelight. Ethereal fairy lights twinkled in every corner. The tablecloth was a starry night sky of purple velvet beneath a silvery crochet overlay. So vintage. So Spellmeyer.

Mom had set the table with Nana's wedding china, something we never did, and in the center of every dish stood an island of lasagna surrounded by a ring of spinach salad, not a single piece wilted. Every wine glass sparkled with something bubbly, tiny red and blue fruit pieces bobbing inside the flutes. Cannoli sat on tiny saucers at precise angles to the dinner plates. Everything identical. Everything exact. Everything so perfect while my life was a living nightmare. The room screamed *happy*.

I hated it on sight.

Then it registered that, unlike any other night in the history of Spellmeyer dinners, Mom sat at the head of the table, staring at her plate. No one ever sat at either end of the table. We always scrunched together along the sides, facing each other.

Dad, in a tux I'd never seen before, continued sitting beside her for several long seconds before he stood, cleared his throat, and steepled his fingers on the table's edge.

I groaned. "I know, I know. I'm sorry I'm late."

Dad stared at his fingers. Then at mom. Then back at his fingers. Up. Down. Up. Down. Up. Down.

Mom closed her eyes.

I was livid. Did they not realize I was alone? Without Rickster the Dickster? Did they not wonder what had gone wrong? "Yeah, OK. You guys totally outdid yourselves. Everything looks great. Better than prom."

Mom reached out and pressed Dad's hand flat. He looked at her, swallowing rapidly, his Adam's apple bobbing; still, neither spoke.

Uncomfortable tension clawed my chest, my throat, forcing me to fill the silence.

"Well, in case you're wondering, Rick won't be joining us. Where are Davis and Steve? I need to yell at them."

Mom clutched Dad's hand to her chest, lips moving but without sound. Dad's eyes were wild as they flitted around the room. "There was an accident. Steve was drinking. Davis is gone."

I'll never forget laughing at Dad's robotic voice as if it was a bad joke.

"There was an accident," he repeated. "Steve was—"

"Davis? Steve? I'm home!" I moved toward the living room, certain they lay in wait, ready to jump out, ready to scream "SURPRISE!" I needed a Davis hug. I wanted him to swear revenge on the Dickster for laying a finger on me. I wanted Steve to hold my hand and tell some stupid joke. I wanted Mom to cradle my head in her lap while she stroked my hair off my sweaty forehead. I wanted Dad to tell me nothing about tonight was my fault.

Instead, this man, a man so not my Dad, all explosive and red-faced, grabbed my shoulders.

"Davis is *DEAD!*"

His hands were the only thing holding me up. When he released me, I stumbled into the wall.

He walked away in slow motion, returning to Mom, and started clearing the table.

That's when Mom finally moved.

"Leave it. Leave it alone. *Leave it all alone!*" She clawed his hands and wrenched the lasagna pan out of his grasp. It was long cold and not in need of a hot pad, but she placed it back on the trivet and spun it until it was in the same exact position as before. "Leave it."

The way she whispered it before she walked upstairs... it was the quietest shriek I'd ever heard. As her door clicked shut, in that one flash of a moment, I *knew*. As much as I wanted to rewind, to erase the entire day and start over, I knew everything had changed. Nothing would ever be the same. Nothing would matter ever again.

I was alone.

The dining room smelled moldy for weeks—all rot and decay—until one day, out of nowhere, she cleared all the food. Not the decorations, however. They still covered the walls and chandelier. Fairy lights burned through layers of filth until all but one string died out.

I'd clear the table, clean the room, put everything away if I thought it would change anything. If I thought it would make her care about me, about Dad, like she did before Davis died and took her spirit with him.

"The school phoned today."

Her voice is soft behind me. Barely a whisper. But I jump as though she screamed in my ear and accidentally knock a fork to the floor.

She bends and picks up the utensil, cleaning it with the hem of her wrinkled shirt before setting it back in its place, shifting it around until it's in the exact right spot, equidistant from the plate, centered on the napkin, perfectly positioned like everything else on that freaking table. "Mrs. Pederman says you are failing geometry and may not graduate. I called Steve. For tutoring. Left a message saying he could come to the house for you anytime."

The room spins. "You *what?*" I can barely get the words past the acid cesspool churning in my stomach. Any hunger I thought I had turns to nausea as bile burns my throat. I need candy, but my pocket is flat. Empty.

She bites her lip, and her wide eyes are hopeful when she pushes her limp bangs off her forehead. "Or maybe… I could help?"

The room spins impossibly faster. I've waited for her to say words like this all year. To be my caring, loving Mom again.

But then she picks up the platter I filled with streamer dirt. Closing her eyes, she blows off the excess before dragging it down her pink floral pajama bottoms, leaving a grimy streak down her leg. She puts it back and starts fiddling with the rest of the place settings. She never looks up once.

The cold bile turns to blistering heat, prickling the back of my throat, spreading across my chest, forcing words to fly from my mouth.

"In case you haven't noticed, Dad and I have been getting along fine without your interference all year. We don't need your help. We don't need you at all, Mom."

Little red blotches appear on her cheeks. She opens her mouth, but nothing comes out. When her eyes tear, I steal a move straight out of the Zombie Mom playbook and flee to my room, slamming my door and leaving her alone with her precious china.

I pull my desk drawer open so hard it disengages, clattering to the floor and spewing candy across the carpet. Story of my life: messy and scattered. I drop to my knees and cry out as my shin smashes against something hard. Sliding back to my butt, I see it's a freaking atomic fireball, one of Steve's favorites. I thought I'd tossed anything to do with him in the trash where it belonged, but here he is, showing up out of the blue, causing pain as always. I rub my leg. It will probably bruise.

Who the hell likes candy so hot it melts your tongue off? Steve. That's who. We would shove as many of these inferno candies as we could into our mouths at once, seeing who would cave and spit them into their palm first. I barely lasted a minute, running to the kitchen for water or milk. Steve wouldn't even flinch as Davis sucked cooling breaths into his inflamed mouth, smiling eyes watering.

The fireball cracked beneath my weight. Tearing open the plastic, I give it a firm squeeze along the fissure, breaking off a small shard and popping it into my mouth. The burn is instantaneous, and I spit it out onto the carpet.

Why the fuck am I torturing myself like this? I don't want to think about Steve. I don't want to emulate Steve. I sure as hell don't want to spend tutoring time—or any time—with Steve ever again. But everywhere I look, he's there. My entire life, every incredibly good memory with Davis, Steve's freaking presence overshadows it all.

There's one thing his poison didn't rot though. I pop a chocolate bon-bon—the only non-retro candy in my stash—into my mouth and crawl to the closet. Steve liked 80s stuff because Davis and I didn't really give him much of a choice. If he had his way, we would watch Bond flicks all day instead of John Hughes movies.

I find the battered cardboard box in the back of the closet and drag it across the floor, freeing yet another thrift store relic from it: a bulky stereo, its plastic scratched up with a messy exclamation of *Class of '88 RULZ!!!*

Davis insisted it wasn't just a stereo but a *boom box.* I couldn't get rid of it like Dad did all of Davis's other stuff and I never thought I'd use it again, but I want to obliterate all thoughts of Steve. I want to demolish any thought of two-in-the-morning hot chocolates during thunderstorm sleepovers. The way he could make Davis laugh so hard he snorted. And I really want to forget that he's dating the she-devil bride of Satan herself, is suddenly appearing everywhere I turn at school, and is now my only freaking ticket out of Podunk. Right now, I need Davis, and there is nothing that will take me to him faster than music. I could stream stuff through my phone, but I want to hear Davis's mix tapes. The preparation of the cassettes, the routine of popping them into the deck, the physicality of it all thrilled him as much as, if not more than, the music itself.

I run my fingers over the spine of the tape cases, each one labeled with Davis's tiny script. *Soundtrack Spellmeyer, That's My Jam,* and the best of them all, *Pru/Davis Theme Songs,* an equal mix of both of our favorites. I pull it out of the case, noticing the tape sagging at the bottom, and slip my pinky into the center of one of the reels to rewind the slack how Davis taught me. Before I think better about things, I slide the cassette inside, slap the plastic door closed, and hit play.

Each tape is ninety minutes of heavenly hell, but I sit here, rewinding and listening to each one over and over and over until the sun sets and the room turns black. I curl up on the floor and cry myself to sleep with songs of Davis simultaneously piecing me back together and ripping me apart.

"*Prudence!*"

Robo-Dad's pounding my door so hard it rattles in the frame, ready to fly off the hinges and thwap me in the head.

Rubbing sleep out of my eyes, I open the door and…

Mom's limp in Dad's arms.

"She's been depressed. Took some pills. I'm taking her to the hospital. We can get there quicker than an ambulance could get to us. But I need your help."

His voice is steady and clipped, but his eyes are wild and his breathing shallow. Before I can respond, let alone process, he's halfway down the stairs.

"Grab my keys. Open the doors."

For once, I'm grateful for Robo-Dad speak. His words are an anchor that steadies me. Something to hold, directives to follow. Otherwise, I'd stand gaping at the wall like—

Well, like a zombie.

Mom is lifeless as Dad carries her. She doesn't even twitch.

Not when Dad sets her gently on the seat and buckles her in.

Not when he kisses her forehead and whispers, so soft I almost miss it, "Hang on for me, Joycie."

Not when he starts the engine.

"Mom?" I whimper from outside the open passenger side window, but she doesn't hear me or respond. Her skin's so pale against the sedan's dark interior that it hurts to look. But I can't look at Dad either.

Does he know mom and I fought?

Did she tell him all the horrible things that I said before this happened?

81

The streetlamps by our house flicker on, spotlights illuminating the car. I can't see anything but Mom, crumpled and small in her seat. There's a horrible pressure in my chest.

I can't breathe.

I want to tell her I'm sorry. That I didn't mean it. That I do need her. That I'll always need her. But my lips are numb and all the hateful things I said echo in my brain so loud I can't think.

"I'll call with news. Charge your phone. Don't wait up." Dad's hands shake so bad when he pulls out of the drive, I wonder how he'll keep the car straight on the road.

I stay in the driveway long after the taillights vanish. Crickets sing *come back, come back, come back.* All the warmth seeps from my body. My legs stiffen as I turn from the darkness and enter the empty cavern that was once a home. The door's closing *click* reverberates off the walls. I flip on all the lights, but every room's still way too dark.

I should have gone with Dad to the hospital. I should have forced my way into the back seat. He made it all sound so easy. Stay home. Sleep. Wait for the call.

Except sleep's impossible, and I've never been good at waiting.

I've also never handled anything this huge alone. None of us have. As a family, we always used to face things together. Even when Davis died. Mom and Dad were at least always in the house, always around even if we were not speaking to one another. We were at least physically present even if emotionally unavailable.

Maybe, even if that's as good as it gets, it's better than the aching isolation I feel right now.

I can't hear any news about Mom all by myself.

Fishing my phone out of my pocket and slipping it onto the charger, I check the time.

10:52.

It's too late to call Anne-Marie.

WWDD?

Only one answer comes.

Call Steve.

So, before I think better of it, I do.

His phone rings three times before he finally answers sharply: "What?"

I hang up.

The phone isn't even back on the charger when my ringtone goes off.

And it's not Dad.

"Shit." But I answer.

"Why call if you're gonna hang up?"

Shit and double shit. *Why* did I answer?

"Pru, I know it's you. Do you really think I'm an idiot?"

I don't know what I was expecting exactly, but it wasn't this. "No."

"Then talk or I'm hanging the fuck up. I don't have time for games."

Woah. Steve never cusses. Davis and I used to always tease him about it and—

"Whatever. I can't do this anymore."

"*Wait!* Please wait. It's… Mom's in the hospital."

He's so silent maybe he did hang the fuck up on me. I babble on anyway.

"I dunno what's going on, Dad's supposed to call when he knows something, but she took some pills and—and—" I stutter over the words and have to force the rest out fast before the tears come. "She was unconscious when he took her. I don't even know if she was breathing. I—I—"

I think I killed her. It's all my fault.

My voice catches as I sob. I can't bring myself to say the words. If I don't speak it, it won't come true. If it's untrue, then I'm still me. Nothing like the Sleazle.

Oh God…

"I'm on my way."

He texts when he arrives instead of pounding out his signature knock on the door. It feels weird typing *come in* versus singing it aloud. I should get up, open the door, and greet him, but my butt is firmly glued to the kitchen floor. I don't think my legs could support me right now if I tried. I've not stopped shaking since Dad and Mom left.

He lets himself in with a quiet *click*.

"You here?"

You. Not Pru-Si-Q.

"In here." I hate how my voice catches while he's all cool and collected. I hold my breath as he passes the living and dining rooms—Dad's bed and Mom's shrine on full display.

Can I vanish now?

"Da—Larry call yet? I know I'm kinda late."

Was it late? Time stopped the instant I opened my bedroom door. I can't trust my voice, so I shake my head.

"She's at the west side hospital, not east, right?"

Shrugging, I trail my fingers over the checkered patterns of the floor. Waiting's the worst. "It's closest."

His jaw twitches as he nods. He stares into space, and I return to tracing patterns across the linoleum.

When the phone finally buzzes, rattling against the counter like an angry wasp, we jump.

It's Dad.

Steve looks as freaked out as I feel with his curls sticking up at odd angles, cheeks red and forehead sweaty. He looks anywhere but at me or the phone.

BD, he would have been glued to my side and holding my hand instead of hanging half out of the kitchen into the hall, but I'm still grateful he's with me, regardless.

Pressing speakerphone, I swallow hard and ask the hardest words ever.

"How's Mom?"

"In the clear. Dehydrated. On an IV and sleeping. She'll be released tomorrow."

My shoulders drop away from my ears. "Oh, thank God!" The way Steve's stance relaxes too calms me even further. "What time?"

"By noon. But go to class. Need to talk with you after."

"But—no! I wanna be here when you guys get home."

"Promise me, Prudence."

I gnaw my lip, promising nothing.

"Please?" His voice cracks. He still sounds so stressed, but I don't understand why. Mom's *alive*. She's coming home, and everything's gonna be OK.

"OK. Fine. I promise. But Dad?" The heavy weight of near tragedy has gone featherlight. So light my head floats. "Thank you. You know… for saving her."

He coughs. "Go get some sleep. It's late."

"You too, Dad. Kiss Mom for me?" It's something I would have said BD. It feels strange to say now after all that's happened this past year. But I still mean it. With all my heart.

"You bet. Night, Pru."

Relieved, I spin to face Steve. "Can you believe it? She's—" But he's not there behind me.

"Steve?"

I hear the front door open. I race down the hall.

"Steve! Wait… where are you going?"

"Back to Maddi's."

It's like he's kicked me in the stomach. All lightness in my brain sinks like a rock deep into my gut. "But—I thought—" I try to get control of my voice. "Didn't you hear? Mom—"

"Joyce is fine. I heard. Now I can go."

"Back to Maddi's, right?" He's abandoning me. For *her* of all people. Mom's barely stable and he can't spare a millisecond more of his time. I want to ask him to stay but stare at my feet instead. We aren't friends anymore. I can't expect more. But I do. And my heart shrinks for it.

The sparkling chrome of his new truck glints beneath the street lamps. The truck door doesn't squeak like his old one as he climbs inside the cab.

The quiet house looms behind me, oppressive, suffocating. Empty.

I'm tired of being alone, and the words shoot out of me before I can pull them back. "Hold on! You could stay. I've probably got some ice cream, or we can order your favorite— Chinese. I won't even complain about the vegetables or cringe when you eat the hot peppers. We could watch movies. We could study."

Once the words start, I can't seem to stop them. I keep going on, talking about his favorite things, about geometry. He shakes his head, his AD hairstyle falling over his eyes. I can't see their color, if they are blue or green right now, if they are angry, sad, indifferent.

But I'm guessing indifferent because he still cranks the engine.

He's still leaving.

Anger helps me muster strength. "We're meeting for tutoring. Study hall. Tomorrow."

He gives me a thumbs-up out the window, engine revving as he peels away.

I'm not sure he even heard me.

6

A Million Miles Away ~ The Plimsouls

My snores wake me up. They're loud. So loud the students sitting closest snicker. Which of course alerts Mr. Luna.

I slide down in my seat and press my hand to my knee to stop it from bouncing against the underside of my desk. Everyone stares when all I want is to be invisible.

"Prudence Spellmeyer! How kind of you to rejoin us." Mr. Luna crosses his spindly arms over his bowed chest and frowns.

I knew I shouldn't have slept on the sofa last night—if you can call staring at the ceiling until you black out as sleeping. And worse, no Davis dreams. Just a stiff neck. My skin prickles, and I run my cold palm across the back of my hot neck. I know Mr. Luna expects me to sit straight at attention. What I want is to succumb to gravity and let it pull me under the desk, preferably through the floor and deep into the center of the earth's molten core where I could properly disintegrate into ash and nothingness. It takes all my willpower to fight through this half-asleep, sticky molasses brain fog to move.

I wish I were home. Why did I promise Dad I'd slog through classes today? All I can think about is Mom.

"Miss Spellmeyer, did you fall back asleep?"

I never saw him move from the podium to my desk, and I jump at the proximity of his voice.

With an impatient sigh, Mr. Luna runs his knobby fingers through his white, thinning hair. "Well?" he asks, and I realize he expects an answer. To a question I never heard.

Normally, I love Luna's class. History is all things known, all things safe. Yet Luna's class is also challenging. He is stingy with his grades and the tests are an absolute bitch to pass. Some of the most exciting events since the beginning of time have died a dullsville death in this classroom. But he takes his history seriously. And his teaching style? It's a totally glorious one-sided thing. Purely lecture. No sad song and dance where the teacher asks the stupid student a question only to have the stupid student give a stupid answer. If they even have one at all. The whole ridiculous event snowballs until the entire classroom needs to stop and consider the question, holding the lecture up until the blessed bell rings.

And right now, *I* am that stupid student. "Um… what's the question again?"

The quiet chuckles grow into outright laughter.

Mr. Luna shakes his head. "What ended in 1896, Miss Spellmeyer?"

My mind is blank. I know I should know this. But all I hear are Dad's urgent knocks on my bedroom door and my cruel words thundering through my brain in an endless earworm I can't silence.

"We don't need your help. We don't need you at all, Mom."

"Miss Spellmeyer. Your answer."

"Uh… 1895?"

The class explodes.

Mr. Luna struggles to regain control and quiet the students while I pray for the floor to swallow me whole. The bell answers my prayer instead. I'm out the door faster than a speeding spit-wad. This day can't end fast enough.

Today's block period—Spanish class—is buried at the back of campus. I take my sweet time walking there but instantly regret it. I should have booked it and gotten there early.

Steve and Maddi block the entrance, hanging all over each other, thirsty and pathetic, as though it's been fifty years since their last suckfest. Like he didn't spend an entire night at her house. Stopping abruptly, I search for a way to slip past them unnoticed, but in my sudden stop, someone slams into me from behind, pitching me forward.

Steve and Maddi jump and pull apart. Steve steps forward, reaching out to stop my clumsy ass from slamming into Maddison.

"Careful." His hands are as warm and gentle as his voice when he squeezes my shoulders. Then he looks me in the eyes. "Hey, how are you holding up?"

Did he really ask that? I'm transported to BD times by the way his brow furrows with concern, his eyes shifting from green to blue and back again, mesmerizing.

But his lips are all swollen and smeared with Maddi's bubblegum-pink lipstick. I resist the urge to wipe them clean with my thumb, then check over his shoulder for the clout demon herself. Her face is so red her head might explode. Flipping me off, she turns and stalks into the classroom. The little zing running through me at her response would make me smile if there were a valid reason for her to hate me. I don't know why she's so pissed. It's not like Steve actually ditched her for me last night. He crawled right back over to the she-witch after staying with me a total of ten lousy minutes.

I step back, widening the gap between me and Sleazle.

His hands drop to his sides, and his eyebrows shoot beneath his bangs.

"I'm fine," I finally mumble, staring at the floor. "I'll be fine. Everything's fine."

My words don't sound fine even to my ears.

Steve runs a hand through his hair and tugs his earlobe like he always used to do when he was frustrated or confused. "OK. That's good. Um. Tell Joyce I am thinking about her. See ya."

He turns and I watch him move stiffly down the hall till he disappears around the corner.

I rub my shoulder where the loss of his hand on my arm has my skin feeling cold and achy. If we can't look at each other or talk freely, how are we going to manage tutoring?

When I enter the classroom, the only seat left is the one directly in front of Maddison. The second I sit, she starts kicking my chair. No bueno, bitch-o. My temples pulse in time with her stomps, but if I grab her foot, turn around, or say anything, things will get worse. Slinking low in my seat but keeping my eyes on the teacher, I unzip the main pocket of my backpack and dip into my open bag of Jolly Ranchers, quietly slipping one out of the wrapper and onto my tongue. Sweet watermelon bliss helps me endure the remaining hour.

When the bell rings, I slip on my earbuds. They are purely for show, not music. Maddi's lips move to say something, but I shrug, pointing to my ears.

"Can't hear you," I yell in her face, giving her a forced smile.

She rolls her eyes and stalks out the door. Thank God I don't have to see or deal with her the rest of the day. Tossing two extra candies into my mouth, I hang in the doorway to make sure Maddi is gone before I head down the hall.

I arrive at geometry in time to hear the words *pop quiz* leave Mr. Roderick's mouth. The candy on my tongue turns sour and my head pounds as fast as my heart.

He has the test positioned on my desk before I even sit.

"Um, Mr. Roderick? I've got a real bad headache. I think I might throw up. Nurse pass?"

He hands me the overflowing trashcan from beside his desk. Fabulous.

Squeezing the back of my neck, I shut my eyes against the image of Steve pulling from the driveway in his truck, his unclear response to my tutoring demands hovering on the air. Before me, the quiz is a riddle, some unintelligible language I'll never decipher.

"When you're done, find your test from last week." Mr. Roderick points to a pile of exams on the corner of his desk.

Even more fabulous. Let's let the entire classroom see I can't solve a single freaking problem in geo-hell. Who puts everyone's business out on display anyway, Roderick? There should be a law against this or something.

I look back at the quiz. It's no more decipherable than before. My stomach clenches and I spit my half-eaten candies into the garbage. You know it's bad when sugar makes it worse.

I'm the last to finish, big surprise, so my test's all alone, front and center on Roderick's desk, the big, fat, red F taking up more space than my name at the top of the page. Beneath that in big block letters is *TRY HARDER!* Like I haven't been. Like I'm somehow capable of pulling an A out of my ass. Like I've been completely faking my ineptitude this entire time. I wanna crumple it into a ball and heave it in the trash

While Mr. Roderick drones on and on and on about finding sine and cosine in triangles, I torture myself by thumbing through the stapled pages. The note on the front isn't the only one. Page two is riddled with some kind of pen-explosion fallout—red slashes everywhere punctuated by *NO!* and *???* and *SHOW YOUR WORK!*

Page three, he's actually taken the time to write something more. *You're close on some accounts. Your thinking is on the right path. If you applied yourself, you would find better results. Aim for a passing grade. Surely, it's within your reach if you study. APPLICATION IS NECCESARY TO PASS THIS CLASS!*

I slouch in my seat and stare out the window. Sunlight glints through a crack in the pane, and within the rainbow prism of glass, I imagine the outline of city skyscrapers. Then the sun drifts behind a cloud. I watch as the hopeful visions, my well-laid future plans, vanish. The distorted reflection of my shocked and hollow eyes stares back, and the feeling that I'm forever falling through darkness overwhelms me. My thoughts are an old cassette that keeps getting recorded over until everything left is blurred gibberish. Pass this class... pass this class... pass this class... All their voices repeat at once: Mom's, Mrs. Peterman's, Mr. Roderick's.

When the bell rings, Roderick glances my way and crooks his finger, but another student steps between us to ask a question, enabling me to rush out the exit while staring at the floor and pretending I didn't notice.

I haven't set foot in the cafeteria for years. Davis, Steve, and I always left campus to eat at home or at Giallanza's. All winter long, the popular crowd takes the cafeteria over, but when the sun comes out like today, they crawl out of their snake pit and scatter. AD, I feel awkward and conspicuous eating alone in a room swarming with noise and friendship, so I'm usually outta dodge the second the lunch bell trills, no matter the weather. But when I see the mass of bodies clumped at the front doors, I backtrack and follow the stink that is definitely *not* pizza toward the lunchroom.

Lucky me. It's Kung Pao crap day. I hate cafeteria-ized Chinese food with its too many unidentifiable vegetables submerged like bad surprises in viscous sauces. And those little red peppers are *nasty* hot. Steve could binge eat all of mine, his, and Davis's and barely sniffle. I tried one once and cried for days. I can still taste that bitter burn in my mouth.

Grabbing a fistful of teriyaki packs and a little fried rice, I take up the seat of power against the wall near the back door. It will do. With my feet in the chair across from mine, backpack and all its contents sprawled across my table, head down, elbows out, earbuds firmly in place, you'd think it's obvious this table seats one.

But no.

Bruce is short but mighty. The air crackles when he moves as though his aura is consuming it. He's quirky and different, the kind of person I have always been in awe if not a little jealous of. He is true to himself, comfortable anywhere and with anyone. He doesn't upset or embarrass easily; in fact, nothing ever seems to get to him. He isn't exactly popular, but everyone knows and loves him because of how easygoing he is and how quick he is to make others laugh.

Basically, Bruce is everything I am not.

"Hot, hot, hot!" Bruce chants, and sets his tray on the table, pushing my pack aside. "Your shirt!" he points, practically jabbing me in the chest, and pulls the chair out from under my feet, which hit the ground with a *thump*. "The Cure, right? I love that song!" And then he *stands* on my former footrest and *belts* the lyrics at me in some twisted version of a serenade. He sings the *hey, hey, hey* lines with an exaggerated growl, head thrown back and fists pumping. On the *hot, hot, hot* lyrics, he swivels his hips.

Oh God. This isn't happening.

I'd bolt out the door, but the few people in here are standing, staring, and blocking the nearest exit. All eyes on Bruce means all eyes on me. I slide down in my seat, watching him through splayed fingers and wishing for spontaneous death.

On the last line, he slips his hand under his shirt and pops his fist in and out, mimicking a heart hammering out of his chest, then jumps off the chair with a low bow.

Everyone laughs and claps. Bruce sings well—he even sounds a lot like Robert Smith—and his theater antics are nothing abnormal. For Bruce, anyway.

He peels my hands from my face. "Oh, c'mon, Pru! Don't wear it if you don't wanna sing it, right?"

I groan and start emptying pack after pack of teriyaki into my rice bowl. I don't know how to tell him 80s music depresses me now despite my being a walking ad for it. Despite having been the one to introduce him to all my favorite songs last year.

He sits and stuffs an egg roll in the corner of his mouth, gnawing on the end as he studies me.

"So, is all that retro music too yesterday for you or something?" he teases.

I don't really want to be the sad, depressing girl who only talks about her dead brother. Besides, whenever I try, my tongue gets frozen and my brain ties itself into knots. Everything comes out backward and awkward. Either I become a sharp-toned snarky bitch or a blithering idiot. "I'm just a little tired. That's all."

"I get it," he mumbles as he chews. "Happy Crap-iversary."

"Crappa-what? You mean this mystery food masquerading as lunch?"

"Ha. No. Crap-iversary—the anniversary date of your world turning to shit. Mine was a few weeks ago. Yours is coming up. But usually, those of us unlucky enough to have a crap-iversary wallow at least the entire month." Bruce puts the half-eaten roll back on his tray. "It's allowed."

He slides his glasses off his nose and rubs them with the hem of his shirt. His ragged fingernails blur as his thumb spins around and around and around the lens. I'm not sure, but he may be crying. The sight is strange. I've known him since kindergarten, and he's always been the same ole happy-go-lucky guy.

"Bruce? Are you OK?"

His voice is soft, and I have to lean forward to hear him better.

"Derek and Donny. My cousins? They lived three and a half hours away, but we were close. I spent many summer breaks at their place. They lived off a lake and we would spend most of our time swimming, fishing, and floating on inner tubes for hours until we were so sunburned and waterlogged we could barely move."

Bruce stops cleaning his glasses, looks up, and smiles. His eyes are misty as he stares out the window with a faraway gaze, lost in some memory I can't see. I am acutely aware of his use of the past tense though, and my arms turn hot and cold at the same time—sweaty and prickly yet covered in goosebumps.

"Seven years ago, late spring, Derek was chasing Donny across the icy lake, except it wasn't fully frozen at the center. Donny fell through when the ice cracked beneath him, and Derek jumped in to help him. They both drowned. They were twins. Only eight years old. My aunt and uncle blamed each other. They couldn't get past it, got a divorce, moved away out of state. Both live as far from here and each other as possible."

When Bruce pauses to take a drink, I smile and nod in a way that's hopefully encouraging but then realize that normal people never smile when discussing the taboo D-words: death and divorce. Yet here I am, an idiotic grin plastered on my face, lips lodged against my teeth so tight my cheeks ache as much as my heart. I suck in a shaky breath that rattles louder than I intended.

I know I should do something—anything. Lay my hand on his forearm, say something profound or helpful. But as I sit here, overthinking everything and unable to budge or speak, Bruce surprises me by reaching over and patting *my* arm in comfort instead. Then he settles against his seat, limbs all loose and fluid and way more relaxed than I ever could be while sharing such a painful truth. I don't know how he can be so calm when his memories must feel like yesterday, same as mine.

"We never heard from Aunt Georgie again, and she was my favorite. I haven't gone swimming since. I can't play sports, not anything involving a ball of any kind—that was Derek's thing. And I swear Donny had a built-in ice cream truck radar, so I can't eat ice cream either. I've tried. Everything gets stuck"—he pats the base of his throat and swallows hard—"right here."

I know I should say something, but what?

"We *maybe* get a Christmas card from Uncle Marcus once a year? I miss him too, you know? But he told Mom he can't see us, can't bear the *knowing* in our eyes. The grief, I guess. Maybe one day." He shrugs and slips his glasses back onto his face. "So. Yeah. I get why music sucks for you now. Again, Happy Crap-iversary."

I do the math on my fingers. "Wait, so you were... ten when they... when..." I can't bring myself to say it.

"When they d-d-d-died?" He grins as he purposefully stutters the word to tease me. "Saying it won't make you keel over. Or maybe it will. That would be kinda funny actually. I hope I die doing something ironic like that."

Sorry never fixes anything and canned responses are tacky, but my brain spins in hyper-overdrive. Hundreds of words I should say collide with images of Davis, Derek, and Donny. Everything blends together into one kaleidoscopic blur till only the lamest words slip out. "I... I'm sorry for your loss."

My friendship skills have thoroughly rusted.

"Nah. No worries. Live hard, die fast, no regrets. Life's too short to be anything but happy." He holds up his hand expecting a fist bump and I reluctantly mash my knuckles against his. It's hard to live when your happiness died. Bruce makes it sound so easy.

He polishes off his egg roll and starts on another while I dribble wads of rice off my fork, watching it form goopy brown mountains in a teriyaki swamp. I'm afraid if I look up, I'll cry. Or worse, I'll accidentally give him the sympathetic pity stare that would only make him feel shitty. My mind whirls with questions. Was Bruce able to shrug things off and be happy because he was so young, or did it take seven years to grow numb? I want to feel now what Bruce seems to feel—content, happy-go-lucky, healed even. But every time I think of Davis, I shatter all over again. I don't think there's anything whole left inside of me to even piece back together.

"Pru, oh, my God. I am so glad I found you. We really need to talk."

Oh my God is right. I should have been watching. I never saw her coming.

Maddi doesn't ask; she just pulls out a chair and sits. Batting her eyes and twirling her glossy hair around her finger, she smiles. Bruce looks from her to me and back again, chomping the end of his straw.

"So, a little Stevie-bird told me that you were having trouble with geometry."

It's like she kicked me in the stomach. All my air rushes out in a groan I didn't intend to make, and my eyes bug out in surprise before I can narrow them. Maddi smiles bigger.

"Trouble is…" She leans forward, crossing her arms on the table and dropping her voice in a conspiratorial whisper as though we gossip together all the time. "Stevie and I have plans after school every day. There's no time for him to help. I would totally hate it if you couldn't graduate because you can't pass one simple class. Your perfect parents are accountants; aren't they supposed to be good at math?" Her voice is as sing-song sweet as her smile, but her eyes flash dangerously sharp and bright.

"I think accounting and geometry are two totally different things, Maddison," Bruce answers for me the same way Davis would have done. I am grateful because I'm sure all that would come out of my mouth if I opened it right now is the scream ringing in my head. Instead, I clamp my lips tight, stare at the table, and remember to breathe while the room spins. Did Steve really tell her… everything?

Ignoring Bruce, she reaches past him and pats the table in front of me. "Besides, spending time with someone who can't stand the sight of you would suck, don't you think?"

She stands, planting her palms on the center of the table, leaning in, and towering over me. "Seriously, Pru. Find someone else to tutor your sorry ass."

Her smile vanishes as she pushes my lunch toward my lap. Reflexively, I throw my hands up to block the bowl.

The tray flips up into the air.

Maddi's eyes widen and Bruce lets out a low "Oooooooo" as mounds of teriyaki splatter across the tabletop—and Maddi's sweater.

She screams. "This is *cashmere*, you cow!"

Everything stops. The room is *still*. So still I can hear Bruce breathing.

"Just—just—" Her face is pinker than her sweater. *"Just stop fucking up my life!"*

The door slams behind her as she runs off outside. The room springs back to life. Chairs scrape loudly across the floor as everyone rushes to watch her out the window. It's the perfect opportunity to grab my crap and leave before the attention returns to me.

"Gotta go, Bruce." I toss my uneaten lunch in the trash and eat another Jolly Rancher instead.

Bruce laughs. "Hey, you can't really take Maddi seriously when she's wearing those pink-rhinestone combat boots."

But Bruce is wrong.

Steve hasn't called or texted me once to talk about geometry. He drove off when I tried to schedule our first tutoring session. He's conspiring with the enemy, betraying me when he used to be the keeper of my secrets.

I should take Maddi seriously.

Because Steve's not the guy I remember him being.

7

Secret ~ Orchestral Manoeuvres in the Dark

After classes finish, I consider sticking around to see if Steve has bothered showing up for tutoring. But as I cut across the back lot, heading toward the tin-can mobile home they call study hall, my stomach churns and my palms sweat. I wouldn't normally believe a word that comes out of Maddi's lying mouth, but everything she said about Steve checks out in my mind. I don't think he intends to help. The more I think about it, the heavier my legs feel and the harder it is to trudge across the grass. Even if he's there—which he likely isn't—I can't bear to see her truths written across his face.

Ten feet from the door, I pivot and leave. Besides, it's like Bruce said—no regrets. And Mom is at home. Fixed, feeling better, and waiting for me. For the first time in forever, she might have the motivation to sit with me, talk with me. She might have a solution to my geometry woes; after all, she did offer to help yesterday. And BD, she was great at finding the solution to anything—at brainstorming, puzzling, making everything work...

And despite my worry that she might hold what I said about not needing her against me, I have hope. My steps are stronger, lighter, the second my feet hit the sidewalk.

There's a strange car parked behind Dad's in the drive—a boxy SUV the color of grape cough syrup with a bumper sticker that says *I BRAKE FOR BOOKS* and a stick-figure family of five plus a dog in the corner of the rear windshield. The cooling engine ticks beneath the hood as I pass.

"We're in here, Pru." Dad calls from the living room when I open the door.

Dropping my bag, I run down the hall, ready to see Mom, but nearly bowl over a string bean of a bald guy blocking the entryway.

"Pru, this is Mr. Devin McKittrich."

"Hello." Mr. McKittrich stares down at me, chomping and popping a huge wad of gum. "Nice to meet you, Prudence." His hot, sweaty hand dwarfs mine. I resist the urge to pull back the second his slick palm wets my skin.

Craning my neck to see around him, I take in the spotless living room. All of Dad's clothes and blankets are gone, the freshly vacuumed carpet, the room smelling of fake pine. Mom is scrunched up in one corner of the couch. She's in fresh clothes, her hair is brushed, and she even has a touch of makeup on. She looks up briefly to smile and nod at me but then returns her gaze to some colorful pamphlet clutched in both her hands. She opens and closes it in time with Mr. McKittrick's gum snaps.

Dad stands stiffly behind the sofa, one hand in his pocket jingling his car keys, the other on Mom's shoulder. He only plays with his keys or pocket change when he's overthinking stuff.

Something's off.

I want to go sit with them, but this McKittrich fellow blocks my path.

"Pru, Mr. McKittrich asked you a question," Dad says

For someone so big, his voice sure sounds small. I obviously didn't hear his question, and I hardly hear him when he speaks again. "No biggie. Prudence can take a minute to adjust to my being here."

Dad's frown says it *is* a biggie. He's jingling his keys again, Mom's wrinkling the brochure. They both look stressed. So, instead of serving up the daily dose of cow pie that's my entire scholastic world, I lie.

"Senior year's a good year." I tack on a smile and shrug for good measure.

Mr. McKittrich blows a small bubble and snaps it with his oversized buckteeth while he stares at me. "We spoke with the school. It seems you're failing geometry." He rocks back on his spindly spider legs. "And frequently skip class?"

"She went today," Dad announces, and Mom grabs his wrist, shaking her head.

My tongue is dry. I reach into my pocket for a candy, but they are all in my backpack by the front door. It's hard to force any words. "I'm here to see my Mom."

"And I'm here to see you." Mr. McKittrich's eyes bulge when he smiles.

"Why?"

"Necessary family services protocol for suicide attempts."

He crosses the room to where his briefcase is open on the coffee table and slides out a clipboard with papers and a pen attached. Sitting in the recliner, he stretches and crosses his impossibly long legs at the ankles. "Let's start with your grades."

Mom and Dad exchange nervous glances. Neither looks so good. Both are pale. Mom is squeezing Dad's hand so tight I can see the whites of her knuckles, and Dad's pulled the keys clear out of his pocket now, gripping them tightly.

"My grades are passing." I swallow hard around the lie and tick off my wins on my fingers. "Cs in history and English, an A in art—"

"My concern is your F in geometry."

"Actually, I have a plan for geometry."

Mr. McKittrich clicks the end of his pen. "Go on."

"Well, first off, I knew I needed… *help*, so I went to the counselor's office, and they set me up with a tutor." I make sure to look him in the eye to sell the lie. I don't twitch, I don't chew my lip, I don't blink. "We've created a solid study plan already."

"You and this… tutor?"

"Yes. Me and this tutor. Steve Nolan, actually. If you need to write down his name."

And he actually does, nodding and scribbling notes on his paperwork. "It's a start."

It's unclear if he actually believes me. At least Mom does, I think. She sits up straighter at the mention of Steve's name, a small smile bringing a soft glow to her gaunt cheeks.

Mr. McKittrick's jaw must be sore; he hasn't stopped snapping his gum once since I got here. "My main job is to ensure your safety and well-being. Not just scholastically, but here. At home." He glances toward the sofa before leaning forward. "Tell me, Prudence. How have you been holding up since your brother passed? I know. I know. Terrible question, right? But in light of the current situation with Joyce, I—"

"That was a mistake," Mom blurts. "An accident."

The small hairs on my neck rise. Mom's voice is a whine I've never heard from her. She doesn't sound confident or calm. She doesn't look fixed or better. The makeup, the pressed clothes—all of it is fake. A disguise hiding the ugly truth: BD Mom is still gone.

McKittrich ignores her, his bugged-out eyes stuck on mine. "Suicide attempts are taken seriously, Prudence. I'm afraid we can't risk—"

Dad steps forward and hands McKittrich the brochure mom had been holding. If McKittrich didn't bring the pamphlet, then why do Mom and Dad have it ? What else is going on?

"Joyce is receiving help and will be staying at Oakmont for a few weeks," Dad tells him. "Pru will be fine here with me."

McKittrich takes the pamphlet, snapping his gum. "An outstanding facility." He drags a folded paper from between the pages. "Contract signed? Done deal? She starts tonight?"

"Yes." Dad clears his throat, jangles his keys again. "We are heading out as soon as you're finished talking with Pru."

What the heck is Oakmont? What does dad mean by *heading out*?" I look to mom for answers, but she's hugging her knees muttering, "An accident, an accident, an accident."

"There was an accident."

I slam my eyes shut. Open them again. Mom's eyes are scrunched tight, blocking the room out. Blocking *me* out. Moving to the sofa, I sit as close to her as I can, but still she rocks. Her whimpers grow louder. I rub my forehead, instantly lightheaded. I don't know what she needs. I don't know what to do. When I lightly touch her back, her muscles tremble beneath my fingertips.

McKittrich clicks his pen again, chewing his gum vigorously. "Prudence? You feel all right with this?" he asks.

All right with *what*? I'm not sure what I'm agreeing to, but Dad is nodding, so I do too. My focus is shot. Words and images fly through my head, but I can't stop to digest any of it. All I am left with is more questions and zero answers and a sickening dread in the pit of my stomach.

"OK then. I'm not recommending foster care. However, my influence and thus leniency in this is limited. Larry, it's imperative that you monitor Pru's schoolwork and attendance. To stay in your household, she must remain non-truant the rest of the year with a focus on geometry and graduation. If she misses any classes, I'll be contacted. Infractions will result in a placement, and there will be little I can do to prevent it. We can reassess things when Joyce returns."

Handing the brochure and contract to Dad, he stands, puts his clipboard in his briefcase and closes it, then pulls a bent business card from his shirt pocket and hands it to me. "If you ever need to talk, call my office. My secretary will schedule a therapy session."

I do not respond.

He shakes my hand, then Dad's. He looks to AD Mom. "Good luck, Joyce. If anyone can help, it's the professionals at Oakmont. Best facility in the area."

Dad walks him to the door. When I hear it close, Dad reappears pulling a wheely suitcase from the hall that I hadn't noticed in my rush to see Mom.

She's really leaving. And the sad part is that I don't know if it will feel any different here with her gone. Mom has been gone all year. But will this really bring her back?

Dad sits beside me on the couch. He lets out a gush of air as though he'd been holding his breath this entire time. Then he takes one of my hands, and Mom takes the other.

I should feel comforted, but I don't. Mom's hand is cold and frail. Dad's grip is overly tight. I feel small and insignificant sandwiched between them.

I want to fall into the cocoon of their embrace, especially after craving this for so long. But I can't tolerate their attempts at comforting me when I know they need it just as much themselves. How am I supposed to make them feel any better when I am stuck in the same mess as they are?

Mom reaches out and draws a heart on my cheek with her shaky finger. "Shh," she whispers. "Don't cry."

Was I crying? I didn't realize. But as soon as she speaks, as soon as she touches me, it's exactly like BD times. I sag against her, ugly sobbing, leaking snot and spit all over her clean, checkered blouse while she holds me and Dad rests his warm hand on the top of my head.

"Why do you have to leave?" I manage to huff out between hiccups.

"I just need to get my footing, Prudie," Mom whispers as she stands. "But I need you to do something for me. Study hard with Steve. Go to all your classes. And *be here* when I get back."

"Pru, I'll be getting a room near the facility and staying the night, but I'll be back before school is over tomorrow. Call me if you need anything. There's pizza money on the kitchen counter."

He'll be gone all night? The last thing I want right now is to be alone. But Dad is helping Mom into her coat. This is really happening. My body goes numb, my head and heart empty and heavy.

"Mom…" It comes out as a scratchy whine, and I bite my lip to stop from crying again.

"I'm so proud of you, Pru. I want to be as strong and brave as you. I *will* be," Mom says.

Dad puts a hand on her back, guiding her toward the door. When they leave, he glances over his shoulder. "Call me. For anything. I mean it, Pru. Go to class. I'll see you tomorrow after school."

The door clicks shut, but I stand there staring at the floor until I hear the muffled engine sounds vanish down the street.

I turn around to face an empty house. Again. I wander, unsure what to do with myself.

Passing the dining room, I yank a dusty streamer from the wall. Then I feel bad, knowing this would hurt Mom, so I tape it back up.

I need chocolate.

In the kitchen, I'm reaching to pull a bowl down from the overhead cupboard when I bump dad's open briefcase with my elbow. The case crashes to the floor before I can catch it, spilling all Dad's work folders across the floor.

Crap.

Thankfully Dad's pretty organized, and I am able to match most papers to their proper client folders. I even take the extra time to sort things by date for him. The repetitive motions are surprisingly calming. Until I spot a bunch of letters addressed to Dad. I don't really want to read them, but I see mentions of Mom…

Dear Larry,

Over the years we have been more than pleased with your agency's accounting skills and customer service. The attentive care you and Joyce always provided made your agency stand out above the competition.

However, it's not without notice that Joyce no longer works with you at Spellmeyer Accounting. We feel it's best to move on with a firm that provides the same or similar service you used to give.

We understand how challenging it must be to run the firm alone during your time of need. Unfortunately, the lack of Joyce's eyes and hands on this year's filing resulted in costly errors. We will need to re-document, correct, and re-submit everything to the IRS along with requesting an extension—something we haven't had to do before. We hope to avoid an audit.

It is our sincere hope your family finds the support you need.

All our best,
Matthew and Marci Emmons
Emmons Dry Cleaning and Catering

Errors. Something absolutely unlike Dad and Mom. It hurts to see that. It hurts to know it happened even though it makes sense. But also, what the hell? There's six more *sorry not sorry* bullshit letters. *Six!* All of them with the same condescending tone. All of them hinting at knowing everything when they really know nothing. All of them apologizing but not really meaning it. Instead, they judge, they abandon Dad, they blame Mom.

I'm sure Dad hasn't shown her any of these letters. They would devastate her.

Mom has to get better. For herself, for me, and for Dad.

I scout the living room for that Oakmont paperwork and, finding it, skim the bold text.

...top-rated facility... first-class care... elite accommodations... award-winning therapy programs... privately funded... minimal occupancy... individualized attention... focus on grief and healing... suicide prevention ... intensive but loving environment...

Flipping through the pages shows photos of their cozy bedrooms and therapy areas. Spacious and colorful gardens. Plates of rich meals and heaping desserts.

OK. So not a hospital at least. But the relief only weakens my limbs.

Mom was wrong. She should know I have never been brave or strong. I have always leaned on her, on Davis, on Dad for every little thing.

Pulling the contract out from between the back pages sends a small scrap of paper fluttering to my feet. I lift it up and smooth it out.

My appetite vanishes.

My gut twists.

This isn't happening.

But the truth stares back, taunting me, no matter how many times I close and re-open my eyes.

Dad is selling the Monte Carlo.

I re-read the advertisement. Each pass-through sharpens the tang of bile on the back of my tongue, the taste of my AD shitty luck. The rotted flavor of secrets and loss.

When did we go from being a family that shared everything to one divulging nothing? To one deciding on life-changing moves without consulting one another? I can't find Davis without the Gherkin. I can't lose him again.

How could Dad do this?

And then I notice the cost for Mom's stay at Oakmont, printed in bold black ink at the bottom of the contract: ten grand.

For *one week*.

The grand total is the exact amount Dad is asking for the Monte Carlo. And he's likely to find someone who'd buy it for that much too, working or not working. It's rare.

But to me, it's priceless.

The room's so quiet I hear my ragged breaths through the tinnitus in my ears.

I drop the papers. They flutter into Dad's case as my vision blurs, and I slam the vile thing shut. Push it so hard across the floor it bangs into the fridge and bounces back. My head understands. But my heart? It's tearing in two, ripping under the force of an impossible choice.

Keep Davis? Or fix Mom?

WWDD?

The answer doesn't come.

"Come on, Davis. What would you do? *What would you do?*"

Screaming the question aloud doesn't summon my brother or bring answers. It only tightens the killer band crushing my chest.

My hands shake as I pace the floor. I can't sit still. There's only one way I know how to help—and that's to stop screwing everything up. The one thing in my control is to pass geometry. Which keeps me living here and takes the pressure off Mom and Dad. And who knows, maybe Steve has a surprise solution for the Monte Carlo too. Time to suck it up and force him to tutor me. Tonight.

Steve's rambling ranch-style house stands watch on the hilltop of Fowler Lane and North Circle Drive, nestled under the limbs of a towering ancient oak. The wraparound porch looks out onto the elementary school playground across the street where we used to spend our weekends and summer days. Except for the rhythmic *thump-a-thump-a-thump-a* of someone dribbling a basketball behind the low brick building, the schoolyard sits silently beneath the dusky glow of the tangerine sunset lighting fire to the sky in its final gasp before surrendering to the night.

A glow spills from Steve's bedroom on the corner, blue and white lights flickering behind the half-open glass. The rallying cry of what I'm sure is some movie sports team in their final playoff moments drifts out to welcome me.

My chest tightens.

You don't have to do this, my mind taunts. *You don't need him, you'll figure it out alone, same as always.*

But I haven't figured anything out, and I'm running out of time.

I drag my rubbery legs up the front steps. The cool wood of the door chills my hot forehead as I rest my throbbing head.

Come on, Pru. Knock already.

But I can't lift my head nor my fist to do so. My limbs are weights, and it zaps every ounce of my energy reserves just forcing my lungs to operate.

I could go home, try again tomorrow...

The door opens, and I stumble into the house.

"Oh my God, were you spying on us, you disgusting creeper?"

Fuck. It's Maddison. Of course.

Her voice is so shrill and loud I'm sure the entire neighborhood heard her scream. I failed to notice her tiny candy apple red sports car hiding in the shadow of Steve's new hulking truck. I should have realized she'd be here. She did admit to monopolizing all his time...

Steve appears behind her, tugging on his earlobe and frowning at me. "What are you doing here, Pru?"

This was a bad idea. It's like Maddi said. He doesn't want to help.

But I keep seeing Mom. The letters in Dad's briefcase. The newspaper advertisement for the Gherkin.

I blink against the pressure building behind my eyes, swallow hard, and hold up my backpack. "Geometry." It's all I can manage to stutter.

"We were supposed to study after school. I waited over an hour, but you never showed up. So you might have guessed that this wouldn't be a good time."

My checks burn. Maddi curls her body into Steve's side, burrowing her face against his neck and twirling a golden lock around her finger. Further showcasing how much of a bad time it is for me to be here, she pulls his skin to her lips, her tongue darting out in small circles.

A hot flush spreads from my cheeks, across my face, and over my scalp when he emits a breathy sigh. I can't bear to watch them, but the living room visible behind them is worse. Maddi's stuff is everywhere. School books sprawled on the sofa, puffy pom-poms on the coffee table, her cheer uniform draped over the back of a chair. I don't belong in his world anymore. The realization makes the room spin and blur.

But no. None of that matters. Mom, Dad, and graduation matter. Not Steve. And definitely not Maddi.

Stick to the plan, Pru.

Maddi whispers something in his ear but all I catch is the mousy squeak of her giggle.

Steve shakes his head, gently pushing her back. "Later, OK?"

Maddi's laugh dies and so does her smile. "But Stevie," she whines, grabbing his hand and thrusting her thumb under the cuff of his navy Henley to rub his wrist. "You promised!"

His blue eyes fire to green. He slips from her grip, pulling his sleeve down and shoving his hand into his pocket. "I said later," he snaps. "This will take an hour tops. You and I can always go tomorrow if—"

"Whatever," Maddi interrupts. She stalks to the kitchen and scoops her phone and keys from the counter. "Don't bother."

She shoulders me into the wall before storming down the porch steps.

"Maddi, wait." He chases her outside, but the *bleep-bleep* of her ruby roadster followed by the car door slamming is the only reply.

"Maddi!"

Her tires squeal, kicking up gravel. I breathe a sigh of relief as she vanishes down the street. But then Steve spins back toward the porch.

"What is going on, Pru? This immature bullshit isn't you."

The motion-sensing light over the garage flickers to life, bathing him in an eerie glow. He looks pale, washed out. Ghostly vapor trails curl past his lips in quick, shallow puffs. I've seen Steve blazing mad only once before. He wore this same expression right before he punched Jake Gunderson in the mouth for calling me a fugly, frizz-headed, bossy bitch in eighth grade.

He'd teased me later just to make me laugh. "You may be bitchy sometimes, but you're far from ugly." When he wrapped his arm around my shoulders, pulling me tight to his chest, I felt safe. His fingers running through my hair made me feel pretty, treasured—something I haven't felt since.

"Are you even listening?" I jump as his voice pulls me out of my reverie. "You can't expect me to drop everything for you. Meet me halfway, Pru. This has gotta stop."

He shoves both hands through his hair, pulling back his curly bangs. His eyes are still an angry green. I want to say something—anything—but my brain shuts down and my throat closes, chocking off my words.

Steve shakes his head, pulls keys from his pocket, and opens the truck door.

He's going after Maddi.

"Mom tried to kill herself." The words burn my throat on their way out, but they root him in place. "There was a social worker who wanted to take me—to take me from Mom and Dad. But Mom's leaving instead. Going to some fancy ass non-hospital hospital in the city. And Dad's selling the Gherkin to pay for it."

"Where? Can she have visitors?"

"I don't know. And it's called Oakmont. Dad said she'd be gone a few weeks."

Steve stares at me, chewing his lip. "OK. Thanks." He opens the door and cranks the engine.

"Hey wait, what about—"

His high beams and poppy rap crap that could only be Maddi's bad influence blast me as he backs down the drive.

"—geometry."

I'm alone. Again.

In his rush to get to Maddi, Steve left the front door open. I should close it, but I can't stop staring. So many memories live in Steve's house. Aside from all things Maddi littering the front room, everything looks exactly the same as it always has. I can still smell food wafting from the kitchen, picture Mr. Nolan sweating at the stove, attempting some new recipe. I can hear Davis's laughter echoing down the hall. I can see Steve's huge smile as he greets us, always happy to see me.

Well, not anymore.

I slam the door shut, closing down that train of thought. Davis would advise me to focus on graduating, on family, because nothing else matters. And Steve isn't family anymore. Wiping my eyes, I sling my pack over my shoulder and begin the chilled walk home. Back to the garage and my beautiful Gherkin, ready to hold me with open arms and whisk me away to the only person left on the planet who hasn't left me.

Not fully.

I won't lose hope on him. I will keep Davis.

8

Wishing (If I Had a Photograph of You) ~ A Flock of Seagulls

P ru crouched in the kitchen of Davis's apartment. Her fist ached as she clenched her t-shirt in a crumpled knot against her chest, pinning her erratic heart in place. She scanned the walls. Peered under the cabinets. Searched the floor. Light streamed from the hall, illuminating the corners, flowing through the room, and warming her skin. No lurking shadow monsters lunged from the cupboards.

Rising on shaky legs, she peered over the edge of the counter. A rhythmic *thud-thud-thud* sounded, raining plaster from the popcorn ceiling and coating the living room carpet in a fine white dust.

"Hey, you made it!" Davis tossed a football into the air, spiraling it into the exact same spot against the ceiling as he had with his last throw. Pru marveled at his precision. "Pru-Pru, go deep."

He lobbed the ball in her direction. Pru cried out as it soared overhead and smashed into the corner of the kitchen. Scrambling to retrieve it, she pressed her hand on the wall as she scooped up the pigskin, but the plaster crumbled beneath her palm. Tarry sludge reeking of rotted meat gummed her fist from fingertip to wrist. Gagging, she ran to the faucet. The sink trembled and the pipes groaned as Pru rammed the handle back with her forearm, but none of the expected water poured from the spout—only flakes of powdery rust.

"Toss it back!" Davis grinned at her, oblivious to the mess.

Pru frowned and pitched him the ball. "Davis, your plumbing isn't—" Her eyes widened as warm water gushed across her clean palm. The slime-free silver basin sparkled and shone as the wet spray danced against her skin and splashed across the counter. Pru glanced over her shoulder at the intact wall, then back to her hand, wiggling her fingers, but she couldn't find a speck of muck anywhere, not even beneath her nails. She closed her eyes and drew a shuddering breath. When she opened them, her hand was the same. Unglued and gunk free.

"What's with this place?" she mumbled.

"Isn't it perfect?" Davis's grin split his face in two as he bobbed on the balls of his feet, unable to stand still. "It's all ours, Pru. Don't you love it?"

When she turned off the faucet, her hands were dry. Pru walked to the corner where her hand had disappeared, pressed her fingers against the hard surface, and scratched at the paint. Music played, soft and muted, as she scraped and prodded. The wall remained sturdy and immobile save for the pulsing bass thrum tickling her fingertips.

"I'm so glad you're here." Davis tugged her sleeve until she turned, then pulled her into a hug. She sagged, limp with comfort in the fog of his cologne. The music swelled. Oingo Boingo. "Where Do All My Friends Go."

"I've been calling and calling, and you finally came," he whispered in her ear. "Come on, let me give you the tour."

"But... this isn't my first—"

He dragged her into the living room. "It's small, but there's enough room for all of us. Steve and I can share the larger bedroom, and you can have the guest room all to yourself. There's only one bathroom, but we can make it work, right? What do you think?"

A rolled bath towel lay jammed into the crack beneath the guest room door, yet light and sparkly glitter motes seeped toward them through the splintered jamb. Pru reached for the knob, but Davis pulled her hand back.

"It's not ready for you yet. I'm still working on it."

Pru traced the swirls on the knotted wooden door. "Davis, why are we here?"

He blinked rapidly. "I live here."

"What's…. here?" Pru pressed.

"Our apartment… Do you feel OK?" His brow wrinkled in concern as he chewed his lower lip.

"You know I'm dreaming, right?"

He reached out and pinched her arm, grinning when she gasped and rubbed her reddening skin. "Does that feel like a dream to you? I called. You came. Took you long enough, but now that you know the way, nothing's lost. If it's a dream, who cares? We're together. Everything's perfect. As it should be."

"Everything *was* perfect… when you were alive. Have you forgotten?"

Davis shuddered and his eye twitched. The song stuttered, a needle skipping across scratched vinyl. "I remember." He collapsed against the wall and ran his hands through his hair. "Sometimes. When it's too quiet and you're not here… that's when I know I need to work harder to make things right." He gestured around the room, and Pru noticed the tremble that rippled across his shoulders and down his arms. "Everything ends, but I'd rather focus on living."

The halo surrounding the guest room door dimmed to a trickle as a blanket of shadow crept across the floor, chilling her ankles. Pru yelped as the shadowy fog climbed her calves, and bolted for the safety of the kitchen.

"You hungry?" She called over her shoulder as she yanked open the fridge, looking for normalcy and sugar, but the interior was crammed with white cardboard Chinese takeout boxes. Bowls of teriyaki-soaked rice filled the freezer.

Pru jumped when she closed the freezer door; Davis had materialized beside her. She never heard or saw him move. But there he was, golden skin shimmering, heat radiating off him in waves. She resisted the urge to pinch him for permanency.

Davis grinned at her over the fridge door, dimple popping. Gently, he shut it. "Close your eyes and hold out your hands."

"Davis, I—"

"Do you trust me?"

"Of course."

"Well?"

Holding her breath, she looked toward the hall expecting inky darkness, but the gentle glow was back. She let the air escape her lungs with a shuddering hiss and let her eyelids droop shut. She sucked her lower lip between her teeth and held out her hands, fingertips brushing the nubby cotton of Davis's t-shirt. His heart beat through the cloth, a gentle metronome that dulled her worries about him, about this place. Her stomach knots unfurled, her muscles relaxed.

Something weighty dipped her hands forward.

"Careful!" Davis laughed, his hands warm and soothing, steadying her grip. "Now open."

Rainbow light pulsed, a flashing strobe that interrupted her vision. Then Pru saw it. She almost dropped the fishbowl materializing in her grip.

"Sampson!" she squealed as the plump golden fish spun in circles and blew bubbles that burst against the glass in rainbow fractals. Water sloshed over the edge, dyeing Pru's skin and the shag carpet a sparkling violet, teal, crimson, and silver. "I forgot about him."

"He was our test drive for a puppy."

"That we failed because we overfed him."

"*You* put chocolate chips in his bowl!"

Pru shrugged and blushed. "I was cheering him up. He was sad that he couldn't hike with us."

Davis ran his fingertip along the rim of the bowl and a low hum rose from the glass. "I think you're forgiven." He winked as Sampson's scales and fins morphed into a rich, thick pelt, floppy ears, and long, fringe-covered legs. The lights shone and the room wavered, the walls fading in and out of focus around them. Davis laughed. A wheezing, breathy gasp.

The fishbowl vanished as the full-sized retriever bounded over Pru's shoulder and zigzagged through the living room. In the middle of the floor, Sampson vigorously shook his strawberry-gold locks, spraying the walls with watercolor splotches. The apartment reeked of wet dog.

"I wish he were real." Pru buried her nose in the dog's musty neck, laughing when he smothered her cheeks with his wet nose and dripping tongue.

"We create our own reality, right? We wanted a dog, we have a dog." Davis pulled Pru to her feet, panting as heavily as Sampson. "Come on. There's more."

He moved closer to the gallery of photographs nailed to the wall, staggering along the way. Concerned, Pru steadied her hand at his elbow as Davis wobbled, but he batted her away and pointed. Before them, row after row of rectangular black-and-white prints were housed beneath glass, each in identical, minimalistic frames. The more Pru tried to count the rows, the more they shifted out of focus, melting into the plaster, merging into a singular movie screen, breaking into hundreds of Mini-Mini-Chicles-sized squares and shifting back again. The effect was dizzying. Pru gripped the counter and turned her focus to Sampson, but the dog was missing.

The music stopped.

Davis bent his angular body toward the pictures, cupping his hand to his ear. Hunched, he shuffled from frame to frame, listening in the heavy silence. His forehead smoothed and his eyes widened. "Yes," he breathed to himself. "Let's start here." Pru gasped as his body stretched like pulled taffy, elongating into something inhuman.

Legs lengthening to the top rung of prints nearest the popcorn-textured ceiling, Davis tapped his finger along the base of the highest black lacquered frame. The pixilated image sprung to life, bulging and scratching beneath the glass as swirling grey fog poured from the corners. Behind the mist, the sparkling flashes flickered like fireflies.

"Davis?" Pru swatted at the moist clouds weaving between her legs, around her shoulders, and through the apartment. She blinked and scrubbed her eyes with her balled fist. The kitchen vanished and the Gherkin sat where the counter and appliances had stood. Pru swallowed hard. Lightning crackled across the ceiling, a spiderweb that pulsed with life as it spread. The engine growled and the car glowed. And then…

The Monte Carlo carved a path through the living room.

Screaming, Pru dove sideways, rolling across the floor. It wasn't far enough. But the phantom car glided through her tensed body, dimpling her skin into chilled gooseflesh despite the building heat of fear.

Belly-down on the carpet, she screamed for her brother. "Davis? Where are you?"

His muffled reply—dampened and distorted as though underwater—was everywhere and nowhere all at once. The fog thickened. She couldn't see Davis anywhere but felt his touch in the clouds that brushed her skin with feather-like fingers.

"With you, same as always. Watch."

Pru squinted into the smoky haze. The scene hovered before her, superimposed over Davis's dreamland apartment, transparent yet vivid and flashing and bright. She could make out the scraggly carpet, the walls, the ceiling, but the apartment visage wavered, shimmering in and out of focus. Pru softened her vision and relaxed…

The Gherkin idled by the side of a damp, dark road. The windows unrolled and the room blossomed spicy-sweet, the air ripe with rain-soaked pine and earthy forest greens. The steady drumming of drops on the hood echoed louder as the engine died. She could make out the three of them—Davis, Steve, and herself lounging in the seats, rolling down the windows, breathing in the sweet humidity. She watched as Davis flung his head out the window like a puppy, closing his eyes in bliss as the rain pelted his face. Pru swallowed past the lump forming in her throat, but the band tightening her chest only further constricted her heart.

"Join me in the car, Pru. Just focus and clap your hands. Try it." His voice echoed from outside the memory.

Pru clapped.

Nothing.

"You have to mean it, Pru."

Of course she meant it. She wanted to be with Davis. She clapped again.

Nothing.

"Hurry!" He coughed, and the image undulated before solidifying again.

She would not lose him. She clapped, hard and solid. Her body bowed and jolted. The room turned black. Each hair on her head and arms rose as she somersaulted through darkness before landing against the slick leather seat.

"Holy shit!"

Inside the car, Pru kneeled, hugging the seat back, and found Steve sprawled across the back bench, his peacock-colored eyes an equal mix of blue and green, heavy-lidded, and locked on hers. His infectious smile, soft and lopsided, lit a fire in the bowl of her belly, warming and filling her with joy and belonging. Beside her Davis sang out of tune to the radio, but his words were staticky white noise.

The apartment vibrated. Pru looked out the Gherkin's windshield. Fog spun in twisting eddies. A pressure built at the back of her neck, and her body lifted off the seat and passed through the roof of the Gherkin. The room glimmered in a wavy haze as the scene changed.

A crowd bellowed.

An announcer's voice rang from some distant corner of the ceiling. *"The tigers are going to the playoffs!"*

The team encircled Davis, hoisting him onto their shoulders. They paraded him up and down the field while the losing opponents slunk to the locker room. The scoreboard flashed in the night sky. Pru raced down the sidelines, grass spongy beneath her shoes.

From the edge of the group, Steve spotted her. He started running, flung his helmet to the field, and lifted her into the air. Round and round they spun, cheeks flushed, hearts hammering, his arms tight around the back of her thighs, suspending her effortlessly. Autumn leaves crunched beneath his feet. The world smelled of foot-long franks, hot charcoal, and triumph. As she slid down his chest, she wrapped her hands around his neck and squeezed. His eyes darkened. For a moment, she thought he might kiss her…

Light flared. Steam hissed across the floor, a twisting cyclone that swallowed the memory and spat out another.

"Slinging high the pizza pie!" John Giallanza's exaggerated Italian accent sent us kids busting up laughing. Especially the Mario 64 bits. *"It's all-a in the wrist-a. Mama-Mia, let's a-go!"*

John and Anne-Marie babysat a preteen Davis, Pru, and Steve while their parents worked. Pru kicked the floor, and the hologram-dream overlay flickered. Musty taupe shag from the apartment poked through the red and black checkered diamonds of the restaurant linoleum. Flour slicked the avocado-green countertops.

Pru watched as Mr. G's round of pizza dough soared into the air, spinning and undulating, the edges dancing. He caught it with the knuckles of his fingers before flipping it toward the ceiling again and again and again.

"Show off," Anne-Marie teased, standing over a bubbling pot of ripe tomato, fresh garlic, and robust spices. The more she stirred, the more Pru's mouth watered.

Davis and Steve mimicked Mr. Giallanza's movements, tossing their little pizza rounds as high as their foreheads.

Pru could go higher. As high as the sky.

"Slinging high the pizza pie," she sang, heaving the dough into the air.

She caught it... with the top of her head. While her memory-self peeled the dough from her forehead, blazing sun glared through the apartment window. Giallanza's faded to mist, drifting with the clouds across the room.

The Nolans' living room solidified in its place. Steve's knee knocked against hers beneath the table as he wriggled in his seat. Pru cringed when he popped yet another pickled jalapeno into his mouth; she sucked harder on her butterscotch candy, scraping it against the back of her loose front teeth. Steve smiled and stuck his tongue through the hole where his were missing. He could shoot milk and soda through his gap. Pru couldn't wait to do the same.

"What's it going to be, Pru? Fold or call?" Mr. Nolan smiled patiently, and Pru returned her attention to the oversized cards clutched in her small hands. He'd told them poker was sorta like Go Fish. She remembered she needed matching numbers, but all hers were different. And she didn't have a single A or even one with a person on it, which Mr. Nolan said were the best ones. High cards, he called them. Her eyes skimmed her low cards. Two. Three. Four. Five. Six. She mouthed the numbers as she read. Steve snickered, and Davis rolled his eyes, running his fingers through the towering pile of black and gold plastic discs Mr. Nolan called chips even though you couldn't eat them. Scrunching her lips tight, she pushed her last three chips into the center of the table. Mr. Nolan folded, but he didn't bend his cards. He just laid them on the table face down.

Davis dropped his cards and dragged her chips to his pile. "Lookit all my threes! I'm the five-card stud!"

Mr. Nolan laughed so hard the table shook against his round belly.

"This one's gonna be good, Pru. The best one yet," Davis's voice boomed behind her, but when she spun, no one was there.

"Davis?"

The fog coalesced into a single dripping wet cloud that drenched the apartment floor.

"Come on, climb inside."

Flashes burst from inside the cloud. The Nolans' living room vanished as Pru stepped forward into the storm…

Metallic streamers dripped down the walls in a waterfall of colorful braids, glittery dancers in the flickering candlelight. Ethereal fairy lights twinkled in every corner. The tablecloth was a starry night sky of purple velvet beneath a silvery crochet overlay. Pru trailed her fingers over the delicate weave. Mom scooped goopy cheesy slices of lasagna into the centers of everyone's plates and Dad clanged his fork against his champagne flute, raising it into the air for a toast.

"To family. And another glorious year of a solid roof over our heads, great food in our bellies, cash in our wallets, and joy in our hearts. To family."

"To family!"

The holographic scene rippled when they clinked their glasses together.

Pru smelled dust and decay beneath the rich meat sauce she licked from her fork and dropped her utensil to her plate.

Steve and Davis still chowed down, silverware scraping loudly against Nana's special china.

Pru blanched.

Ricky Morgan, her dating mistake, materialized beside her, sucking the filling out of a cannoli with loud slurps that bordered on obscene.

Her cell phone vibrated against her leg, sending shocks through her body. The tabletop billowed and bowed as Davis's disembodied voice crackled through the speaker, clipped and monotone: *"He did what? Where are you?"*

Her dress drooped around her waist in tatters.

The Dickster polished off his cannoli, smacking his lips. "Bet you taste even sweeter, babycakes."

Davis roared as he stood, pushing his plate across the table into Ricky's.

The walls moaned. The low, throaty rumble ended with a keening wail as glass detonated from every photograph, the empty frames hurling the shards deep into the carpet.

The fog lifted, carrying the jagged shards and battered frames out the open bay window. Outside, they fell and melted into the uneven front walk. With one final flash, the blinking lights cut out.

The apartment was just an apartment again.

Davis crumpled, wheezing and clutching his chest as he slumped against the wall.

"Davis!" Pru screamed, running to his side. "It's OK. We're just dreaming, it's OK."

Davis scoffed. "We aren't dreaming. We're thriving! Didn't you notice every detail? Don't you remember every moment?"

"I'm barely surviving," Pru mumbled, staring at the floor.

"Fresh beginnings appear when you stop embracing endings. Can't you feel it Pru?" Davis tapped his finger over her heart. "Our new start is right here. In our apartment. Right now."

"I miss you, Davis!" She sucked her quivering lower lip into her mouth, batting impatiently at her tears.

"I'm right here, doofus." He nudged her shoulder with his in their old teasing way. "I'll always wait for you. Right here." He patted the carpet, releasing plumes of fetid dust into the air. "I'll mend the pictures. I'll clear the guest room. I'll rework each memory until I get them right." He winced and rubbed his temple. "Everything's under control. We have it all. Nothing has to change."

Pru nodded and chewed her lip. Sure, Davis was right here with her as he stated, but everything was different than her life with him before. She wasn't sure this new beginning he was so excited for was something to embrace. The apartment was dark. Creepy. The memories off and twisted. Still, the thought of losing him and this dreamland raised a cyclone of fear that spun up from her stomach, tore through her heart, and ravaged her brain.

Maybe she could help him get it right. Keep him with her forever.

Pru sneezed and wiped carpet fibers from her face, shook dirt from her hair. "Housekeeping's gotta step it up. This place is falling apart. Where's the superglue?" Pru asked, but the joke felt weak.

Even so, Davis's eye twitched and the lights flickered. His hands shook as he clapped them. "Music. Music is the glue stick that makes memories stronger. Better." He coughed—a dry, rattling rasp. "But you've stopped listening." On the third clap, the song started. Faster than normal, then slowed way down. It took Pru a moment to make out the words. "Don't You (Forget About Me)" by Simple Minds. The tune drifted from the street below, ruffling the moth-eaten curtains, filling the apartment with discordant notes.

In the corner, Davis rocked, singing along off-key. "Don't, don't, don't, don't. Don't you... forget about me..." He twitched and bolted upright when she touched his shoulder.

The lights zapped out. A piercing screech emanated from the roof as the ceiling peeled back, exposing a star-filled sky.

"Hey, Pru!" Davis grinned, pulling her into a tight hug. "You finally came!"

9

Last Night I Dreamt That Somebody Loved Me ~ The Smiths

A low screeching pulls me awake. Takes me a second, but I realize the driver's side door is opening, and there's a large shadow climbing inside the car.

Screaming, I rise and pummel the hulking form with Davis's letterman jacket.

"Woah—it's me, it's OK, Pru. It's me!" He scrambles backward out of the car. Pushing the seat forward, I follow.

"Steve? You scared me to death."

"Sorry. Didn't know you'd be out here."

"How'd you… I thought I locked the garage door…"

"You did. I still have a key." He shakes a keychain, and a clanging rattle sounds.

The open car door stands between us, the dim glow of the dome light accentuating the chiseled lines of his face. Through the smudged window, his body wavers and distorts, reminding me of my dream. Of Davis. Loss burns on the back of my tongue.

I don't want to be awake.

"What are you doing here anyway?"

"I... um... when you said your folks were selling the Gherkin... I had to see it. One last time." He holds my gaze, his eyes deep and piercing. My twisted mind flashes to my dream of Steve holding me in the air, eyes locked on mine. Warmth washes over my skin and I look away, busying my fingers by fishing out my cell.

"At 2 a.m.?" I wave my phone screen at him.

"Yeah. Well. After all your games today, I couldn't sleep." He turns and paces the garage, dragging his hand down the hood of the Gherkin.

A slow blaze sparks low in my stomach as I slam the car door shut. He flinches before the shadows swallow us.

"What do you mean by games?" My voice sounds thick with sleep, but every nerve ending in my body activates.

"You call me with family emergencies but avoid me at school. You need tutoring but can't be bothered to show. You arrive on my doorstep unannounced and expect the world to stop spinning. What the hell do you want from me, Pru? We aren't exactly buddies anymore."

The word *buddies* comes out hard, sour. His voice is sandpaper scraping me raw. My cheeks sting and my entire body aches. I squeeze my eyes shut and see Davis. Dreamland. All the happy memories he showed me. All of it gone. Steve's presence is a weighted anchor dragging at my limbs. A chronic depression reminding me of the present, ripping me from Davis, dragging me underwater.

I can't breathe.

"Well, I am alone, aren't I? You made sure of that when you killed my fucking brother."

The room's so quiet I can hear him swallow. Twice. His footsteps shuffle forward. His voice is raw as he speaks, as he reaches for me, fingertips grazing my temple before dropping to his side. "It was an accident."

I can't make out his expression in the dark, but I see him shift his weight and run his hands through his hair before tugging on his ear. He's nervous. Or hiding something. I hear Dad's words ringing in my head: *"Steve was drinking. Davis is gone."*

Steve's lie ignites a fire in my core. It was not an accident. Why did I think I could trust him again?

Pain and pressure build behind my eyes. "Bullshit. You made a choice."

"*Choice?* What *choice?*"

"You *chose* to drink. You *chose* to drive. Dad told all about it. Do I have to spell it out for you, you freaking assaholic!"

He sags against the bumper. "Is that honestly what you guys think of me?" His breath catches in uneven hitches. "After all this time?"

As he cradles his head in his hands, Davis's false memory of prom night plays in my mind so vividly I smell lasagna. Davis wanted something different, tried to make a change. But nothing can erase reality. No amount of wishing can alter the fact that Steve destroyed my life. My family. Him and me. Frustration obliterates the urge to smooth his wayward curls. To still the tremor rippling down his arms.

I take a step backward, clasping my hands tight behind my back. "It's the truth."

He cocks his head in the same way he always does when he's worried or concerned about someone and moves closer, tension and body heat filling the gap between us. "Pru, I wasn't drunk."

I snap. "Is that the story you tell yourself so you can sleep at night? I'm not stupid. My parents don't lie."

"You aren't the only one who lost everything," he growls. It's deep, throaty, and angry. His stance is rigid and stiff.

"Maybe one day you'll wake up and realize it's not all about you before it's too late."

"It's already too late!" My face is inches from his as I scream. "Davis is gone. There is no one else to blame but you. And I hate you for it!" He catches my wrists when I strike his chest. His touch is firm yet gentle. His hands are cold, but my skin tingles where he touches me and my trapped pulse quickens beneath his fingers. I'm hyperaware of the proximity of his mouth in relation to mine, and my head spins.

What the hell is wrong with me?

Squirming from his grasp, I shove him and run to the garage door opener, jamming the button. "I think you should leave."

The outdoor light clicks on as the motor whirs and the door rises. He stands there staring at me open-mouthed and clutching his chest. Tearing my gaze from his wide, glossy eyes, I stare at the floor and kick a fallen screwdriver near my shoe. It scratches and clunks across the cement.

Steve picks it up and places it on the corner of Dad's workbench. He nods without looking at me. Shoulders rolled back and head high, he marches stiff-legged to his truck.

The engine roars as he blazes down the alley, taking every last happy moment from my past with him. It all vanishes in darkness and dust.

I clamor inside the Gherkin and sprawl across the back bench. Sleep doesn't come. I'm too upset and wired. Pulling Davis's jacket over my face, I breathe the comfort of his cologne. It crushes me as much as the first time I smelled it. Curling into a ball, I dig my fingers into the plush leather. But it's Steve's presence I feel more than anything. My skin still alive and thrumming where he touched me.

I don't want this. My focus needs to be on Mom and Dad. On Davis and dreamland. Not stupid Steve, the root of all my problems.

I sit back up and grab my journal, markers, and a bag of peanut M&Ms, ripping open the corner and pouring half into my mouth, letting the savory sweetness settle my shaking hands before drawing. When in doubt, draw it out.

After flipping to the last page, I turn the book upside down, figuring I can keep my ongoing Davis and dreamland designs separate from my waking-hell sketches this way. Every second my pen transforms the creamy paper brings calming peace. It's the best thing ever, letting my heart bleed across the page.

Mom in a puddle on the ground beneath a black storm cloud raining colorful pills.

The Gherkin split in two, Dad straddling the broken halves while clutching his empty, turned-out pockets.

My house with the roof blown off, mirroring the Tower card in a tarot deck, and a red-devil Steve riding a lightning bolt over the disembodied chimney.

And Davis to the rescue. Driving his angel-winged Gherkin through the stars, straight into a glittering portal bringing us together in his perfect dreamland apartment.

10

So Lonely ~ The Police

Everything was dark as midnight, and Pru could only make out the shady outlines of the kitchen. The deeper into the apartment she went, the blacker it became. Each step across the stale, dank carpet shot out music, but the songs played slowly in reverse, the words and notes discordant and garbled.

"So nice of you to finally make it."

Pru jumped at the voice and the staticky hiss that followed.

"OK. This is my second time here tonight, and—"

Davis clapped and his palms sparked. Blood-red light cast rough, stained shadows across the sunken, angular plains of his face.

"I've not slept for days and days waiting for you." He frowned. "Where is everybody? I thought you were bringing Mom and Dad. Steve. The Giallanzas."

"Davis… I'm dreaming. I don't think that's possible." Or was it? Everything about this place defied logic, but maybe she could try. She'd do anything to keep him smiling. Do whatever it took to stay with him forever, happy and close. As if they'd never been separated.

"Anything is possible." Davis cocked his head and smiled but it didn't reach his eyes. They reflected nothing but crimson in the eerie glow.

Pru shivered.

"Just look at this apartment!" He flung his arms wide above his head. Crackling pops drowned out the creepy music. A dim glow radiated from Davis's outstretched hands, illuminating the space.

Pru cringed. It was worse than before.

Every flat surface was coated in ashy black grime. It smeared the walls. It swallowed the carpet. It dripped from the ceiling. A scratching sound emanated from the living room. Pru backtracked and froze when she reached the wall where the photographs had hung.

Hundreds of roaches swarmed over the plaster, picking holes in the paint with sharp, oversized mandibles. The metal D, P, and S lay on the ground, chipped and rusted.

Pru screamed and ran backward, slamming into Davis. His hands on her shoulders were ice, but the burn down her arms was fire.

"W-what's happening, Davis?" She shivered against his chest, and he wrapped a protective arm around her, pulling her tight against him.

"It's better when you're here, Pru." He was whispering in her ear, but the words sounded far away. Even so, his breath hung heavy in the air, pungent, ripe, and reeking of formaldehyde.

Of death.

"I got this." He gave her a reassuring squeeze before crossing to the infestation and punching his fist into the center of the roach horde. They scattered. Pru gasped as they morphed, thinning into long, oozing, putrid trails of liquid smoke. Some crunched solid, falling to the crusty carpet.

"Dammit, I won't let you take them all," Davis howled as he smashed.

Tentatively, Pru stepped up to Davis, trailing her hand down his back, rubbing in small circles the way their mom would. "I think they're gone," she whispered, grabbing his raw, skinned fist in hers.

"Yeah. They are, Pru. Memories and family"—he poked his finger through a hole in the plaster—"are everything." He pulled his goopy finger free and painted a sticky, upside-down frowny face with the muck across his shirt.

Swaying into the wall, Davis slid to the floor, a mushroom-cloud of dust surging from the brittle shag. Pru plopped next to him, wiping grit from her face.

Davis clapped, and the dirt cleared from her clothes and skin.

"I got you." Davis smiled, but his lips rose only halfway. His eyes drooped heavily. "I won't let anything hurt you. Not ever." His voice was thick. Sluggish.

A sob rose in Pru's throat as she dropped her head onto Davis's shoulder. He sighed and slipped his hand in hers.

"I feel everyone's pain all the time. The teeth are so sharp it eats my heart, Pru." He shuddered. "I feel it right now. So be happy for me, Pru. I need that happiness."

Pru snuggled closer to her brother and closed her eyes. Despite the stench, he felt warm and real. Like love she could hold in her hands. It helped her drift through her mind, let her conjure being with him when he was alive. The joy of their friendship.

"This is what matters—right, Pru-Pru? Us, together?"

"Yeah, Davis. It's the only thing."

"You remember, right? How everything was perfect? I've been so alone, just waiting for you. Waiting for everyone."

11

The Ghost in You ~
The Psychedelic Furs

I 'd fallen asleep beneath my art supplies, and the tin and markers clatter to the floor as I startle awake. Sun filters through the grimy garage glass and into the Monte Carlo. Stretching my neck, I angle my head away from the light when it hits me.

I search for my phone to find the time.

8:37? Stupid freaking Steve screwing up my sleep! Thank God I didn't miss geometry.

Good luck's still on my side when I make it to campus during passing period and slip through the hallway without alerting the lemming herd. Slinking to the back of the classroom, Mr. Nelson tells us to pull out our notebooks and starts droning on and on about literary devices. Motifs. Foreshadowing. I'm way too jazzed to take notes, so I sketch instead, hunching tight over the notebook so no one notices.

I'm doodling little cars in the margins of the paper, Davis foremost on my mind. I wish I could spend the day in the Gherkin. Live in dreamland. I need to find a way to save it.

And the magical car that takes me there. But I only have a handful of ideas, none of them good.

Trash the Monte Carlo so that no one in their right mind will consider buying the old hunk o' junk? Talk the Giallanzas into letting me be a live-in nanny, complete with hefty advance? Rob a bank?

The fourth option involves massive amounts of pizza as payment for the football team heaving the car onto their shoulders Roman palanquin style and carrying it into the woods where I could secretly escape to it. But that requires asking for help from the jocks, which is a slightly worse fate than prison time for armed robbery. Besides, that was Davis's crowd, not mine. I was always an afterthought. They wouldn't help me even for pizza.

I'm totally on my own.

The announcement speaker squeals to life, and I jump.

"Hiya gals and dolls! It's me, Maddi, with a very important reminder. It's our favorite time of year!" She shrieks and giggles too close to the mic, setting off an awful reverb. "*Prom!*"

My stomach drops.

Prom. Fucking prom. It can't be time already. I drop my head to my desk, wishing for spontaneous sleep to whisk me back to Davis where I belong.

"This year's theme is A Flashback to the Past: Delish Decades. Dress up in your fave fashion from your fave era: 50s sock hop, 60s hippies, 70s disco, 80s big hair and neon, or 90s grunge. Be sure to vote for royalty and donate your artistic and creative talents. We still need an amazing artist to help decorate the gym. So stop on by and show us what you got! The cheer team booth will be in the cafeteria all week, so grab some grub and let's get those votes in! Can't wait to see ya!"

Well then. Giallanzas for lunch it is. Fingers crossed Anne-Marie's working today. Her smile—and pizza—makes everything better.

The bell rings and most of the school swarms the cafeteria. They clog the hall like marching insects scurrying top-speed to an all-you-can-eat-buffet, so I wander the long way to the back of the school and slip outside by the football field.

The air is autumn crisp, but the hint of ozone reminds me it's spring and rain could drop any minute. Water-gorged flannel-grey clouds with dark bellies hang low in the denim sky.

By the endzone, I pause even though my stomach twists in knots. Davis lingers everywhere. I try to force a smile—to be happy for Davis like he asked me to in last night's dream—but how is that possible when every memory stabs my heart and steals my breath?

I shut my eyes. The crowd roars in my ears. Pride wells in my chest. *That's my brother! The future of football!* I squeeze my eyes tighter, hyper-focused on that fickle joy that I know will vanish the second I re-open them.

I think they forgot to bury me in the casket beside Davis.

Voices sound behind me. A heap of letterman jacket–clad jocks spills out of the school doors, lumbering toward the field. I hear Ricky's obnoxiously loud voice and laughter before I spot his unruly red hair. My throat closes and my palms sweat.

I take off running before he notices me.

I'm panting when I get to the restaurant, but when I step inside, there's no sign of either Giallanza behind the counter.

Bummer. But my favorite quick-escape seat is open, and when I see the pepperoni mushroom on the daily slice menu, I know its fate. If only all the world's problems could be solved with pizza. I'm not convinced they can't. That or chocolate. It might be debatable if not for the Giallanza pie. That stuff's medicinal. Truly. End of story.

Order placed, I wedge myself tight into the brick corner and pull out my journal as I wait.

I sink into the pages, each pen stroke healing the broken fissures in my heart with vibrant color. By the time I notice my order sitting on the table, it's cold. It's OK. The need to record everything dreamland before I lose the Gherkin gnaws at my stomach way more than hunger.

The seat shifts beside me. I jump and a hand reaches out to steady my teetering soda cup that I've bumped.

"Sorry, Pru, didn't mean to startle you." Anne-Marie's tinkling laugh pulls me out of my head and back to reality. "I'm so glad you're here; I've got something for you." She reaches into her apron's oversized front pocket and pulls out a framed photo. "It's my all-time favorite. I found a copy and thought I'd share."

She slides it upside down along the table, looking expectant but gnawing her lip. Her nervous stare makes me hesitate before flipping it over.

When I do, I wish I hadn't.

It's the photo from Anne-Marie's book, the one that fell out in the kitchen the last time I babysat. The one of me, Davis, and Steve. I want to shove my thumb over Steve's face, but with Anne-Marie watching, I force a smile that I'm sure looks more like a grimace.

"Do you remember this day? You three were always such a help in the kitchen. But always so messy!"

Messy is an understatement. Every appliance littered the countertops. Sauce painted the pristine cabinets. Sugar coated my chin. Flour dusted our navy aprons white.

I remember our food fight. How it started with me flicking flour at the guys and ended with puddles of marinara on the floor and in our hair.

I run my finger over Davis, but my focus is drawn to Steve. He stands behind us, laughing. With one hand, he thrusts bunny fingers over Davis's head. The other rests on my shoulder. His grin is bigger than mine or Davis's, but he isn't smiling for the camera. He isn't glancing at Davis. He's staring directly—*only*—at me. His intense eyes practically glow through the glass...

I realize I'm lost in my thoughts too long when I feel Anne-Marie shifting uncomfortably on the seat.

"I'm sorry if it's too soon. I thought—well, I wanted you to see how you still have love and support in your life. Not only with your parents, or with John and me, but with Steve too." She runs her finger lovingly across the black shellac frame directly above Steve's head. "You know, he always looked at you that way. Like you were better than pizza." She coughs, her face rosy-pink, and snags my journal off the table. "Whatcha drawing?"

I know it's only Anne-Marie, but I want to reach over and slam my palm over the drawings and grab my book back. I squeeze my knee to stop my leg from thumping and bumping the underside of the table while she flips through the pages.

At first, I think she's looking just to change the subject from the photograph, but then she hunches closer to the pages, fingers trailing across the ink. "These are lovely, Pru," she whispers. "So real and lifelike. Do you mind?" she asks, even though she's already at least half a dozen pages in.

Apart from Davis and the rare occasion of Steve or my parents, no one has ever looked at my art journal. Cold pepperoni-and-shroom sticks in my throat.

"This is a stunning collection. I especially love how the early images are colored differently. How did you do that? Different mediums, yes? Ink and... what's the other?"

"They're all the same," I mumble after dislodging a mouthful of pizza from my throat. I dabble with other things, but fine-tip markers are where it's at. Maybe if I shove enough food into my mouth, I can avoid further conversation.

"Wow. Even if I didn't know you lost Davis, I could still read the story being told in your work. How do you achieve the faded effect?"

I lean closer, squinting and eyeing each pen stroke, trying to see what she does. At first, I don't see anything, but then...

The ink outlining Davis, filling him in, it isn't as vivid as everything else. Me, the apartment, all the surroundings are comic-strip bright, but Davis fades into the paper, a watercolor nothingness.

My nails dig into my thigh as I turn to my latest sketch. It's fresh—the ink smudges when I touch a corner—but as I flip through the earlier pages, my heart sinks. Davis is part of each one, but the farther back I go, the harder he is to make out. Davis is so washed-out in the first drawing he looks almost invisible.

My hands turn clammy as my throat constricts. These images are all I have left, especially once Dad sells the Gherkin. How am I losing them too? I don't understand.

Anne-Marie hands me a napkin from the dispenser, then glances at the drawings again as I stab at my stupid eyes.

"You didn't paint him that way, did you?"

Feeling another surge of tears, I can only shake my head and press the tissue to my eyes.

Anne-Marie studies every picture, her frown deepening as she turns the pages. "Where do the ideas for these drawings come from, Pru?"

My head's buzzing. I can barely hear her, and match her tone whisper for whisper. "Dreams. They are all scenes from my dreams."

The paper crackles way too loud as her fingers rush through the journal. Rifling backward, forward, backward, again and again and again till the room spins. Every time she winces and shudders, my temples pound.

Words cyclone through my head, ballooning and buzzing and suffocating until they flood out of me in a torrent I can't stop.

I blubber everything. How sleeping in my bed leaves me alone and dreamless yet always in the Gherkin I dream. How magical yet realistic my Davis dreams are. How incredible yet strange and unsettling the dreamland apartment is. How familiar yet eerily Davis behaves.

I'm describing the sealed guest bedroom, how light shines past the door but can't fully chase away the darkness or the shadows or the decay, when she gasps.

Her grip on my hand is sudden and tight. "What did you say?"

Her eyes are wide and hard, and I have to look away. "No, n-n-nothing," I say. "Forget it. It's stupid. Just dreams."

But she clamps down and asks me to repeat myself.

I stare at the awkward wrinkles forming on my hand beneath her unyielding grip. My fingers ache.

"His apartment always changes. Sometimes, it's perfect. Rundown and old, but clean. And sometimes it's filthy and falling apart. He is often dirty himself too. Maybe there's no such thing as soap in dreams." I mean it as a joke, to lighten the mood and the somber look on her face that makes it hard to breathe, but Anne-Marie doesn't blink or crack a smile.

"That explains a lot."

She drops my hand. Blood rushes hot to my fingertips and my entire hand tingles. After closing the journal, she pushes it back over to me but rests her palm on the cover.

"Remember how I told you I dream about Abri and Nonna?"

I nod, grabbing my soda to cool my arid throat. Sugar, give me strength.

"My dreams are like yours—vivid and realistic. Electric. But the setting is consistently indistinct. Abri and Nonna are clear as a bell. They're either surrounded in bright white light or a candle flame's yellow glow. I can never tell if we are indoors or outside. Everything around them blurs. This is how I know their spirits have moved on—that I am visiting them some-where that is not our own world. I don't think we are supposed to see or know what the afterlife looks like until it's our time to pass on. But I do believe that our perished loved ones can visit us somewhere in between. The fact that Davis *always* meets you in such a physical place, one where the features remain markedly the same every time but age and deteriorate... Something else is going on..."

Every word she speaks smothers my thoughts and squeezes my heart. My face burns no matter how much soda I guzzle. I can barely follow along she's talking so fast. Something about a ghost. A shadow soul. Unfinished business. Free will and wrong choices. Ignoring the light. My ears ring and my temples throb. I chew my straw.

"...trapped for eternity, decaying until nothing of their recognizable soul is left."

I think I'm going to be sick.

She slips her trembling hand in mine.

"He made the wrong choice, Pru. But he can fix it. There's not much time left. Get him into the guest room. Help Davis find the light."

"The—what?"

"Anne-Marie!" John waves his arms from behind the cash register as though drowning.

She gives me an apologetic smile. "If you need to talk, call me. You aren't alone in any of this." She plants a sticky coconut-scented kiss on my forehead and hustles to the kitchen.

Throwing my journal back in my pack, I spot last night's half-eaten bag of M&Ms. Caught beneath my math textbook, the packet rips when I pull it, and the colorful candy shells tumble into the lint-filled bottom corners of my pack. I fish them out and eat them anyway.

In the blinding sun, the trees, buildings, and sidewalk blur into one big blob. Same as Davis in my journal. I'm numb as I race down the street to the sound of Anne-Marie's words buzzing in the back of my head. I want so badly to skip the rest of the day—to sleep in the Gherkin and stay with Davis until we untangle this mess, whatever the hell it is. But no. The bell rings as I near the base of the embankment, forcing me to cannonball uphill.

Out of breath, I slump into my seat right as Roderick slaps my latest quiz on my desk. He taps the big red F at the top.

"Speak to me after class." He sighs and moves to the next student.

It's all I can do not to cry. Or throw up. Or both. I can't focus on anything but Davis. Every word churning out of Roderick's mouth is as unintelligible as the geometry itself. An AD world beyond my comprehension, same as always.

I'm prepared to bolt when the bell rings, but Roderick's propped against the corner of his desk, watching me while everyone else escapes.

"How are your tutoring sessions going?" he asks.

"They're not."

"What do you mean?"

Same as a kid pretending they have the superpower of invisibility—if I can't see you, then you can't see me—I close my eyes.

"Pru?"

Dammit.

"This is beyond serious. What do you mean 'they're not'?"

"I mean I've tried to set up sessions, but he's too busy with his girlfriend to help." It's not a complete lie, but Roderick cocks an eyebrow. I stare at my shoes, missing Davis and knowing if he were still here, none of this would be happening.

Roderick clears his throat. "I'd help you myself, but clearly, if you could learn from me, we wouldn't be having this conversation and you wouldn't require a tutor. Clear your day tomorrow."

AD, I never have plans, but doing nothing all day is better than geometry. "But tomorrow's Saturday!" I whine and kick his table leg. The Muppet clamped to my shoestrings bounces and my heart skips. I won't ever stop missing Davis.

Immune to whiners, Mr. Roderick pounds his fist on his desk. "Meet me outside the study hall building. 9 a.m. Don't be late. Steve and I *will* be there. This ends now."

The social worker's car is parked in the driveway and Dad's body fills the living room window as he watches the street. When he spots me, the curtains billow closed and the front door flings open before I can dash to the safety of the Gherkin.

Dad's necktie is crooked. The lopsided knot wilts, loose at his neck, the fabric crimped and wrinkled as though he's been tugging on it for hours. His fingers work through his short hair, massaging his scalp. I'll never get used to either: Dad in a tie or sporting short hair.

"Why'd you skip school today?" he hisses, glancing over his shoulder. He tries to shut the door and join me alone on the porch, but the popping of Mr. McKittrich's gum stops Dad cold. He shuts his eyes and breathes through his nose. My pulse speeds up.

Dad still doesn't open his eyes. Not even when Mr. McKittrich steps behind him and pats his shoulder. "We'll be inside in a moment."

McKittrich nudges the door wide with the toe of his caramel-cream wingtip and brushes Dad aside. "It's a gorgeous day. Let's all talk outside." He blows a large blue bubble and I resist the urge to smash it with my finger before he sucks it between his teeth with a loud crack. "This won't take long." As though to emphasize, he checks his wristwatch. "I'll get to the point. What happened with your attendance today, Prudence?" He rocks on his heels, hands clenched behind his back.

How can he be so calm when Dad is so stressed? I slip a squished bon-bon from my pocket and pick at the gold foil wrapper. "I overslept and missed art. I attended the rest of my classes, including geometry." I don't mention the failed quizzes, tests, and lack of tutoring.

"We talked about the importance of avoiding truancy the last time we spoke. Remember?"

"Yes, and I haven't skipped school."

"You skipped art, correct?"

"It's an *elective*!" My voice rings sharp, and Dad shakes his head, a barely perceptible movement unless you know to look for it. It's a sign he always gave me when I was younger and got overstressed and near to bursting. *Slow down, Pru. Ease up.* I cram the chocolate into my mouth to slow my words.

"Every class is important. Right, Larry?"

Dad's eyes narrow and he clears his throat, a low, guttural growl McKittrich probably doesn't hear over the snapping of his gum. It doesn't matter though, because he doesn't even wait for a response.

"Whether you miss tree climbing one-oh-one or trig, both are equal to the state."

"It won't happen again," I mumble around the wad of melting chocolate coating my tongue. Sugar, the only thing holding me upright. Dad slides the knot up and down his tie like he doesn't know what to do with his hands. I don't either, so I shove mine in my pockets.

"Can I go to my room now?"

I'm asking Dad, but McKittrich answers. "Remember how remaining at home depended on perfect attendance? One class—one *skip*—matters. I can't stop state policy. But the good news is that your new living arrangement is only temporary until your birthday. Larry's arranged for you to stay with a family friend, and we can reassess where things stand afterward."

"I'm not staying with the Giallanzas. I'm staying here."

"Pru—"

Mr. McKittrich smiles weakly. "There isn't a choice here, Pru."

I swallow the bon-bon; the sweetness burns my throat. If I can't be at home, maybe staying with John and Anne-Marie is the next best thing. I'll help Anne-Marie during her pregnancy, watch the kids, be there when Giovanni is born. I need a distraction. Maybe this is exactly the kind of distraction I need.

"Fine."

McKittrich snaps his gum and taps his watch. "Go pack. I'll be back in an hour to take you to the Nolan residence."

Wait…

What?

I can't find my words. My brain is numb and all I can do is stare as McKittrich's long spider legs close the distance from our porch to his car faster than the speed of life-altering light.

"Dad?"

"Come on. I'll help you pack. We don't have much time." His voice is strained and husky. Same as when he gave the eulogy at Davis's funeral. I'd only ever seen him cry that one time in my entire life.

"This isn't fair."

Dad's eyes are dry as he holds open the door, but his voice cracks when he says, "Tell me about it. But rules are rules, kiddo."

His hand is warm and steady on my back as we trudge up the stairs. My door's shut, but I can't bring myself to open it. I don't want to leave Dad. I want to be here when Mom comes home. My eyes burn when I realize how impossible it will be to sneak to the Gherkin and be with Davis when he needs me most. I gulp in a breath, but it catches on a sob.

"Hey," Dad whispers. "It's Steve and Tim. You'll be okay." He pulls me into a hug.

I want to tell him about the Gherkin, the dreams, Anne-Marie's warnings, but then I remember all those horrible client letters I found in his briefcase and the cost of Mom's treatment. So I don't.

"I could stay with Anne-Marie and John," I suggest hopefully instead.

His chest vibrates against my cheek when he chuckles. "I called and spoke with John. I don't want to worry you, but Anne-Marie has been struggling with her pregnancy. Her sisters are flying in tonight to help with the restaurant and kids until the baby's born. Anne-Marie starts bed rest as soon as they land. I did start with them, Pru. But they have far too much on their plate, so I didn't even ask."

This is just like Anne-Marie not to have mentioned anything about this. Always putting everyone else first. I can't believe I was so wrapped up in my own issues that I never thought to ask how she'd been feeling lately. A wave of guilt, sadness, and anxiety washes over me, and I can't help but shiver.

Dad squeezes me tighter in response. "Tim's more than happy to help. It'll be good with the Nolans, Pru. Like when you were kids." He reaches around me and opens my door. "The alternative's worse."

Pulling from his grip, I stare at the black wall of clothes glaring back at me from my closet. This will be far from good. We aren't innocent kids anymore. Without Davis, Steve and I are nothing. Without Davis, I am nothing. My stomach knots chain into a band across my chest. "I don't know. This is so messed up. Living with the guy who… I can't, Dad. Please."

"I think we need to talk."

There's nothing to talk about. Everything's been clear since AD day one. Ignoring him, I pull a suitcase from the back of the closet. It snags on the dirty pile of clothes on the floor. "Fuck my life," I snap, sharper than I mean to, and yank the handle.

"Hey, language," he reprimands, but his voice is resigned, not angry.

"There's nothing to talk about," I blather. "Life sucks, and then your BFF kills your brother." The suitcase flies free, launching into the wall, and Dad catches me before I fall on my ass.

"Work with me, Pru. I'm doing the best I can." He opens the suitcase and sits on the floor. "You know that, right?" His soft, pleading eyes lock on mine. "I get it. I understand your reluctance to live with Steve, I do. But you think something about him that's completely wrong, and that's my fault." He drags his hand down his face and sighs. "Come on. Choose your outfits. Drop them in the case. I'll fold and pack while I explain."

Maybe in the next millennia, when thinking of Davis doesn't annihilate my insides, I can forgive Steve. But today's not that day. I know there's *nothing* Dad can say about Steve that changes anything. Besides, forgiveness doesn't mean including the person who wronged you in your life—unless you're moving in with the bastard.

Dad's eyes, ringed with deep, sad wrinkles not there a year ago, droop. Uncertain, he stares into space. His fingers tremble and he fumbles with his tie. His nervousness rattles me. BD, Dad's eyes remained bright and confident through any challenge. They held the answers to all life's difficult mysteries.

But he's trying right now. For once, he isn't talking to me like he's a robot.

Swallowing hard, I turn and start pulling outfits off the hangers. "OK. I'm listening."

Dad clears his throat and ruffles the buzzed hair on the back of his head as though seeking his missing ponytail. When his hands come up empty, he grips the back of his neck instead. "I really don't know how to do any of this without your mom."

I drop a wad of clothes into the suitcase and join him on the floor. "Me either," I whisper, dropping my head to his shoulder. We've not sat this close all year. His hand hovers over my leg before dropping and giving my knee a squeeze. Same as BD times, we just *are*. Sitting in silence. Together.

He groans as he gently untangles his hand from mine. He grabs a pair of jeans. I snag a shirt. Together we fold.

"Davis was sick." His voice breaks the comfortable silence and my heart kicks up. "Ever since that game where he was sacked—twice—and the second one knocked him out awhile? He had headaches."

I remember. We'd make plans for the weekend, and then Steve and I'd be off scouring the thrift store or playing Frisbee in the park by ourselves while Davis was stuck in bed. Sometimes, he'd miss school. He'd sleep it off and be fine the next day though. He always said it was nothing, so I believed him and let it go.

"Doctor said it was migraines. That he'd probably have them for life. He suggested Davis give up his football scholarship and stop playing. Then he put Davis on all these different medications."

This I don't remember. Davis never mentioned pills.

"The side effects were horrible. He hated taking them, so we suggested"—he pauses, voice hitching on his next words— "*I* suggested he stop taking them, told him we'd find another solution. He didn't get migraines often, but that night, when Steve told us how much Davis was blinking and twitching before blindly missing the turn, I *knew*. If Davis had been on the meds, if they had been in his system... And your mom, the look on her face, her disappointment and disgust... in *me*... She knew. She knew and she'd never—and I—"

The room is suddenly too bright. His words too loud. I close my eyes, like shutting out the world will stop the room from spinning.

This isn't right. I remember everything though I wish I could forget.

Dad's horrible words ring in my head, clear as if spoken yesterday. Words that have haunted my life ever since.

"There was an accident. Steve was drinking. Davis is gone."

I grab and squeeze Dads hand—for me as much as him.

"No. No, Dad. It was Steve—"

And it was me. I was the reason they were on the road in the first place. Davis was coming to save *me*...

Uncertainty churns in my gut as Dad shakes his head.

"No, Pru. It wasn't Steve. He called us immediately. We could hear the medics in the background, could hear them as they helped Steve, as they mentioned the... deceased driver. And still, I *shamed* Steve. He needed me, and I blasted him for drinking. Told him if he'd been sober, Davis never would have driven, never would have crashed. I begged him to leave my family alone after all he'd done to wreck it. Even though he'd done nothing wrong and was the only son your mom had left. I still don't think she's forgiven me for losing both of them. For everything."

"Steve wasn't..." My lips feel numb. "He didn't drive drunk?"

"No. I'm so very sorry that I gave you the impression he was at all responsible. It was me. Be angry with me."

Dad snaps the suitcase closed, stands, and carries it to the door. He pinches the bridge of his nose, breathing deep as he struggles to get his Robo-mask back in place. His jaw tightens. His lips press together. His chest rises and falls with shallow breaths.

All the same as me.

We are alike in the saddest of ways.

The doorbell rings and we jump.

It can't be time. I'm not ready. I'll never be ready.

Dad opens my bedroom door. Instead of pressing past him, I throw myself into his arms, same as when I was little and scared and didn't want to leave his side.

His hands are soothing on my back as I cry. "Shh, shh," he comforts. "This is only temporary. I'm close. Call me when you need me. You're always my girl."

His words soothe but still I feel lost inside. My stomach floats into my chest, my heart sinks into my stomach, my head disconnects from my body. I have nothing left to anchor me anywhere.

McKittrich smacks his gum when we open the front door. "Ready?"

No, I'm not. But I shrug, and Dad grunts.

Tucking me into the front seat, Dad pulls me into another hug, tugging on the back of my ponytail like I always did his. I wonder if he will grow his back. I rather miss it. "Call me. For anything. I mean it. I love you, Pru."

We may be a supportive family, but we've never said those words often, BD or AD. A lump sticks in my throat as big as the one that looks lodged in Dad's. His throat bobs as he swallows and swallows again.

"I love you too. Tell mom for me." My voice squeaks.

McKittrich cranks the engine. Dad shuts my door. I watch him shrink in the side-view mirror until he's a dot in the distance and I'm vapor trails on the horizon.

My hot head pressed against the cold window, the world blurring by, I'm numb, lost within the lo-fi hip-hop beats streaming from the radio and within the crackling of Mr. McKittrich's gum.

Mr. Nolan rolls my suitcase down the hall, and I follow. He pauses outside the door beyond the bathroom and Steve's bedroom. His breath hitches and his hand hovers over the knob, trembling a little. I remember from BD times how rarely he enters this room. It's storage for all of his wife's old things. Similar to Mom's dining room shrine but with stacks of packing boxes, overflowing dressers, and steamer trunks; messy clutter instead of organized chaos. Where my dad got rid of everything Davis, Steve's dad kept it all.

The door creaks open with a jittering sigh, and I can see it's not too different than before.

"Here we are." His voice booms, boisterous, but he slumps, long limbs limp against the doorframe. "It's not much, but it's something. Do know we're glad to have ya."

As kids, we crawled along the floor, weaving like snakes between the unsteady cardboard pillars dominating the back half of the room. Now, they're stacked floor to ceiling along every inch of free space against every wall and stuffed inside the walk-in-closet. A rumpled futon sits alone in the cramped space. Matted square and rectangular indents pattern the carpet around it, a checkered minefield of smooshed and scraggly fibers. My shoulders feel just as dented and weighed down.

All that monotone brown creates a 70s paneling vibe. The effect is claustrophobic and dark even with the last of the sunlight streaming through the small open window. And despite the light breeze, everything reeks of mothballs. At least the window and the two doors leading into the bathroom and hall are clear of boxes.

It's weird, being here without Steve, seeing Mr. Nolan after an entire year, talking to him as though nothing happened. Like no time has passed and my stay isn't due to my unstable home life but some fun sleepover like when Steve and I were kids.

Mr. Nolan sets my bags next to a tall dresser and pats the top two drawers. "These are cleared out for you. If you need more space, let me know. I've also got this desk for ya." He points to a card table and folding chair I hadn't seen squeezed between towering cardboard spires. Everything's clearly a rush, a thrown-together afterthought. Same as me.

"Dinner's just you and me tonight—spaghetti and salad. While the sauce is simmering, I'll cook the noodles and brown the meatballs. You can help chop lettuce, tomatoes, and cucumbers for the salad, OK?"

"Sure. Sounds good, Mr. Nolan."

"Tim. After all these years, Pru, it's Tim." He smiles and winks. "Come. Let's cook. I bet you're hungry."

My appetite's shot, but I nod and remember to smile as I follow him out the door.

Salad fixings are already strewn across the counter. I grab the knife and cutting board and start chopping the head of iceberg. Mr. Nolan gives the sauce a stir; fragrant basil and rich garlic permeate the room. He hums and flips on the front burner. Meatballs sizzle hot in the pan.

"I used buffalo meat. Flavorful and lean. I hope you like it." He delicately molds more tiny, bite-sized meatballs with his large, squared hands.

"It sounds great, thank you."

We fall into an easy, quiet rhythm. Every repetitive slice of the blade through the veggies settles my nerves. I didn't realize I needed this. My mouth actually starts to water. And with no sign of Steve, at least tonight won't be so uncomfortable and strained. I don't know what to feel when I think of him. I'm still angry. Humiliated. My jaw clenches, a scream building in my throat. If I start, I won't stop, so I push the thoughts away, focusing instead on chopping a tomato into precise chunks, on cutting rounds of cucumber the exact same thickness.

We settle in at the table. Tim takes off his baseball cap and rubs his bald head with his palm. I've never seen Mr. Nolan with hair. Steve said when his mom went through chemo and started losing hers, his dad shaved his off and never grew it back. The memory sets my cheeks ablaze. I move my eyes onto the sprinkling of Parmesan melting into cheesy goodness atop my mound of noodles.

"Dig in," Tim says, spinning noodles around his fork and pressing them tight to the tines with a spoon. I remember him teaching me that trick as a kid. He smiles as I chase a rolling meatball across my plate.

"Thank you. For dinner and, uh, you know. All of this. Letting me stay here…"

"After all your family has done for Steven? It's the least I can do. The best thanks you can give me is to go to class, study, and pass geometry."

I wonder if he realizes I can't pass math without his MIA son. And that Steve and my family are no longer close.

"Working on it." I remember to smile although it's forced. I hope my cheeks don't look as plasticized as they feel. I'm unsure he notices. Mr. Nolan's gaze is as fixed to his plate as his fork.

The rest of the meal flows on autopilot. We eat. He lets me know the house rules: curfew of ten on a school night, midnight on the weekends, some nights he will work late, text if there's an emergency. It should feel comforting that the protocol is the same as always. Instead, it's a watered-down and depressing déjà vu. Too much has changed to ever bring back BD moments.

I carry the dishes to the sink, rinse and put everything in the dishwasher, and Mr. Nolan stores the leftovers. He invites me to watch TV after, but I tell him I need to be alone and decompress.

"Make yourself at home," he chirps, and I head back to the cardboard guest room, plotting my escape route to the Gherkin. While I'm grateful to Tim for the help, I don't plan on sleeping here. Lunch feels like a lifetime ago, but I still hear Anne-Marie's words screaming in my brain as though she's in the room shouting at me. No way am I letting Davis turn into some soulless nothing.

Slipping my cell on the charger, I see it's 7:23. Later, I'll slip out the window, walk home, and sleep in the Gherkin. If I set an alarm, I'll be back early in the morning before anyone notices I'm missing. All I gotta do is wait it out a few hours till Mr. Nolan goes to bed.

Worried about Davis as I am though, I can't focus, let alone study. I drag out my journal and try to get comfortable on the futon. Ink flies across the parchment. My calm. My refuge. My great escape.

I draw the Gherkin so it fills the entire page, Davis centered behind the wheel with his outstretched arm hanging out the open window, palm wide to catch the wind. Complete with angel wings, the pickle-mobile soars through the starry sky, straight toward the dense, velvety purple glitter portal on the opposite sheet. I imagine the car lifting off one page and diving into the next. Over his shoulder, Davis is laughing. His smile reminds me of better days when everything was simple.

It's gonna be OK, Davis. I'm coming. I promise.

My phone reads 10:02 when I'm jumping out of my skin, unable to wait another second. Leaving my drawing to dry, I flick off the light and listen at the door.

Silence. Beautiful silence.

Stuffing my pillow under the futon quilt probably won't fool anyone, but I do it anyway.

It's easy breezy popping out the screen and shimmying through the window. My ninja feet don't even make a sound as I drop onto the grass. To celebrate my prison break, I slide a bon-bon from my pocket, picking at the foil as I move slowly through the dark.

I don't notice the occupied hammock until I slam into it. When I do, it steals my breath.

I'd forgotten the hammock was here, but the memory's as vivid as yesterday. Davis, Steve, and me crammed inside the woven fibers, side by side on our backs and moshed so tight we didn't have individual beginnings and endings. In a jumble of sun-pink limbs, we'd laugh and talk for hours. I loved being the one stuffed in the middle. Safe, warm, protected. Baking beneath the hot summer sky, surrounded by birdsong and laughter. We'd link our arms together and Davis and Steve would take turns pointing out the silliest things they saw in the clouds. They held contests to see who could make me giggle-snort first—something I hated but they found hilarious—and would gang up with me to push the loser off the side.

The loud *oomph* isn't Steve though. And it certainly isn't Davis.

It's Mr. Nolan I've almost toppled out of the hammock.

"Hey Mr. Nol—ahh, Tim. Didn't see you there. Sorry."

"I was stargazing. What's up?"

A hot flush fills my cheeks and I'm grateful for the darkness. Even though he didn't call me out on it, he must know I'm not out here to admire the sky. I go with the truth.

"Dad's selling Davis's Monte Carlo. I was hoping to go see it and be back by morning."

"Hmm. Not sure that's part of the state's plan."

"Right," I say.

"But my rules count too. So you can go if you take Steve with you."

That's as good as a no. "He's not here."

"It's Friday night. He's with his girlfriend."

"Girl-*fiend* you mean." The words are out of my mouth before I can stop them.

Mr. Nolan chuckles, but he shakes his head. "Maddi's great."

I snort. Loudly. "You don't know her very well."

"What I do know is she's been there for Steve during one of the worst times of his life."

His unspoken words—*unlike you, Pru*—hang between us.

"He's been good for her too. They have so much in common. Only children, parents that are… neglectful." He clears his throat. "I've been working hard on fixing that. Being around more. Losing his mom so young, then losing Davis…" His voice trails off and he goes quiet for so long I think it's a dismissal. I'm not sure what to do: head back inside or flat-out race for the Monte Carlo right now. I wonder if he can run as fast as Steve. Could he tackle me before I vault over the fence? Would he call McKittrich and revoke my stay?

"Life's way too short to live without people who see and accept you for who you are at your core. Those who stick beside you are a rare gift. Maddi is Steve's glue. She's the only thing holding him together these days. She's been there for him when no one else has. When someone shows you who they are, believe them."

My cheeks tingle and my stomach clenches. I can't make out his eyes, always as intense as his son's, in the dark. Still, he sees through to my soul, my insides exposed and scraped raw. If I'd known the truth about Davis's death sooner, Maddi never would have sunk her claws into Steve. I want to hate her for it. But really, I hate myself. All I've shown Steve this year is blame and anger. Is that who I am? Who I've become? What I show the world? Maybe she's not the super villain I've always known her to be.

Maybe I am.

"Talk to Steve about the car. Maybe he can take you after study hall tomorrow."

He shifts onto his side. Definitely a dismissal. Mr. Nolan never was a big conversationalist. He sighs heavily as though he expended the last of his energy sharing his insights. But then he lifts his head for a final few words.

"Oh, by the way? Feel free to use the front door from now on. And fix that screen before you go to bed. Those are a pain to put back in."

Busted.

Mr. Nolan wasn't kidding. It takes ten times longer to seal the screen in place than it did to kick it out. After, I slump onto the bed with my journal, clutching my drawing to my chest. Those treacherous tears, always hiding and at the ready, fill my eyes. I'm so damn tired. Tired of crying all the time. Tired of being angry. Tired of worrying. But most of all, I'm tired of being alone.

I think about what Mr. Nolan said earlier: *"When someone shows you who they are, believe them."* But I can't help thinking, what if people show you someone different than they show everyone else?

In elementary school, Maddison showed me her mean side by teasing me till I cried, laughing, then pointing my tears out to everyone else, humiliating me—even when we were friends. In junior high, she showed me her cold side when she joined the cheer squad and told me that since she was now popular— and I *so wasn't*—we couldn't be friends. Now, she's evolved into the queen of backhanded compliments and downright pissiness. She's nice to the popular crowd, and to parents and teachers, but never to me. So of course Mr. Nolan and Steve would get a different version of the Maddi I always do.

It never used to matter. I had all the friendship and love I needed, so nothing she did hurt for long. But everything's different when you're riding solo and there's no one left sticking up for you.

I still don't understand how Steve can be with her when he knows our horrid past. Guess it's what I deserve though. I threw everything away AD, allowing Maddi to swoop down and gobble the leftovers.

Maybe there's truth to what Mr. Nolan says and she is there for him in ways no one else can be. I see the way he looks at her—and she him. As though he hung up the sun, moon, and stars himself, just for her. Steve used to have that effect on me too, back when he gave two licks about my life.

Before I forced him out of mine.

If she cares for him, if he laughs and smiles with her, I guess it's a good thing. Maybe Maddi and Steve do belong together. My opinion's meaningless in his world now though. BD, I wanted the best for Steve. Now that I know the truth about that night, I find I still do. But it's too late for me to fix anything. I don't think I'd accept my apology if I were him.

Flipping to a blank page, I draw Steve and Maddi in formal garb, dancing on a cloud high above the world. Even though prom night is Davis's death anniversary, I bet Steve will still take her to the dance. Maddi gets what Maddi wants.

Thinking about prom reminds me of Rickster the Dickster, which makes me want to hurl. Instead, I draw out my nightmare to purge my system. Me in the gym beneath pulsing strobe lights, hair a swirling mass of electrified frizz standing on end, my dress in tatters with my hands clasped tight over my exposed chest.

Drawing always helps me work out the bad stuff. I may not have Davis to confide in anymore, but at least I have this.

Breakfast is frozen waffles with Mr. Nolan; still no sign of Steve. I don't even know if he came home last night, but if Mr. Nolan ain't sharing, I sure as hell ain't asking. He must have at least spoken with Steve though, because he knows enough to tell me to hurry when he catches me drawing syrup swirls across my plate with my fork instead of eating, stating he needs to drop me off at school on his way to the auto shop.

Yippee.

Snarfing down the last of my meal, I grab my stuff and take my time walking to the truck. Mr. Nolan already has my door open and the engine roaring. "Come on. Let's move," he hollers down at me from inside the towering cab. I toss my pack across the worn leather bench and hoist myself through the door instead of running down the road like I want to.

The gigantic Nolan Tow and Repair truck takes up half the block, so of course Roderick sees me when we pull up to the curb, preventing any hope of escape. As Mr. Nolan and I traipse across the grass, Steve looks anywhere but in our direction.

Roderick unlocks the door, informing us we have the room until 3:00. Mr. Nolan hands Steve a wad of cash and tells him to order Chinese for dinner, as he'll be working late. Blech. Could the day get any worse?

Once we're alone, Steve's all business, his face buried in my geometry textbook to pore over the pathetic handful of failed tests Roderick told me to bring. That's when the door bangs open.

"Never fear, the calvary's here! Man, I thought Roderick would never leave. Maddi will be here in five with the dough-nuts, bro."

I turn, already sick over the voice, and then my heart plummets at the sight of him.

It's the Dickster.

Steve startles, his forehead crinkling as his eyebrows shoot up behind his curls. His mouth hangs open as a strange grunt escapes his lips.

Ricky's eyes meet mine, and I watch in horror as they darken while he stares. His gaze is so intent, I can feel his body pressed hot against me, octopus hands groping everything they shouldn't all over again.

I can't breathe.

"Wow." The Dickster's voice drops an octave, and he licks his lips. "Lookin' great, babycakes, though I really prefer you without your shirt on."

I don't see Steve stand, clenching and unclenching his fists. "Back off, Rick."

"Woah, hey, come on, man. I was just being friendly. There ain't nothin' wrong between me and her. We were only reminiscing. Right, babycakes? Wanna go to prom again? I remember how you taste sweeter than candy."

Steve's a blur when he flies across the room. His punch is so hard, the Dickster stumbles and falls on his ass.

Steve's on him in an instant, hitting him again and again and again.

It's unreal. I hover on the fringe—disconnected and cold. I want to move but my head is underwater. Steve's punches flow in slow motion, grunts and blows sounding muted and far, far, far away.

Until Maddi shows up, screaming.

"What are you doing? Get off him! Stop!" She smacks the oversized pink doughnut box across Steve's back and the lid pops open, maple bars and chocolate glaze rings spilling across the floor.

Steve's eyes are wild. He stands over the Dickster, panting and re-clenching his fists, eyes narrow slits so dark blue they're almost black. Maddi pushes him out of the way to kneel beside Ricky.

"What the hell happened?" She touches her fingers to Ricky's swollen, bloodied lip.

"No clue. I was flirting with Pru, asked her to prom, and lover boy here jumped me outta nowhere."

"Oh, shut it!" Steve growls. I'm pretty sure he'd deck Ricky again if Maddi weren't there.

"Seriously?" Maddi's voice drips venom, her eyes shooting lasers first at Steve, then at me. "Come on, Rick. Let's go." She drops the empty box on the ground and helps Rick stand, draping his arm across her shoulders and shuffling him toward the door. "Thanks for spoiling the surprise," she snaps, looking over her shoulder at Steve one last time. I'm surprised to see she's crying. "Why is it always her?"

Before Steve can answer her, they're gone.

"I am so sorry, Pru. I did *not* invite them. I told Maddi last night I'd be tutoring you all afternoon, but—hey." He stops before me, eyes wide as he watches me shrink against the cold bricks.

I don't remember crossing the room and plastering myself to the corner.

It's prom night all over again, me shoved against a wall barely holding me up as I shake so hard my teeth chatter audibly. Feeling so naked and exposed, I can't tug my shirt down tight enough around me.

The Dickster's gone, but I'm still trapped.

Steve touches my shoulder. I jump and he winces.

"Okay. I won't touch you. I'm sorry. Let's clean up and get out of here, OK?"

All I really want is to bolt out of the room and run to the end of the Earth, where I'll never see the Dickster again. But Steve starts picking doughnuts up off the floor and tossing them in the trash. I gather up my math crap and shove it all into my backpack, test papers crunching beneath my textbook. Even once we're outside, I'm shaking.

"C-c-can you t-t-take me to the Gherkin? P-p-please?" I hate that I'm crying. Sobbing actually. The Dickster isn't worth a single snotty tear, but I can't stop.

Steve raises his hand as if he might touch me again but doesn't. I can't read the expression on his face, but his eyes are still dark, so it's gotta be disgust. 'Cause yet again, I've gone and totally fucked things up for him and Maddi.

He helps me into the truck, reaches inside the glove compartment, and hands me a packet of tissues. I go through half of them on the silent drive to the garage.

He uses his key to unlock the door and I practically trip over my feet racing for the back seat. My numb legs give out as I tumble across the cool leather.

Steve starts to climb in with me, but I stop him.

"You… you should go find Maddi."

Steve draws the center of his upper lip, a perfect Cupid's bow, between his teeth.

"She's been there for him when no one else has."

Mr. Nolan's words and Maddi's face override my desire to ask Steve to stay. She looked crushed, not cruel. Maybe she has a heart where Steve is concerned even if that's the only time it's used.

They really are good for each other.

Outside the Gherkin, Steve's eyes swirl, dark blues lightening to soft greens as he studies me, gnawing furiously at his lip. Shaking his head, he reaches for me, but the thought of being touched by anyone right now turns my skin clammy and sends my stomach flipping.

I slide further down the seat. "Really. I'll be fine. I just need a nap, OK? I'll be home for dinner. Go. Fix things with Maddi. She really does love you."

He opens his mouth, ready to add something, then closes it and nods before shutting the door with a quiet click.

12

Cry Little Sister ~ Gerard McMann

L ightning flashed inside the apartment, a blinding flare searing Pru's eyelids red and gold before engulfing her in darkness. Sooty air reeking of carnations—a smell she equated with funerals and death—clogged her nose and lungs.

Pru fumbled for the counter, the slick Formica crumbling in her grip. She fell as thunder rumbled and the walls moaned.

"Davis, where are you?"

Hot breath prickled her cheek. Inches from her ear, the darkness howled in reply. A low guttural growl that picked up speed and shook the floor. In splattering chunks of soot and debris, the roof ripped apart, spinning up into the midnight sky, and the walls crumbled to the carpet, melting into a river of molten mud.

The gelatinous black ooze writhed beneath Pru's feet, its surface bubbling and boiling as it surged upward. Waist-high mounds of skeletal insects with cracked, fungus-coated shells and decomposing claws undulated around her. Rising and falling, they skittered and scraped, blazing a path down the hall.

At the end of the carved-out walls, Davis's room was alive and pulsating.

Large, misshapen swaths of light flickered and sizzled before extinguishing with a pop. Weighted piles of filth overfilled the corners. Water dripped from yellowing ceiling stains. Wallpaper peeled in long, ragged strips, falling continuously to the bed in dense streams, burying the quilt beneath fetid piles of pulp. The air buzzed, crackling in blazes of charred smoke and violet-tinged lightning that illuminated everything in purple, the dreamland a bruised and rotted plum.

Weighted with mire in the center of the bed, Davis, eyes closed and dreaming, thrashed and wheezed as a tide of shadowy roaches swarmed his face, suckling his skin, sliding into his ears, consuming his mind. Pru saw his memories rising— greyed-out images resembling those in her journal, visions of herself and Steve and their parents, each contained in separate fuzzy clouds hovering over his forehead. Greedy, the shadows breached them like killer whales soaring through the air, swallowing the figments whole.

"Pruuuuuu." Davis's wail creaked, strained and desperate, echoing through the apartment.

"Davis! I'm here. Hold on!" Pru screamed, and the shadows thickened, rising from the floor as she scrambled on hands and knees toward her brother. Elbow deep in sludge, her skin chilled and tingled, arctic cold. The puddled surface rippled with the shadows swimming beneath, black as pitch, stinging her skin as they nipped and gnashed. She gagged, her pulse throbbing in her throat. With every inch forward, the floor slipped and pulled her back. As she neared the bedroom door, the air stuttered. Hot, rancid breath blew across her cheeks, blowing her hair from her sweaty forehead. Twin orange orbs blinked then flashed with hunger. Something huge, something hulking. An ebony mountain filled the hall and blocked her path to Davis.

Pru closed her eyes. But when she opened them again, the darkness swelled. A hazy gloom crept across the ceiling, scraping and skittering as it slid down the walls. The foundation shook. Pru's hair stood on end.

Ooze dripped from above in chunks, rancid and stinking of spoiled fish. With wet plops, they coated the scaled talon tapping the ground before her.

The floor sagged beneath its hulking weight, denting and cracking with each slow scrape of the beast's thick, massive claw.

Pru's mind screamed for her to run, but she froze, muscles paralyzed, airflow to her lungs and blood to her brain restricted. The dull pounding of her heart filled her head with cotton.

Inky shadows undulated, a fluid, vibrating smog. Breathing. Expanding. Solidifying into a smoldering, ashen mass that clicked and growled and huffed as it sniffed and searched the air.

Pru whimpered as the towering beast lowered its head from the ceiling. Unblinking soulless eyes latched onto hers, and the beating *whoosh* of dense feathers filled her ears. Enormous wings blackened the last dim glow of light flicking from the hall.

Sharp as spikes, the beast drove the tips of its feathers into the ground. The floor buckled and quaked, pitching Pru backward. She rolled into the gathering icy fog filling the apartment that rose in a wispy, acidic vapor reeking of sulfur and immolated dead things.

The gloom followed, sinister and ugly and far too real. Its forked tongue tasted her tears, coating her skin in noxious drool that burned as it dribbled down her neck. A hooked, cavernous beak unhinged to swallow her scream.

Pru tumbled backward. *Can you die in dreams?* she wondered as thickening clouds obscured her view, dissolving the shadows and erasing the apartment walls from view. Not seeing wasn't an improvement. Clacking talons and a fusty stench haunted the opaque fog. Haunted her mind.

Pru clutched her chest, willing her heart to slow and her stomach to cease churning, but she vomited on the carpet anyway.

The beast screeched, a piercing, keening howl with Davis's voice as the hazy cloud of buzzing dirt and grit parted to reveal the Gherkin. Idling, it hummed beneath a rain shower of thick violet drops. The glowing liquid trickled down the hood in venous rivulets while music pulsed through the open windows.

Dear Prudence... Won't you come out to play...

The beats slowed and warped. Pru's skin broke out in goose-flesh, yet she ran for the car when she caught sight of a shock of blond hair behind the steering wheel. But as her hand brushed the cold chrome door handle, the Monte ignited, burning her fingertips. Flames sparked and licked the ceiling. Lightning flashed. The apartment glimmered in a wavy haze. Shadow roaches scuttled across the floor, devouring everything they touched before their bloated bodies sank into the loamy ground.

The scene changed, lifelike yet dim and gray as though under layers of dingy plastic sheeting.

Da-vis! Da-vis! Da-vis! With a jubilant roar, the football team encircled Davis. Hoisting him onto their shoulders, they carried him to the ring of dancing cheerleaders, depositing him in the center of the fray.

Davis smiled wide. And then his grin shattered his face in half, a pixilated explosion that hovered in flickering static, overwriting his features.

Pru screamed.

Two brothers, one housed deep inside the other, stood before Pru. One confident and proud, the inner one small and shaking. Squealing cheerleaders surrounded Davis in a greedy, fumbling circle. While they took turns kissing his cheeks and ruffling his hair, one Davis laughed, but the shimmering, smaller Davis trapped within frowned. Pru squinted as the dual, blurred Davis faded in and out of sight.

A too-heavy emptiness emanated from Davis's chest, a nothingness that consumed her, weighting her limbs and squeezing her skull. Beneath his celebratory façade, the diminutive inner Davis, slumped and listless, picked at his lip with his teeth. *Why can't you see me?* he called, the words uneven and coarse, strangled by the external Davis's jokes and laughter. He clutched thin, trembly arms around his middle, staring at a ring of putrid methane bubbles rising from the curling mist. The saturated carpet quivered. Mud slurped Pru's ankles and murky water rose in waves, seeping inside her shoes. She prodded the saturated floor with her foot, and something bumped her leg—scale, bone, and slime parted the shag carpeting, slinking toward Davis.

Spears of lightning cracked the ceiling above as fanged jaws burst the ground apart. A monolithic mass of primordial night arose. Growling. Ravenous. Solid as stone. The scene before Pru exploded in a shower of muck and decay that splattered across her face and dribbled into her open, screaming mouth.

Gnashing teeth gobbled the scene whole before spitting out another, the shadow roaches scurrying behind to slurp lost and leftover fragments. In smoky plumes, another scene rose from the carpet, the wavering streaks of unsteady light floating as discordant chunks before settling into place like pieces of a jigsaw puzzle.

While Pru struggled to catch her breath, Giallanza's Pizzeria materialized.

Steve and Pru tossed rounds of pizza dough into the air while John Giallanza sang in an off-key, over-exaggerated Italian accent and Anne-Marie stirred a pot of sauce. Davis hovered at the fringes, chewing his inner cheek and watching. Above his head floated two indistinct bubbles. They bobbed and bumped against his head and shoulders. Every time they did so, Davis winced.

Straining, Pru noticed the talking heads of her parents within the filmy spheres.

A chittering, gravelly speech slithered inside her ears…

Be polite. Take care of Pru. Watch over Steve. Don't make a mess. Do more than what's asked. Be a good son. A good son. A good son…

Davis crushed a ball of pizza dough inside his fist while Steve and Pru tossed theirs in the air as they sang along with Mr. Giallanza. The dough bled through his fingers, dripping to the floor. Gasping, he scooped the mess from the linoleum. Davis shut his eyes and ground his knuckles against his temple.

When John called his name, Davis's eyes popped open and a smile snapped into place. Liquid smoke rolled off Davis's shoulders in dense, black mushroom clouds bitter with the tang of rancid sweat. The apartment shuddered. Glancing at the floor, he ran the tip of his sneaker over the dirty smudges still decorating the red diamond tiles. The harder he pressed, the more the dirt smeared. The more the apartment shook.

A keening locomotive noise crashed into Pru with a force that knocked her off her feet. A windy cyclone of grit and shadow sped across the floor, shattering the memories into splintered bits. The inky carpet teeming with roaches was sucked up along with Davis's memory into the black and starless sky, leaving a soulless silence in its wake. A dusty haze settled.

The Nolans' living room crystallized within the pallid mist.

Precise stacks of blue and gold poker chips lined the table edge. Davis carefully sorted his playing cards by color, diligently separating the reds from the blacks. He fanned them wide, then pressed them back together tight so only the very edge of the numbers showed, each exactly spaced, one after the other, within his hand.

Pru giggled and Davis glanced up to see Steve stick his tongue through the gap where his two front teeth used to be and wriggle it at her like a lizard. Pru elbowed Steve, and Steve dropped his cards on the floor. Clutching his own cards tight, Davis reached out toward Pru's messy pile of chips that were sprawled across the tabletop. He stacked six of her chips into a neat and tidy pillar, pulling his hand back when she smacked him across his knuckles. He chewed his thumbnail and frowned as she knocked the pile over and laughed at him.

Beside him, Mr. Nolan sat stiff and straight. He glanced at Davis and wagged his eyebrows but didn't smile. *Poker face,* Davis thought, the sound of it echoing through the dreamland apartment as though giant speakers were broadcasting the warbled, discordant words. Sitting taller in his seat, Davis focused. He paid attention. *If I play my best, I'll be my best.*

Ogling the numbers, Davis's heart raced. The beat of it radiated from his chair where he sat, shaking the floor. Rattling the table. Bouncing off the walls.

Four threes and a king. Counting them with his finger to be sure, he bumped the center cards, nearly dropping them, and had to stop to press everything back together and then spread them out again with the exact same spacing as before. His temple pulsed, and he rubbed the back of his neck.

Above the table, a storm gathered and grumbled. Rain pelted the now frozen scene, flattening it into the dark, drenched ground of the dream apartment. Pru gaped as the images bled, sank, and vanished into the floor while shapeless shadowed specters rose to take their place around a different table.

The Spellmeyer dining room shifted into view.

Dull lifeless streamers clung to the wall in grey, threadbare clumps. Mom scooped moldy slices of lasagna and dropped them haphazardly onto chipped china plates, splattering curdled cheese chunks across the moth-eaten tablecloth.

Grey and indistinct, Dad stood on unsteady feet. He clanged his fork against his champagne flute, raising it into the air. The clink of it distorted, a deep and low *thrum*. A pulsing, erratic heart.

Darkness fell, and a rasping croak grated in her ear.

"Hey, babycakes."

The voice was everywhere. Rattling in her head. Ringing from the walls. Oozing down her skin and crawling beneath it. Darkness hissed, pressed against her face, hot, stale and suffocating.

Just beyond, in the bedroom, Pru reached for Davis's bed as it slid across the floor, gouging deep ruts into the carpet. Ebony wings spread and cloaked the ceiling. The floor bucked and rolled, the quaking earth tossing Davis's bed around his room and out the door. The black wings curled over Pru, an imprisoning dome that stalked and followed, growling and scratching.

The apartment tilted. Pru tumbled into the hallway, slamming into the base of Davis's bed. She clawed her way up the splintered posts. Rotted tentacles reached from the carpet, groped at her waist, squeezing, constricting, slithering over her skin, dragging her back. Pulling her under. Above her Davis moaned in his sleep. The mattress jerked and twitched, pitching her over the side.

Her body sank into murky water that flowed into her mouth, coating her tongue and crawling down her throat. "Davis! Please! Help me!" Her voice gurgled, a muffled, water-logged cry.

Davis's slick fingers brush against hers. His eyes popped open as her palm slipped across and off his. He blinked his eyes as he yawned—and noticed his flailing sister.

He screamed.

Davis extended his hand, but Pru couldn't make a fist, couldn't hold on. His slick fingers slipped through her limp ones. The darkness laughed, squeezing, suffocating, choking her screams as it dragged her kicking and squealing beneath the watery surface.

Pru was alone. Blind, deaf, numb. Floating beneath the world in a vast, empty space. *I'm dreaming, I'm dreaming, I'm dreaming,* she chanted, but the words, silent on her lips, only rattled through her mind. She struggled to wake up, to swim toward the surface. Her skin itched and crawled with the sensation of millions of clawed feet that scraped her arms and legs, dissolving her fingers, erasing her limbs.

With a roar, dark detonated into light. A hand—solid, bright, and rosy-hued—plunged through the oppressive night. Vice-like fingers found her neck, entwined in her hair, and yanked her upward as she sputtered and gulped.

The darkness hissed as Davis ripped Pru from its grasp and gathered her into his arms. The apartment snapped into place. The roof slammed down. The walls creaked and reformed. The lights clicked on one after the other. The odors faded and the water receded. The clean kitchen sparkled, the scent of baking cookies wafting from the oven.

Davis rocked Pru while she sobbed, eyes wide and body shivering. "It's OK. I'm here," Davis soothed, rubbing her back with trembling hands. "I've got you. I've always got you."

He wiped a beaded line of sweat from his face with the back of his hand and smiled. From beneath the ratted knots of hair matted to his forehead, shadow antenna quivered. A roach. It crawled along the outside of his ear, clicking and suckling.

Then it wormed its way inside.

Davis twitched and tilted his head. "Why are you crying? You made it, you're here! I've been calling and calling, and you finally came. This is my new apartment. Isn't it great?"

Davis's knees buckled, eyes rolling into the back of his head as he fell. Beneath the yellow walls, dark stains coalesced, sliding, creeping, dripping from the ceiling.

"Davis, no!" Pru dropped to her knees, pressing her palms to his chest as he bucked and convulsed. Her fingertips brushed his clammy skin.

The contact connected them, pulling her under and into his mind...

Like ink sinking into parchment, Pru and Davis merged, spirits entwined. Pru squeezed her eyes tight, overwhelmed as their connection roared to life. Every atom of his being flowed hot, spreading through her, awakening her mind.

She was Davis. She was Pru. They were one.

Loud synth music thumped, and Steve danced across the room. Davis followed beside him, jabbing his fist in the air at an offbeat to the erratic bass. The crowd parted around them. Pru felt their shared stomach flip-flop and tighten. They rubbed and squeezed the back of their neck. Their vision blurred for a second, reforming so sharply everyone at the party glowed with rainbow auras.

"Hey guys, taste this!"

An overflowing red cup changed hands around the room. Everyone took a sip. But right before Davis's turn, when it got to Steve, he slammed the remainder and crushed the cup in his palm with a whoop. Then he jump shot the crumpled plastic into the trash. "He shoots, he scores!"

The room erupted. *Steve! Steve! Steve! Steve!*

Pru felt Davis's smile fade as he fished his vibrating phone from his pocket. "Hey sis, sup?"

Their eyes went wide, their face hot.

"He *what?*"

Davis and Pru jammed one finger deeper into their ear.

"*Slow down.* Where are you now? Pru? I can't hear—*PRU?*"

They shook his phone, willing it to reconnect, then shoved it back in their pocket. Their temple throbbed, the knots in their neck aching even as they reached back to squeeze and massage the base of their pounding skull.

Colors swirled. The walls, the floor, the people around them ripped apart and fell back together into mismatched forms. Their shared vision rippled and distorted as Davis elbowed his way through walls of drunk bodies, his thoughts an angry whirlwind.

Don't believe this.

Not my sister.

I'll kill Ricky.

Where the hell is Steve?

His thoughts rang sharp through Pru's head. Too loud. Too hot. Somewhere, her fingers—her own fingers—pulsed, sweaty against her brother's writhing body on the floor of his apartment.

She could see it if she focused. Could see Davis's fear, a tangible thing. It seeped through his skin, rising in wisps that grew into inky, flowing shadows. Uncoiling from the corner, Davis's fears slithered underfoot, weaving through their ankles to slide up Davis's back and drape possessively across the span of his shoulders. Pru shivered as the shadow beast entered their melded mind.

"*NOLAN!*" Davis screamed over the din, and the sea of dancers parted.

Crouched in the back by the bottles and keg, Steve played bartender. His smile dropped as Davis neared. "Is it Pru?" he asked.

Davis nodded, his tongue too thick and swollen to speak.

They raced to the townhome parking lot. Half the room followed.

A static hum filled Pru and Davis's shared headspace, muffling sounds and fragmenting thoughts as pressure built. The stink of booze permeated the crowd.

Davis held out his hand. "Keys, Nolan."

Steve closed his fist around the keys. "I'll drive. It's my truck."

Davis blinked hard and fast. Steve blurred in and out of vision. "You've been drinking. I'll go, you stay."

"Like hell I'm staying. I care about her too. I barely had anything, I'm fine," Steve growled before sliding into the truck. He revved the engine.

Davis stumbled. Pru felt the world tilt. *We don't have time to argue. Pru needs me.* The ground appeared to rise and dip when he walked. His head throbbed, splitting his skull with sharp, hammering impacts with every step. Bile climbed Davis's throat.

"Rules are rules, Nolan. You drink, you ride shotgun," Davis said, jumping into the passenger seat and body-slamming Steve out the still-open driver's side door. Davis slid across the cab, slamming the truck in reverse before Steve could pull himself off the ground.

"Get in," Davis yelled out the window. "Hurry up!"

Davis and Pru's heart flew as fast as the truck. But Davis's impatience coursed faster. They weren't going fast enough. He pressed on the accelerator.

"I'm *not* drunk," Steve growled.

"You were drinking. I was there. Remember?"

"I'm barely buzzed."

"Buzzed driving is drunk driving."

Steve scrubbed his nose with the back of his hand and nodded. "OK. I understand. I just don't trust anyone with my ride. But we got this."

The road trembled. Split in two. Half faded in while the other half faded out in a hazy, wavering aura of melted crayons. Pru shivered as fear ran a talon down Davis's spine. Rapidly he blinked, frantic to pull the road into clear, solid view. His pulse jackhammered and their hands gripped the wheel to stop them from shaking.

"Davis?" Steve. Worried, not angry.

Davis gagged. His mouth was open, frantically panting while fireworks shot through his head, exploding before Davis and Pru's eyes.

God, no. Not again. Please no. Not now. He moaned.

"What's wrong? Pull over, I can—"

"Let me focus. I'm fine. Now, shut the fuck up!"

But inside, he was screaming even louder.

Pru couldn't tell where her scream started and Davis's began. Their merged head was cracking like an egg, the painful pressure an axe cleaving their skull. Then everything shattered from the inside out, and Davis's vision winked into blackness.

No way out. No way back.

"The turn, Davis. The turn. *DAAAVISSS! TURRRRRN!*"

The old truck was soaring...

Davis's hands fumbled for his unfastened seat belt.

Too late... too late...

The old truck still soared...

Weightless, Davis and Pru lifted from the seat. Hovering. Flying.

KSSSSH!

"Make it stop!" Davis screamed in the apartment. "Make it stop! *MAKE IT STOP!*"

Pru gawked as her brother rolled across the floor, their connection severed. In the corners, the shadows groaned.

"Shh, shh," she comforted. "It was just a bad dream."

"Trapped. T-t-trapped." Davis shook so bad his teeth chattered.

"No, Davis. You're awake now, you're safe."

She patted his back, and a sick sense of déjà vu washed over her. Like a movie on fast-forward, the images from the nightmare raced through her head in a dizzying blur.

Davis screamed, grasping his head in his arms and rocking.

Pru pulled back her hand. "Davis! What's happening? I don't understand!"

Drool coated his chin as gibberish flew from his lips.

Each time she dared to touch him, she was thrust back into the center of the accident, dying alongside him over and over again. His body convulsed, eyes rolling into the back of his head. No matter how hard she tried, he wouldn't fully wake. From the depths of every corner, the shadow beasts crept closer, rolling across the floor. The apartment shook, the walls dissolved, the ceiling vanished…

13

Time After Time ~ Cyndi Lauper

I come to screaming with my head in my hands and my heart thundering so hard in my chest I think it might explode. I feel my brother's presence in the Gherkin, a heavy weight on the seat beside me, pressing through the stuffy air. My palms tingle and throb like they did in the dream and I long to touch him again, but I'm fearful for the horror it brought.

Oh God, Davis. What the hell is going on?

Am I really losing him like Anne-Marie forewarned?

I need to check my journal and see if the pages are still fading, to see if—heaven forbid—he's vanished from them entirely. But idiot that I am, I left it at the Nolans' house.

I stumble out into the darkening garage. The setting sun, slung low across the horizon, casts long shadows along the concrete floor. Shrinking against the hood and struggling to breathe, I fish out my phone from my pocket to cast light around the room.

Tree branches bent by the wind scrape across the side window. Shadows twitch on the workbench and walls. Pack secure on my back, I bolt outside into the crisp dusk thick with ozone and the promise of impending rain. Dark, dank clouds drift over the sunless sky. Around me, the day's final shadows ripple down the street, outstretched and flapping like feathered wings.

I don't stop running until I see the sanctuary of Steve's house standing on the hill.

The driveway's empty; no sign of Mr. Nolan or Steve. I slide my key into the knob and open the door with a quiet click, hesitating on the porch while peering inside. I've done this a million times before. Walked up these same steps. Unlocked the door. Raced to the fridge to grab us all snacks. But today it feels like the first time ever. Like I'm an unwanted stranger breaking into a place where I don't belong.

A criminal.

Every light was left on and the kitchen reeks of China Castle, Steve's favorite restaurant. Dirty dishes dotted with specks of rice and sticky splotches of soy sauce sit unrinsed beside the sink. I spy a twenty and a note on the table waiting for me.

Ate early. There's an untouched container of combo fried rice for you in the fridge, but order pizza instead if you want. Back late. Don't wait up. ~Steve

As I run my thumb over his old, familiar handwriting, I hear Mr. Nolan's words in my head.

"Life's way too short to live without people who see and accept you for who you are at your core."

Steve and I had that magic. We did. Then Davis died, and I blamed Steve for everything, vanquishing it.

My head swims, and I lean against the counter to steady myself, legs rubbery and weak from running all the way here. My dream confirmed everything Dad told me. Steve drank, but Davis was driving with a migraine.

Because of me.

It was never Steve's fault, it was all mine.

If I'd called Mom and Dad instead of Davis, if I'd stood up to the Dickster myself, if I'd made a single, dependable friend who could have driven me home, none of this would have happened. I'd still have my brother. I'd still have Steve. Everything would be normal and not this terrible upside-down reality I've been lost inside all year. That same unwanted yet haunting pressure I can never seem to escape builds behind my eyes. The dreams should be helping... but they're not. They rip and scratch at an already festering wound I don't think will ever fully heal.

I shove the bill into my pocket for later when I might actually bother to have an appetite and fold the note from Steve gently in half.

Rounding the corner to head to my room, I smack into...

Fucking Maddison.

"Oooooh!" she squeals, and almost drops her phone before stuffing it into her pocket. "I thought Steve was kidding when he said you were newly homeless."

Of course she knows. I mean, she was bound to figure it out sooner or later. But still, this is beyond awkward—way worse than I thought it would be the first time Steve brought her around after my Nolan home relocation. Except he's not even home.

"Steve's not here. So why, exactly, are you, Maddison?"

She flashes a gigantic, toothy smile, but her eyes narrow into catty slits. "I dropped off a fabric swatch so Stevie can match his tie and cummerbund to my dress. You know. For prom?" She tucks a perfectly lacquered curl behind her perfectly tiny ear. Jutting her chin, she widens her stance, filling the entrance to the hall so I can't sidestep past.

Maddi lives to push buttons, but I'm done giving her that power. I flash a fake smile back, pretending just like I do any other day that I'm fine while on the inside I'm crumbling. "How'd you get inside anyway?" I make the words bite, but they sound as forced to my ears as they feel to speak. I have zero sway at the Nolans' house; it's not my home. Maddi is wanted. Invited. My stay is all about obligation—about Mr. Nolan repaying some imagined debt. I'm not here in some deeper way that actually matters.

My hands shake. Still, I cross my arms over my chest and let my smile dive-bomb into a harsh frown to drive home the point: *We are so done here.*

"With a key," she answers. "Duh. No wonder you can't pass geometry. You can't even put two and two together." Tilting her head with a false sympathetic pout, she pats the top of my head and wriggles past.

I crumple Steve's note in my fist, wishing my brain had some sort of witty comeback. A crisp, cool, I-don't-care-you-don't-bother-me reply. Instead, my head thuds in useless, rhythmic beats, not snappy words, while my skin grows hot and my cheeks turn red.

"You know," she says, glancing back over her shoulder, "it's not too late to find a date to the dance. I'll never understand why, but Ricky still holds a soft spot for you." She smirks and winks, slamming the door as she leaves.

I bang the dead bolt into place, but my stomach knots intensify.

What was she really doing here...

Racing to the hall, I see Maddi left Steve's door wide open.

There it is. A big ole sequined periwinkle square taking up the bulk of his pillow. It looks intimate fanned across the sheets in the exact spot his head rests. My gut constricts. The more I stare, the more the twinkling fabric seems like taunting laughter. Pulling a bon-bon from my pocket, I snap the chocolate shell with my teeth and open my bedroom door.

Thankfully my room looks the same as I left it this morning—unmade bed, dirty clothes in a small pile on the floor, my journal positioned in the exact same spot I placed it on the desk. Letting out a shaky breath and dropping my backpack with a thud, I notice the door to the shared bathroom between my room and Steve's is ajar. But I've more important things to worry about than Maddison spying on me. Or Maddison dancing with Steve. Or Maddison and Steve spooning in his bed.

Groaning, I rub my eyes to wipe away that image and collapse on the futon with my journal, opening it to the first page.

My stomach rolls and ice pours down my spine.

Everything's worse.

Before, Davis's colors were simply fading. Now, all his facial features are gone too.

OK. It's all OK.

My fingers are numb and trembling wildly. It takes three tries to rip open the marker tin. Beginning with the first entry where everything's so far gone I can't even tell the blob on the page is a person, let alone my brother, I touch the pen tip to the faintest of outlines. As black ink soaks into the parchment, I choke on a sob. Relief floods my body. My arms tremble. I have to stop, take in gulps of air, and shake out the jitters before resuming. I won't be able to rest until I get his pictures perfect.

I'm fanning the page dry when I see it—Davis's newly darkened form already lightening as though I've run an eraser over the image instead of cool air. In half the time it took me to recreate the scene, it's evaporating again.

No matter which color I use, which page I fix, the result is the same.

I'm gonna be sick.

I fly to the bathroom and dry heave into the toilet.

My mind and stomach are a ruinous mess, my spine so tight my back spasms. I stumble to the dining room and put the twenty back on the table. I won't be eating dinner.

Instead, I wander to the window. I want Steve's truck to pull into the drive, but the neighborhood is silent. A full moon hangs over the yard, outlining the shadows and bathing the grass in a milky glow. I shove my last bon-bon into my mouth. It tastes chalky and dull.

For a moment, I consider leaving. Consider running home to sleep in the Monte. But as the wind picks up, clouds drift over the moon and shadows swallow the street. The hair on the back of my neck rises. I'm exhausted yet wired. My heavy limbs don't want to move, but my hands shake as though I drank an entire pot of coffee. If the journal is real, then what about the shadows? I know Davis is in danger, but I also know that when I'm awake, the apartment can't hurt me.

I *know* this.

But I'm afraid to go outside alone.

Back in my room, I collapse on the futon, curling into a ball and clutching my stomach. Squeezing my eyes shut, I will myself to sleep and dream of Davis.

My pillow is tear-soaked when I jolt awake even though I didn't dream at all. My door leading to the hall is ajar. It's dark out, late, but a light filters through the crack beneath the door along with the delicious smell of sweet chocolate and warm cinnamon. My stomach growls, reminding me I skipped dinner. After slipping out of bed, I shuffle down the hall, tracking the heavenly scent.

My mouth is on drool overdrive when I spot Steve at the stove.

"Good, you're up. I heard you talking and crying in your sleep. I made some hot chocolate. It always used to help."

I watch him pour the steaming velvety goodness into tall orange mugs with silver spoon handles peeking above their rims. I don't know if it should comfort or terrify me how well he remembers my poor sleeping habits. Where Davis could doze through Armageddon raging in his bedroom, Steve always woke at the slightest sniffle even from halfway down the hall.

"Want to tell me about your dream?"

He turns, mugs in hand—all rumpled PJs, bedhead, and worry. After handing me mine, he pulls out a kitchen chair for me. I'm still so woozy from sleep, my legs tremble as I sit.

Steve is so different from Davis. When we were kids, Davis was a fixer, always looking for solutions and taking action. He worked hard to correct anything that wronged me. But Steve... Steve was always *there*. A safe and solid presence in my world whenever I needed him. Often, that's all I really wanted. An ear, a shoulder, a hand to hold. All that doing and fixing... it was exhausting. When you hurt, having someone sit with you, holding silent space and simply being present... It can be all the fix you need.

I close my eyes and we're eight years old again. Steve is waking me up with a gentle hug after a nightmare. Taking me by the hand and leading me to the kitchen. Making me for the very first time the same drink he made his mom when she became too sick to prepare it for herself. He altered the recipe over the years, going heavier on the dark chocolate and lighter on the cinnamon until he got it exactly how I love it.

He may not be sitting close or holding my hand or propping up my head with his shoulder, but he is still a comfort, as much as in BD times.

And I've been nothing but distant and cruel to him all year.

Clutching the spoon, my hand shakes as I stir and stir and stir, looking deep into the swirls inside the mug because I can't bear to look Steve in the eye. His gaze burns holes along my skin. The clink of metal on ceramic and the soft tick of a clock on the kitchen wall echo loudly in the persistent silence.

"You know you can still tell me things, right? I mean, nightmares suck and all, but they're just dreams. I won't judge you."

He laces his fingers together, cups his hands behind his head, and tosses one long leg over the other. He watches while he waits, but the longer I sit there mute and stirring, the tighter his lips clench.

I take a gulp of chocolate. Then a second. Then a third. All the while, I watch him over the rim while his jaw twitches and his leg bounces.

Plunking the mug onto the table sends ripples across the milky surface that reminds me of the muddied pools alive with darkness in dreamland. Shivering, I push the mug farther away. I can still taste muck on my tongue, and I scrub roughly at my lips. Staring into the dim, yellow bulb over the stove, I let the light burn away the visions in my mind. I wish my dreams were only that, like Steve suggests, but I know something else is happening.

I just don't know what.

"Pru, its late. If you don't want to talk..." He points toward the hall, letting his voice trail off and stating the obvious with his gesticulating hands: *I'm done with you.*

Chewing my lower lip, I shove my hands between my jittering knees.

Steve sighs and uncrosses his legs. The shadows behind him shift and move. No way can I stay here in the growing gloom alone. Fear bubbles through my stomach and the words burble out.

"It's—it's Davis. I've been visiting him in my dreams, but something's wrong. With everything."

He winces at Davis's name but recovers fast, shutting his mouth quickly and nodding as though everything's OK and he wants me to continue. But then, he tugs his earlobe and his eyes swirl, shifting colors. Growing dark. His body language is all bolt and run.

I can't do this. He won't understand. He will never believe me.

I jump from my chair and it squeaks across the linoleum. Steve catches it before it tips. He glances toward his dad's bedroom. "Let's talk outside," he whispers, shrugging like it's a question but already moving toward the front door.

I don't even know where to start. I remember how it felt when Anne-Marie first shared her suspicions. Scary. Surreal and suffocating all at once. My mind screaming, *It's your imagination, it's just dreams.* But after tonight, I can't deny the changing artwork. My journal! The proof is in my journal. "I need to show you something. Be right there."

Before I change my mind, I sprint to my room on tiptoed feet and snag a marker and my artbook before heading back to join Steve.

He meets me on the stoop. I hand him my journal. He drags a sweatshirt over his head and tosses me another.

I finger the worn fabric. This hoodie is his all-time favorite. He's washed it so many times, the white block-letter R in *SANTA CRUZ* looks like a P. Striped red-orange sky and electric blue ocean have faded to pastel pink, yellow, and teal. And the thin, cursive *California* at the bottom has rubbed off entirely, now a scattering of shadowy flecks, a mere ghost of itself.

Kind of like Davis in my journal.

Steve told me once how his family spent three weeks in a cabin nestled in the redwoods right after his mom's cancer diagnosis. She wanted to dip her toes in the Pacific and have one last good vacation before she started chemo.

Warm sandalwood and sweet honey fill my nose as I slide his shirt over my head. My stomach flutters at his scent, how he smells exactly how I remember, and I almost rip it off and toss it back, but the wind kicks up. Resisting the urge to cup the fabric to my face and breathe in deeper, I tug the black hem dangling loose around my thighs.

Steve waits, holding my journal and rubbing his fingers gently across the cover. His intense yet patient stare sends shivers up my spine, as though he is trailing his hands down someone's back—mine? Maddi's?—and not across my book. Heat crawls up my neck, and I pull the hood in place, yanking on the drawstrings to cinch it snug. His eyes darken and his mouth quirks into a half-smile before tugging his lower lip between his teeth. My heart pounds as his eyes dance.

"It—it'll be easier, maybe, if I show you." I wipe my sweating palms on my jeans, take the journal, and sit on the straw welcome mat directly beneath the porch light.

"Scooch. The cement is cold." He nudges his socked foot against mine. Swallowing hard, I slide right. The darn mat takes up only a quarter of the small porch, but we fit. Barely. It's snug. His leg and shoulder brush mine as he leans close to see. I smell sweet chocolate each time he exhales.

I focus on finding the right place to start as a distraction from his eyes. The pages tremble as I flip them. "I've been recording my dreams. This is one of the more recent pictures I drew of Davis." Skipping the images of the apartment swarming in shadow and filth, I show him the one from the football memory—Davis throwing a winning touchdown to Steve in the endzone on one page, celebrating with teammates on the other. Even though it's fairly new, the art looks vintage—aged and worn.

"And this"—my hands shake and the pages rattle—"was the first."

The blurred lump that I know to be Davis stands hunched before the stove in the dreamland apartment balancing a gigantic cookie between his hands while I watch from atop a towering wooden barstool. The vibrant colors of the kitchen, once 80s-era sharp and bold, are now pale and runny like a newspaper left in the rain.

Steve frowns and coughs, shifting uncomfortably. He stretches out his legs, then pulls them back again, draping his forearms across his knees with a sigh. I'm about to slam the book shut and race back inside when, finally, he speaks. "I don't... I'm not sure what I'm looking at, Pru."

"Watch." Uncapping the pen, I touch the tip to Davis's blurry outline and drag it down the page. This time, the ink doesn't even permeate the fibers. I swallow bile.

"Your pen is dry." He flicks the plastic with his finger.

I grab his wrist, scribble a wet smiley face onto his palm, then press the pen back to the book.

"Is something weird with the paper then?"

"No." I draw a line right beside Davis. Then again on his outline. The one not on his body is inky, black, crisp. Nothing appears on the bit that should be Davis.

"And this only happens to the drawings of Davis from my dreams." I turn to the picture I drew in art class of the day I was born.

He lifts the journal from my grip, fingers smudging and pressing the dry, faded lines. "Can I try?"

I nod.

He drags the pen across the bottom of my art class drawing, a thick inky line, then dabs it on the corner of Davis in one of my dreamland drawings of him. Nothing happens. "What's this even mean?"

"I'm not sure. Anne-Marie says... She thinks my dreams might be real. As in, reflect some kind of reality."

Steve clears his throat and tugs his ear.

I stand, pull the entirety of my arms and hands into the baggy sleeves of Steve's sweatshirt, wrap my arms around my middle, and pace the porch.

"There's more." The words scratch my dry throat, and I wish for another hot mug of chocolate to thaw the chill seeping through my skin. "She says if my dreams are real, then he's trapped. That his soul is... deteriorating because he chose to stay. Here. With us. On the Earthly plane or whatever. I know it sounds crazy, but I'm starting to think she isn't wrong. You know?"

I pause before him, tapping and curling my toes against the icy cement, ready to let shame carry me to bed 'cause Steve isn't moving. He isn't blinking. He has flipped to a drawing of morphing shadow overwhelming the living room of the dreamland apartment.

This was a bad idea.

Except… he starts talking.

"We moved here because at our old place, Dad saw Mom in the garden all the time." He closes the journal and caps the marker. His voice continues at a whisper. "At night, the bedsprings would squeak and the mattress would shift as though she'd curled up beside him." He looks right at me now. "It's not crazy."

A tense, shaky laugh stutters from my mouth and I gasp, slamming my palm over my lips. I lift my eyes toward the blinding porchlight and blink, fast. But still the burn and heavy pressure of tears builds, lurking like always beneath my lids.

Steve stands. When he hands me my journal and pen, his touch lingers. "Hey," he whispers. "It's OK. I believe you."

"No. Nothing is OK, Steve. He says he's trapped, and every time I go there, it gets worse and worse. It's dark, and it's creepy, and the shadows are alive and… Davis is changing, Steve. He has these nightmares where he relives his death over and over again. It's breathtaking to see him, but it's scary as fuck. You don't understand what it's like."

"So, show me." Steve pushes the hoodie off my forehead. His fingers trail down my cheek, so soft I'm uncertain it's real, before dropping to my shoulders and giving my arms a warm squeeze. "Let's go to the Gherkin."

"How exactly does this work?"

Now that we're actually here in the garage, Steve looks like he wants to be anywhere else. He didn't bother to change out of his plaid flannel PJ bottoms, and his bedhead hair juts out in all directions as his eyes flick around the room, taking in everything except the car. Or me. He gnaws his lip and his hand trembles over the handle before he opens the door. "We just… crawl inside and go to sleep?"

"Um. Yeah." Gently, I nudge the door wider to wiggle past him. "I usually sleep in the back, but you're taller."

Gripping the top of the door, Steve's knuckles blanch white, and the raw scrapes and bruises dotting his skin from his fight with Ricky darken. I run my fingers, featherlight, across the abrasions. His eyes widen and dart to mine as he pulls his hand away.

"Sorry," I whisper. "I didn't mean—"

"It's nothing. Take the back. I'll get in front. Let's get this over with."

Get this over with? Steve's voice is clipped and hard. I don't understand why when he has been nothing but gentle and supportive all night. Even his silence on the drive over seemed comfortable, like he was simply processing everything happening with Davis and the meaning of the dreams.

Maybe now he's remembering the last conversation we had in here. The one where I called him a drunk. An assaholic. Where I blamed him for things I am starting to realize were beyond anyone's control—not even Dad's despite his convincing Davis to go off his meds.

Not even mine for calling Davis when I needed him most.

And definitely not Steve's, who was in the truck with Davis and—

Images from Davis's nightmare loop race through my mind. Steve's old truck flying into the tree. Davis's body soaring through the windshield. Steve, the ragdoll, bouncing off the side door, body suspended by the safety belt. I hear the shrill, electrified screams as the glass shatters, Steve retching and struggling to breathe before slamming back against the seat so hard his neck pops and cracks. Shards of glass nick and cut his forearms as he shields his head. As he watches a thick branch punches through Davis's airborne face like a knife gliding through a ripe peach and hitting the pit with a wet, sickening smack.

The screams in the nightmare were not Davis's or mine. They were all Steve's.

"I—I thought I could—I don't think—I can't do this." Steve holds his hands up as though I dragged him here at gunpoint and backs out of the car. His eyes are wide, scared, pained—just like the moment the truck went off the road in the nightmare.

I don't think, I just lunge, flying out of the car and wrapping my arms around Steve's neck. I strain on my tiptoes and rest my head on his shoulder, squeezing him so tight the rabbit-fast thumping of his chest pounds against mine.

"I'm sorry. I'm sorry. I'm sorry," I chant, even though *sorry* never fixes anything. I squeeze and apologize, a juddering, skipping record, until finally his hands grip the sides of my sweatshirt, balling it into thick, knotty chunks at my hips. "I'm so very sorry. Thank you, Steve. For everything."

He sags against me. "Don't." He pushes me away, grinds the heels of his palms against his eyes.

I want to reach up and hold his hand, but he's backing away again. "Don't what?"

"Don't thank me. I'm here, but…" He throws his hands into the air. His breath hisses through his clenched teeth. "How do you do it? How can you sleep here every night in *his* car. Surrounded by *him*. Steve reaches out and touches the lifeless hood. Pulls back as though it burned. Shoves his hand deep within his pocket.

I was wrong. Steve isn't mad at me. He's hurting to be here. It hurts me too. But I also need to do this.

"Because I miss him," I answer. "And I really believe he needs me."

Steve stills and tilts his head backward. Shutting his eyes, he draws in long, stuttering breaths that shake his shoulders.

"OK." He huffs the word on a sighing exhale. Then he shuffles to the Gherkin and presses the seatback forward, gesturing for me to climb inside.

Steve falls asleep before I do. His soft breaths hitch in light snores. I can't believe he's here with me. Part of me wants to watch him, but I'm afraid if I sit up, the noise of the motion would wake him. Still, my heart hammers. Not because of Steve's proximity, his radiating body heat warming the cab more than usual. No. I can't think, can't sleep, because I'm unsure this duo dream test will work.

And I'm afraid of what awaits me in dreamland.

14

Stay ~ Oingo Boingo

"Whatcha think, Pru? Plaid or solid? Blue totally looks better than green or red against the yellow walls. 'Course, if you want something more custom, we can have that too."

Davis clapped his hands, and the overstuffed sofa in the living room changed from solid to checkered to black-and-white sketches from Ah-Ha's "Take On Me" music video. Synth keyboard and lively drumbeats played from button tufted cushions. Pru gaped as the band members swirled and danced across the cottony surface while they sang.

"And the seats—beanbags or recliners? Oh, I know! How about something beachy? We can take them outside in the summer." Again Davis clapped, and three wooden Adirondack chairs materialized beneath the open bay window, replete with furry chenille blankets and invitingly plump pillows. Three. Not four for their whole family. Three. One for her, one for Davis…

And one for Steve.

Pru rubbed her forehead. Steve…

She was supposed to bring Steve here. Where was he? Had their experiment worked?

"Things are really coming together now!" Davis's excitement broke her train of thought.

Open-mouthed, Pru took in the fully decorated apartment.

High-end cooking appliances cluttered the counters, and a copper pot rack packed with metal pans dangled from the ceiling above the stove. Quilted placemats dressed a small square dining table perched catty-corner from the end of the horseshoe-shaped kitchen. In the oven, something chocolatey and sweet was baking.

The living room housed a pristine glass-doored stereo system with a radio, an old-timey phonograph, and a duo-cassette player, all flanked by gleaming black waist-high speakers. Patterned throw rugs covered all the bald spots in the freshly vacuumed carpet.

Davis clapped.

Paintbrushes in a multitude of sizes, art pens, markers, pencils, and a rainbow of chromatic paint cans hovered in the air. Pru reached out and tapped one, watching it spin lazily and then float to the floor with a soft *whoosh*. Color passed through the bottom of the jar and sparkled across the carpet, staining the fibers a rich, ruddy-brown ochre.

"I need your artistic expertise." Davis tapped a bare wall. Small, scrollwork letters—D, P, and S—appeared over the sofa. Rectangular picture frames shifted on the plaster and clicked into place, their canvas centers blank.

Davis batted a brush. It tumbled end over end. Pru caught it before it could sail over her shoulder.

"Could you draw…" Davis paused, frowned, and rubbed his forehead. "Something with… someone who… Crap! I had it a second ago." His eyes glazed over, the bold cornflower blue irises fading to a dull grey hue. Swaying, he stared vacantly at the wall. The music from the sofa stuttered, emitting a blaring, discordant note. When Pru jumped, Davis jerked toward her. His head snapped up, his dimples flashing.

"I need your artistic expertise," he said. "Could you draw… something with… someone who…" He scrubbed his hand over his eyes, and his head lolled sleepily on his shoulders. "Us!" He snapped his fingers. "Draw us. Something with everyone. You know, you, me, and… and… and…" He pointed a finger at Pru's shirt as he stammered. Glancing down, she noticed Steve's old Santa Cruz hoodie: brightly colored, crisply printed. Brand new. "Him. And our… our… birth people. Um. Fawn… fim… family! I need you to draw our family photos. I don't have them anymore."

Turning his back on Pru, Davis rubbed a dark smudge from the plaster with the hem of his wrinkled t-shirt. Pru gasped as the stain spread through the fabric, turning it black. She spun Davis to face her. Her hands trembled against his shoulders.

While the apartment looked fresh and smelled lemony clean, Davis reeked—a rotted earth scent that bit her sinuses and stung her eyes. His skin felt icy cold despite the sweaty sheen coating his cheeks and forehead. Deep fissures cut through the tender skin of his lower lip, their edges caked with dried blood. When he smiled, she noticed his top teeth were yellowed, the bottom row crumbling into jagged nubs.

Davis dragged his hand through his hair. Chunks fell out in patches, exposing his skull, grey and mottled with dark oozing sores.

"Davis, are you OK?"

"Oh, hi, Pru, you came!"

Pru gagged. His breath smelled of vomit and rotten meat.

"Check out our apartment!"

Wind howled through the open bay window, billowed the curtains, and raced down the hall to rattle the bedroom doors. The chandelier above them flickered. Glittery dust motes landed on Pru's arms with small zaps of static. Then they rose in oscillating spirals, a crooked finger of warmth and light beckoning her forward. Pru padded after it.

"Where are you going?" Davis asked.

"Come on." Pru swallowed hard and motioned for Davis to follow though she didn't want to lead. The hall was dark, and although the wind had died, the doors still shook against their hinges. "You haven't shown me the rest of the apartment." Her stomach churned on the lie, and she ached with the knowledge that he likely wouldn't remember anyway.

Davis frowned and picked his lip, reopening a crack in it. Dark oil trickled down his fingers. "It's not ready yet."

"But I came with Steve. He might be over here."

Davis cocked his head. "Steve." He mimicked Pru's tone and mirrored her movements. When she widened her eyes and clutched her chest, so did he.

Pru tried swallowing past the boulder swelling in her throat. This thing, this disintegrating, filthy, and forgetful *thing*, was not her brother. Always he was the fixer, the helper, the thoughtful one who remembered birthdays. Who noticed and celebrated minor accomplishments. Who took the time to learn and remember the name of everyone he met. This washed-out shade, hunching when Pru hunched, sighing when Pru sighed, crying when Pru cried… It wasn't even human. It was barely an echo of the brother she used to know.

Pru nodded toward the hall. "Don't you want to see him?" Her cheeks hurt from forcing a smile when, really, she wanted to scream. She wanted to run and escape this nightmare reality.

She also wanted to hang on to it and save her brother. He couldn't live in some freaky, empty run-down nightmare apartment when he could flourish and thrive in the afterlife.

And why wasn't Steve right here? If he were standing beside her, she wouldn't have to face these demons alone. But most of all, he might have helped her figure out how to save Davis and the apartment. No way could she figure everything out by herself. She wished she could stay with Davis in dreamland eternally, revisiting night after night for the remainder of her life. But as *the thing* twitched and convulsed, its spasmodic movements hurling fragments of flesh and hair into the air, an overwhelming sadness erupted within her chest. Clinging to this dreamworld, to her beloved brother, was slowly but surely consuming him, just like Anne-Marie had warned.

Her perfect brother was gone.

Pru held her breath as Davis threaded his bony, skeletal fingers between hers. Crackling husks of skin, as jaundiced and paper-thin as aged onion peels, flaked into the air when he squeezed her hand.

"Pru," Davis whispered, his voice rattling and wheezing. "I've missed you. I'm so glad you came."

Pru ignored the slithering energy writhing beneath the surface of Davis's skin, bubbling and pressing against her palm, threatening to burst as she tugged him down the hall. Anne-Marie's words echoed in her mind, the only thing propelling her forward. The only thing keeping her upright.

Help Davis find the light.

The back of the apartment was nothing like the front. The bathroom door hung cockeyed, sagging precariously from a single hinge. Inside, blackened vines crawled from the toilet, climbed the walls, and choked the sludge-leaking showerhead. Down the entire length of the hall, broken glass and gravel buried the carpet. It bit through the soles of Pru's shoes. Davis, barefoot, didn't seem to notice even as the shards glittered ruby with his blood in the dim, flickering light. Every surface was coated in grime, a bitter, sulfuric ash that swallowed the walls and dripped from the ceiling.

The apartment yawned, and the door to Davis's bedroom at the end of the hall thumped.

Pru staggered closer to the sealed guest room, eyes locked on Davis's bedroom door as it bowed beneath the weight of something heavy pressing from the other side. A screeching emanated from the keyhole like a knife scraping a plate or nails dragged down a blackboard. The door stilled. Then came a knock. An invitation to come inside. A demand to be let out.

Pru's hand slipped from Davis's grasp as he sank to the floor, batting his head with his fists.

"No-no-no-no-no-no."

Black, wispy smoke unfurled from his ears, encircling his forehead in a pulsating ring. Davis threw his head back and screamed.

Lunging, Pru flung open the guest room door.

There was no bright tunnel of light. No white and winding staircase climbing through golden-bellied clouds. No locked pearly gates surrounded by caroling angels.

Equally, there was no fear. No anxiety. No hopelessness. No shadows. All the things that flooded the dreamland apartment and filled her with cold dread every time she visited Davis—gone.

Euphoric bliss flowed through Pru's veins, a contented sigh warming her skin and soothing her mind. Fresh breezes bathed the hallway in a garden meadow burst of cut green grass and fragrant pine. Verdant and mossy.

Pru closed her eyes. Inhaling deep, she stepped through the door. An unseen barrier vibrated and hummed as she did so. Swirling ripples spread out from her, rendering the view beyond hazy and indistinct, but as the world shifted into focus, Pru squealed and clasped her hands to her cheeks.

There was no roof, no walls. An endless expanse of beauty ebbed and flowed, continually shifting.

Lofty peaks of bronze tipped in crystalized diamond snow erupted from the base of deep, shimmering emerald pools. Trees murmured and breathed, swaying and dancing, flush with birds, squirrels, and monkeys—Davis's favorite. Rivers teeming with fish carved paths through lush gardens and dense forests. Smells of pizza and fruit cobbler, ocean brine and musky forest mist, rolled past the door as small rain clouds opened wide to sprinkle gemstone prisms refracting mini-rainbows bursting with color through beams of orange sunlight. Pru spied in the distance a vast football field, the goal posts wavering like a city skyline on a balmy day. Everything thrummed as though alive, glittering with the same golden motes that bounced in the apartment.

"Davis," she whispered, "you gotta see this."

"I have," he muttered, his tone dull and uninterested.

"Then—why didn't you come inside? All your favorite things are in here! I don't understand."

"No. Not everything. Just *them*." Davis flicked a mote from his wrist, glaring as it tumbled back toward the beauty, passing over the threshold with a quiet *snick*. A slender, gilded feather drifted from where the mote had hovered to the floor, sinking into the grimy carpet. "And places. Smells. Things. None of it matters." His voice caught on the words in breathless chokes, and he rubbed his throat as though it burned.

"Them?" Pru squinted and watched as the glitter mote soared over a lake. The reflection mirrored along the glass surface looked nothing like the miniscule dot floating above. A white aura of downy feathers brighter than the sun shone in pulsating rays that vanished as the mote flew overland. "Davis? Is that... an angel?"

Davis slumped against the wall, facing the front end of the apartment and refusing to look at Pru or the guest bedroom. His chest rose and fell with uneven breaths. It took Pru a moment, but she realized he was crying. He made no sound, but large, wet tears streaked muddy paths down his dirt-stained cheeks.

"Why can't I have this instead?" He ran his fingertips down the pocked and broken plaster of his apartment. "I made this for all of us. I worked *so hard*. You finally found me, and now I'm supposed to give it all up and leave? No. It's not fair. I need more time. I'll fix it until it's perfect. Until it's better than that." He nodded without looking at the guest room. "I promise."

Davis clapped his hands and touched the wall, but it remained damaged and dirty.

"I *promise*."

Davis clapped louder.

"I p-p-promise you, Pru."

When the third clap brought no change, his eyes met hers—wet, wild, and bloodshot.

He held out his shaking hand, and she took it, joining him on the floor. "Tell me you'll stay," he begged, the same way she'd begged the universe for him every day and night since he died. "I'm so fucking lonely without you."

Warmth pulsed from the guest room, and Pru glanced over her shoulder. A sense of calm overtook her at the sight of it.

But Davis was right. As perfect as everything seemed, something was missing. The stories people usually told of the afterlife, how all your deceased loved ones would surround and greet you and help you cross over—that didn't exist for Davis. Magical and peaceful didn't matter. Beautifully shifting lands and pitch perfect birds and troops of swinging monkeys weren't enough. Not without Spellmeyers to greet him.

Davis was the first of them here.

He was alone.

"I'm scared," he whispered, as though reading her mind. His hand trembled in hers.

"It's OK," Pru soothed. "I'm here."

Davis launched himself into his sister's arms. Uncertain, she hesitated a moment before pulling him close, patting and rubbing his back in small concentric circles the way he always had for her in the middle of her famously overdramatic meltdowns. He was the strong one, she the weak. This reversal felt as foreign and unreal to Pru as the bulging masses creeping beneath his skin, stinging and burning her palms as she held him.

"I hear you all the time, Pru. I hear you crying in my head, I feel Dad's pain in my chest, Mom's emptiness in my stomach.

Steve's hurt tears at my skin. I feel everyone, everywhere, all the time. How can I leave when my family is destroyed? How? Please tell me you don't expect me to." His fevered skin stuck to hers as she rocked him.

The bedroom door at the end of the hall creaked open, liquid smoke reaching through the crack with long, curled fingers. The door to the guest bedroom slammed shut.

Davis whimpered, pulling out of Pru's grip. His head rolled lazily on his shoulders and his eyes drooped. He groaned, then blinked rapidly.

"Pru! You came!" Davis coughed. His tongue, a black and bloated snake, flicked out to touch his parched lips. "Tell me you're for real, Pru." He laughed, but the sound wheezed and rattled in his chest, and a festering blackness slid up his veins. "I've been calling and calling, and you finally came."

"I… I think we are dreaming, Davis. This place…" She swallowed hard as Davis narrowed his eyes and clenched his jaw. "It's not real."

The temperature dropped. Davis stood. "Why do people think they actually dream when they sleep?" he asked. "How is *this* not also reality?"

His jaw twitched. Black fog filled the hall.

"We're awake. We're real. Can't you feel it, Pru?"

The floor grumbled and the walls shifted.

"We can still have the life we were always meant to live. Bring Steve. Bring Mom and Dad. Bring everyone!"

His eyes danced with excitement and his pallid skin glowed splotchy pink on his cheekbones, raised high with his grin. Pru's anxiety tightened her throat as she grappled with the looming impossibility of it all. She only dreamed in the Gherkin, and soon, it would be sold. Her desperate attempt to reunite Steve and Davis had fallen flat. The truth she hadn't wanted to face hit her like a freight train. They were going to lose the apartment.

They were going to lose everything.

"Nothing has to change. Just stay with me, Pru. Stay, and I promise everything will—"

The ceiling imploded with a thundering crack, exposing a weighted void of starless night. Thick air, stale and humid, pinned Pru to the carpet as she struggled to stand. The walls crumbled, and the floor behind Davis buckled. A wave of shadow splintered the bedroom door.

A torrent of wings landed with a heavy thud behind Davis. Claws scraped the floor. Pru cowered, but Davis didn't flinch. His head bobbed and weaved as the shadow pressed through his body from behind. Davis flung his arms to the sky, and brackish ink flowed across his tensed shoulders. Spiked quills dangled from his arms. Lowering his head, he turned one single, solitary, orange-orbed eye on Pru, opened his mouth, and screeched. A guttural howl ending on a ragged hiss. His features faded in and out of focus as Davis and the shadow beast merged. Clicking and croaking, Davis hunched, stalking Pru down the hall as she fled toward the guest room.

"You—you need to go into the light!" Pru stammered, groping for the doorknob behind her. It slipped in her sweaty grasp as she struggled to open it. "This apartment is a nightmare. None of this is real, Davis. You… you… *you died.*"

The words rose unwanted from the bowels of her stomach, rife with fear, bitter with bile. The thing before her gnashed its teeth and slashed through the air with barbed talons. Pru ducked; the claws missed her head and pierced the door.

Davis howled as light and glitter motes escaped through the cracked wood, racing up his arm. The shadow recoiled, rolling away from his wrist and parting from his back. Davis's eyes flashed open and locked on Pru's. He gasped, wheezing and shaking as he reached for her. "Pru? What's happening?"

"Come on, Davis. I've got you."

Pru gripped the guest bedroom doorframe and thrust out her hand toward her brother as the entire apartment shook. Kitchen appliances tumbled through the air and winked out of existence. The living room furniture swelled then popped, disintegrating into dust. Darkness swallowed the ceiling, the walls, the floor. Hunks of carpet melted into a gelatinous river that absorbed everything.

Wind whipped around her, lifting Davis off his feet and pitching him backward. The greedy darkness of his bedroom welcomed him, a black and icy cocoon.

"*Davis!*" Pru rushed toward his room.

The fetid, cackling wind slammed the door in her face. She yanked on the knob, but the door pulled back, locking in place.

Davis's screams clawed her throat as though they were her own.

15

Poison Arrow ~ ABC

I'm flat on my back, shivering against the cool leather bench of the Gherkin even though it's uncomfortably warm in the car. Davis's jacket lies crumpled in a ball on the floor, and my pillow is soaked with tears. I can't breathe through my nose, my lips are dry, my tongue is parched, and my sinuses feel puffy. I must have cried all night. I'm surprised I didn't wake Steve.

"Steve?"

The front seat is empty. No note, no Steve, no nothing, as though he were never here. His sweatshirt tight around my middle, I collapse against the seat. My entire body aches and shivers, and a dull thud pulses behind my eyes, as though I have the flu. Texting him is the obvious option. Or better, calling so I can hear that calm, reassuring tone in his voice telling me everything about Davis is going to be OK. He'll tell me a story about how he had an entirely different dream. One where he got through to Davis. One where Davis stepped safely into the guest room. He will laugh and call me crazy for worrying.

Or... he'll laugh and call me crazy for trying. Maybe he didn't dream at all. He'll tell me how it was a terrible waste of time, how he slept like shit. He'll call me a liar, saying I made

everything up and the journal effect is somehow fake. That I'm a
total fraud and that's why he bailed early without saying a word.

I put my phone back in my pocket.

I need candy. I need my journal. I left both at Steve's. I
need to know if any dream pictures are even left or if all the
pages in my artbook are now entirely blank. But I don't need to
see it to know I'm losing Davis all over again.

My heart is missing, my legs are numb, my body is sinking
in quicksand. I'm drifting and no longer exist.

I pull my pillow tight to my face and scream and scream
and scream until my throat is so raw it feels gone. It doesn't
help. I still feel all my thoughts and feelings clawing painfully
at my insides. Too jittery to sit still, I get out of the Gherkin
and lock up the garage.

In the backyard, I stare at my house. It's strange watching
it this way, knowing Mom is not upstairs in her room, that
my bed is vacant too. I wonder how Dad's managing and start
moving toward the back door to check on him, but then I realize his car isn't out front.

With nowhere else to go and heavy with disappointment,
I head for Steve's.

Mr. Nolan's gigantic tow truck is the first thing I see as I climb
the hill to Steve's house. Too long to fit in the driveway, it
hulks against the curb, casting thick shadows over their yard.
My heart kicks up in my chest and my brain races to find the
right words to say to Steve when I open the door. Do I play
it cool and act like it's no big deal that he left me alone in the
Monte last night? Do I launch straight into the freaky dream
descriptions and drag him to my room to check the status of
the journal? Do I remain silent and wait for him to explain
himself first?

But as I walk around Mr. Nolan's work vehicle, the drive-way sits empty, concrete glimmering beneath the bright sun. No big blue truck. No Steve.

Inside, it smells like a BD Spellmeyer Sunday morning. Sweet maple syrup and sizzling bacon make my mouth water and my chest clench. I half expect to see Mom at the stove flip-ping pancakes, but it's just Mr. Nolan.

He turns when he hears me, his cheeks flushed, and I man-age a smile and small wave.

"You look hungry." He points to the table with his spatula. "Sit. I'll fry up a few more." He doesn't wait for a response before ladling more batter onto the griddle. While it bubbles, he piles bacon onto a plate and sets it in the middle of the table, snagging a piece off the top. With a sheepish grin, he pops it into his mouth whole.

"Sorry it's only us again," Mr. Nolan says, shrugging his broad shoulders before turning his attention back to the stove. "After breakfast, I need to mow the lawn. I think Steve left some study materials in your room; if you want, you can bring them outside and use the patio table. It's supposed to be clear today. No rain."

He slides a dollop of butter between two perfectly golden pancakes, snaking the syrup in an artistic switchbacking drizzle across both the food and the plate, then decorates the rim with a rainbow of fruit—halved strawberries, chunks of pineapple, round blueberries, sliced mango. It's almost too pretty to eat, but I need the sugar, so I take a bite.

Oh my God, they're so light and fluffy. The pancake dis-solves on my tongue—the perfect ratio of sugar, butter, and griddlecake. My muscles unwind, and I slump against the chair, the most relaxed I've been since before Steve and I fell asleep in the Monte. "Where is Steve anyway?"

"Not sure," Mr. Nolan answers, and I jump; I didn't real-ize I'd asked aloud. I pop a large hunk of pineapple into my mouth as he continues. "I've been letting him do his own thing since…" His voice trails off, his eyes darting from mine to his plate and back. Sitting straighter, he clears his throat. "He goes when and where he needs to, and I only interfere if he asks. He isn't a kid anymore, as he continually reminds me. If I had to guess, he is with Maddi getting things ready for prom. I know she's… excited." He busies himself slicing his pancake into long slivers and sliding them through the syrup ribbons on his plate.

I envision Maddison's fabric swatch covering Steve's pillow, see her face as she stumbled out of the hallway with her condescending smile, and roll my eyes. "How wonderful."

"Hey, if it weren't for Maddi, Steve wouldn't—" Mr. Nolan drops his fork to his plate, pushes back from the table and carries his dishes to the sink. His shoulders tense as he scrubs off the sticky syrup.

"Steve wouldn't what?"

"Sorry, Pru. Steve's business is Steve's business. You'll have to speak with him." He slides the plate into the dishwasher. "All righty then. The day waits for no one. Time to get to work. Coming?" His squared hands rest on his thick hips as he watches me.

"Nah, I think I'll study in my room. Thank you for breakfast."

He nods and pats my shoulder briefly as he heads out the door. After finishing my pancakes, I load and start the dishwasher and head to my makeshift bedroom.

Clutching my journal to my chest, I pace the room, but I can't bring myself to open it and check the artwork alone. I need Steve. Not just for geometry but for all things Davis too. I realize he's all I have right now. Mom's gone. Dad's not home. Anne-Marie's homebound on bed rest…

The power mower revs to life, a deep, drilling hum as Mr. Nolan walks it across the lawn. I watch him through the window. There isn't a single cloud in the sky, and the sun shines so bright everything looks washed out, Mr. Nolan's navy denim and the emerald grass a watercolor sketch. Around and around he circles the mower along the base of the giant oak tree that dominates the Nolans' backyard. Barely budding, its arms brush the sky, searching, but it's an island, all alone. No birds nestle in the branches.

I collapse backward onto the futon and let the gentle drone of the mower lull me to sleep.

On Monday morning Steve is MIA again, so Mr. Nolan drops me off at school on his way to the shop. Inside, a dense crowd gathers a few feet past the double-door entrance, blocking the path to my locker. I elbow my way through the sheep herd and find what's stopped the masses in their tracks.

Plastered front and center on the off-white cinder block wall is Davis.

An image printed from my journal stares back at me—the one of Davis in the winged Gherkin driving to the dreamland portal. Beneath the image, someone's written *Soar to Prom — A Flashback to the Past* in rainbow block letters.

People are pointing and whispering. They may not realize I'm the artist, but they *know* that's my brother and his vintage muscle car. It's a whole-body sucker punch impacting my stomach, knotting every muscle, draining my brain of any coherent thought. Squeezing my eyes shut does nothing. The poster's still smirking at me when I open them.

I can't get out of here fast enough.

Around the corner, it's even worse.

Not only is there a second poster identical to the first, but there's also one using my drawing of Steve and Maddi dancing on a rain cloud. *Vote Nolan & Wells for Prom King & Queen* mocks me in the same colorful print beneath my artwork. My fingers itch to rip the poster from the wall and shred the original in my journal. Even though I feel sick, I can't stop staring. The picture feels alive, as though they are dancing for real before me. Maddi's smile is a sneer meant for me, Steve's eyes secretive and knowing as he winks.

My heart races on my way to class. The posters are pinned to at least one wall—sometimes two—down every freaking corridor.

What the hell?

And then Maddi rounds the corner.

She spots me standing open-mouthed beneath one of the posters of her and Steve. As she nears, she shakes her palmed phone in my direction and blows me a kiss. Her shit-eating grin is so huge it could break her face in two.

Then it hits me. Maddi coming out of Steve's room. Hiding her phone in her pocket. The open bathroom door between my room and his. Of course this was her. She and Steve are the only people with recent possible access to my journal. Steve is as private as I am and would never betray my trust this way.

Right?

BD, I could have said that for sure. But then I picture how his hand fits so firmly within Maddi's claw, how he smiles at her like she is the only person who exists, and suddenly I'm not so certain.

Maddi's laughter floats down the hall as she checks over her shoulder to see me still watching her. "Remember to vote, Spellmeyer!" she coos. One last dig before she vanishes.

What else did she see in my journal? Everything?

The passing bell rings, but I don't care. I still have five minutes before I'm tardy. Instead, I search for the candy bar I tossed inside my pack this morning. The first bite is sharp on my tongue, equal parts saccharine, salty, and numbing like lidocaine on a sunburn. But the ache is still there, the skin damaged and raw. No matter how many bites I eat, I can't wash away my foolishness. And to think I actually felt sorry for Maddi after my talk with Mr. Nolan. To think I convinced Steve she was worth fighting for, forcing him back into her toxic arms when I knew better. It's exactly as Mr. Nolan said: *"When someone shows you who they are, believe them."*

Maddi serves everyone else honey but feeds me steaming balls of crap on a stick. Story of my life. I had hoped she was capable of change. I *wanted* her to change. Fuck. I'm such an idiot.

Classes pass in a total blur. I can't focus during any of them. I can't stop seeing Maddi shaking her phone at me.

At lunch, Maddison is hosting that nauseating prom voting booth in the cafeteria surrounded by her usual popular posse. The room smells of cheeseburgers and happiness. Everyone's laughing and talking at once, milling around the room with lunch in hand, clustered around the tables rather than sitting at them. Bruce walks past clutching a burger in one hand and fries in the other. As he walks, he takes alternating chomps of each. Chipmunk cheeks bulging, he waves at me, flinging ketchup and pickle onto the floor. I think about joining him, but then I spot the Dickster, bruised and pulpy, lurking near the back exit a few feet away from where Bruce's theatre friends have formed a circle. I know that's where Bruce is headed, and my arm freezes halfway up so that I can't return the greeting. Thankfully the Dickster doesn't notice me.

But Maddison does. She shoots me another fang-flashing smile and plasters herself against Steve, dragging black- and red-tipped talons down his back. She watches me over his shoulder and winks.

I wish I were brave. I want to charge through the room, scream in her face, and rip off her smirk. Confronting Maddi always runs smoothly in my head. My imagined self is all fierce lion, knowing all the perfect things to say. I would put her in her place, expose her for the lying thief she is. But now, standing in front of her, my reality is all cowering kitten. I'm pretty sure that mewling whimper came from me.

Maddi cups Steve's face between her hands, leans close, and kisses him. She doesn't fully shut her eyes. I swear she's staring me down through her thick, fake lashes. She digs her nails into his back. When he wraps his arms tight around her waist in response...

Time stops.

The room shrinks and everything blurs. I've fallen into the deep end of the pool, my vision swimming but the rest of me drowning.

Every last clever, snarky retort I've dreamed up fizzles on my mummified tongue.

"Hey look, everyone. It's our famous local artist!"

Bouncing and squealing, Maddi claps her hands. She smiles, barring her teeth, and I shiver. I hadn't seen her break the kiss.

Half the room has turned to watch me, half to stare at her, enthralled. Unquestioningly following her lead, everyone else applauds too. Even Steve. Is he blind? Could he really be this clueless? Or has he just stopped caring?

I die a little inside.

In nature, beauty means danger. You don't touch the sap of an oleander plant, play with the neon dart frog, or cuddle with a male platypus. None are more noxious than Maddison though. Why can't anyone see that but me?

"We all want to thank you for making prom so... unique!" She gestures around the room. "If you don't have a prom date, I want to hire you to draw caricatures of everyone on the big night. We could set up a table right outside the gym."

Steve brings his fingers to his lips and whistles. Cheers of encouragement erupt from the crowd.

"You could charge five bucks a pop or something. Could *totally* help with financials." Tugging the pocket liner out of her skinny jeans, she pops her hip, all perk and flirt.

The world dwindles to me and Maddi. She's just panto-mimed Dad's picture in my journal—the one of him pinching the ends of his turned out, empty pockets and frowning while dollar bills soar out of reach.

Only I see her ugly truth.

"Get your very own personalized Spellmeyer cartoon—only at prom," Maddi calls. "Scream *hell yeah* if you want one!"

The room detonates. *Hell yeah*'s, whistles, catcalls.

Maddi pulls out her phone. "Come on, Spellmeyer, you'd be great. Please say yes? You can keep it light and fun. Like this." Her thumbs glide across her screen. She hits send, cocks her head, and waits.

Over half the phones in the lunchroom light up. A symphony of bells, beeps, songs, and lyrics swells. Mine, too, buzzes hotly against my thigh. She must have gotten my number from Steve.

"Go ahead. Take a look."

She's flushed, excited. Tongue darting across her over-glossed lips. Voice high and breathy.

I glance down at my phone and…

She made a meme.

Of my art.

Of me.

It's my nightmare of last year's prom. My dress in tatters, half the bodice drooped around my waist and half clenched in desperation to my chest but barely concealing my nakedness, my electrified hair standing on end. She's embellished it with a hot pink frame full of bold, black text: *Don't get caught with your pants down. Find a date for prom.*

When I look up, all I see are smiles. All I hear are jeers and laughter. Everyone is pointing and staring at their phones.

At me.

The only non-smiling face in the crowd is Bruce's. His neck whiplashes back and forth, glancing at his phone, then at me. I latch onto his brandy eyes, soft and wide behind his glasses when he catches me staring. Gratitude sparks in my chest but it's extinguished by the bile rising up my throat. Bruce holds out his hand from across the room, motioning for me to join him, but then I see the Dickster's copper-top head cutting through the crowd too close for comfort.

"Hel-*loooo*, babycakes!" he croons, flashing his phone over his head.

I bolt out the door, barely hearing Steve yell my name even though it's so loud his voice cracks. I don't stop.

And he doesn't follow.

What have I done to deserve such a high-effort destruction of my life?

I hide out in the bathroom until class, crouched atop the toilet with the stall door locked. I count three groups of girls pass through—one I'm sure were all freshmen—talking about Maddi's text. I tune them out at the first giggle, quietly sucking on gummy worms and wishing the toilet would raise into the sky like the barstools in Davis's dreamland apartment, whisking me to a place far away, where I'd never have to wake up.

16

The Promise ~ When In Rome

Skipping study hall at the end of the day is a no-brainer. My stupid mind keeps replaying the scene in the lunch-room. Steve backing Maddison. Smiling. Clapping. Letting her hang all over him. BD, he never would have let anyone attack somebody the way she did me. But he couldn't even be bothered to chase after me when I left. He chose Maddi, which means he supports her plans. Did he get close to me explicitly to help Maddi play her little mind games? Did he tell her about my journal? Did he help her print the posters?

Picturing them sitting on my bed laughing as they pore through the pages turns my stomach. So even though it's a long ass hike back to the Nolans' house, it beats suffering through a truck ride home with Steve.

I pull a crumpled bag of half-melted M&Ms from my pack and suck on them one at a time, stretching them to last the walk instead of swallowing them all at once how I want to.

Steve's truck is already in the drive when I'm finally trudg-ing up the hill. Seeing that cheery blue chrome sparkling in the sun on this joyless day knocks the wind from my lungs, and I drop to the curb.

What the hell is he doing home? Shouldn't he be gallivanting across town with Maddi, hatching more evil plans to ruin my life, same as he likely did all those days he's been MIA? Or, fuck, what if she's inside with him right now? Waiting for me to come home so they can ambush me together?

I know Mr. Nolan said use the front door and not the window… but desperate times call for super sleuth avoidance measures. The screen propped gently against the house, I quietly slide open the window… and see Steve standing in the center of my room.

I freeze. My tongue and the last of the candy stick to the roof of my mouth. I didn't expect this aching burn—searing throat, squeezing chest, kicked-up pulse. I want to run, but my disobedient legs go rubbery and won't move.

At the desk, Steve picks up his phone and hits a button. Roxy Music's "More Than This" starts playing, and my heart flutters, erratic against my ribs. The notes release a tornado of dizzying memories at me so hard that I need to clutch the windowsill to keep from toppling over.

In the movie *Say Anything*, John Cusack holds a boom box overhead, blaring the song "In Your Eyes" to serenade his love outside her bedroom window. It's a fine enough song. Appropriately lovey-dovey and sappy. I get why the director chose it versus "To Be a Lover" by Billy Idol as they'd originally considered.

But "In Your Eyes"? It's too on the nose. Borderline cheesy. After watching the movie, Steve asked what song I'd have picked. Without hesitation, I'd swooned, crying, "*Bryan Ferry!*" and dramatically pressing my hand over my heart while Davis rolled his eyes and Steve grinned.

That velvet voice, those bittersweet lyrics of remorse and remembrance. Oh… My… God. I can't even handle how insanely dreamy Roxy Music is. Love songs similar to that

Peter Gabriel one? Basic. Anyone can say "I'm incomplete without you."

"Wanna impress me?" I had asked him. "Be raw and real. Show me how I've flipped your entire world upside down. Tell me we've always mattered most. Choose Roxy Music. Play "'More Than This.'"

The conversation ended, no less, with us in a pile of giggles on the floor when Davis belted the lyrics in a high falsetto. But... that was a lifetime ago. Something we talked about *once*. How could he possibly remember? Especially when neither of them had taken me seriously that day.

Clutching a sheaf of notebook paper, Steve steps in front of the open window before I can get out of sight. He's so close I see the swift rise and fall of his chest, the rosy flush coloring his cheeks. When his oceanic eyes meet mine, butterflies somersault in my stomach.

I'M SORRY

The first note flutters to the floor while the song plays. His gaze, intense and unwavering, never leaves my face as he shuffles slowly through the rest, holding each up a moment before dropping it to reveal the next.

I'M AN IDIOT

MADDI LIED

I BELIEVED HER

I'D NEVER BETRAY YOU
WHEN YOU HURT, I HURT

PLEASE FORGIVE ME

YESTERDAY

TODAY

ALWAYS

YOU MATTER MOST

The fallen papers crunch beneath his sneakers as he closes the short distance between us. It's something straight out of the many cringe-worthy 80s movies we'd watched BD, but his eyes shine with sincerity as they search mine, wet diamond drops clumping along his impossibly thick lashes. Without a word, he leans out the window, pressing his forehead against mine.

I can't move. I can't breathe. I want to yell. Scream. I want to hear his thoughts. Dive into his mind. Find the truth inside the fiction. Pull away, push him away, the same as I've already done a million times this year.

But I'm glued in the past. Glued to him. Hijacked by memories, the dreamy song, his breath as it melds with my own exhalations in soft, uneven hitches.

Guided by the thundering of my unreliable heart.

The song ends, and when he speaks, his voice is hoarse. "Let me explain. Please, come inside."

He helps me through the window, hands steady on my shoulders, electric on my skin. Clearing his throat, he pushes his curls off his forehead. "She told me you showed her your artwork the night she dropped stuff off for prom. I thought you two finally repaired the past because she knows how important that is to me. I also know how personal your art is, so I figured you wouldn't give her access unless you forgave her. But when I saw your face in the lunchroom… and then she sent that text…" He grimaces, glaring at the wall and fingering his cheekbone. It's bruised.

"What happened?" I have to stand on tiptoe to inspect the raised purple lump.

Straightening and angling his head, he catches my fingers in his. "I lost it. It's over."

"What did she do to you?"

"Nothing. It wasn't her," he whispers.

Flipping his hand over, I find the fresh, bloodied scrapes. "The Dickster started something again, didn't he? Did he hit you?"

"The Dickster?" He laughs and smiles, a grin so genuine, so like BD times, my belly flip-flops. "Yeah, something like that. Rick and I are suspended ten days for fighting. And Maddi, too, for circulating that text."

"Shut up! Are you serious? What'd he do?"

"You don't want to know, but it was worse than that day in study hall."

My mind reels. He risked everything for this. Everything for me. My stomach cinches. Suspended means... "What about prom?"

"No prom. We're all banned from campus. Maddi was more upset about missing the dance than the fact I broke up with her. Typical. Based on what I know about her now."

"I don't understand why you were with her in the first place."

He laughs, but it comes out a rough bark, scratchy and humorless. His eyes darken as he diverts his gaze out the window. Dropping my hand, he rubs his thumb across his bruised knuckles and wrist. "Let's just say I made a bad life choice and leave it at that, OK?"

I want to let him know he can talk to me, that he can tell me anything, like he did for me the night I told him about Davis and dreamland and my journal. But when he sighs and tugs his ear, I know he is lying, know he is hiding something. All I can do is whisper, "OK."

"Besides"—he runs his hands through his hair—"this was bound to happen eventually. She knows how I feel…" His voice trails off, his face a strawberry.

Feel about what? About Maddi being a bitch to me? About plunging headfirst into a total whirlwind romance right after his bestie bit the dust?

Turning, he shuffles toward the closet. Slides something out and hides it behind his back. "I, um, bought you some candy in case the apology wasn't enough." Flashing a crooked grin, he empties the plastic bag onto the comforter.

An astounding assortment rains down—jellybeans, gummies, caramels, every brand of chocolate bar. He raided the entire candy aisle of all my faves. Even my new bon-bon addiction is represented. I swear I can smell the sugary sweetness through the wrappers as the candy waterfall floods the bed. It reminds me of all the times Davis dumped his Halloween pillowcase full of treats in the middle of my bedroom floor, gifting me the greatest treasure, year after year after year. A lump sticks in my throat, and when I look up, Steve is watching me, his eyes intense and soft all at once. Heat rises up my neck, flushing my face, and his lips twitch into a smirky grin that sends my stomach spinning. I have to look away.

"These are the bomb!" I point to the bon-bons, desperate to dispel the awkward sensations churning inside me. I pluck two off the pile and toss him one, then peel the wrapping off the other. "I've been newly obsessed all month. How'd you know?"

"Larry told me about them on our way to see Joyce on Sunday." As soon as the words are out of his mouth, his eyes widen and his smile drops.

"Wait. *What?*" I sputter around the melting chocolate stuffed to one side of my mouth.

He crams his candy into his face whole. Gesturing toward his own chipmunk cheek, he shrugs with that universal *full mouth, can't talk* bullshit.

"Dad took *you*... to see *Mom*... without *me*?"

Gripping the back of his neck, Steve ruffles his hair so hard the cowlicks at his crown stand on end.

I sink to the carpet, hugging my knees to my chest. "I haven't seen or spoken to her since..." This isn't happening. I'm her daughter. She hasn't asked to see me once, has she? She certainly hasn't called me at all. "How long has this been going on?"

He clears his throat and looks at the floor. His lips draw into a tight, thin line as he tugs his ear. He doesn't answer. He doesn't have to.

"Get out."

"Pru, it's not like that. I can explain—"

"You excluded me. Explanation unnecessary. Get out."

He doesn't argue, but he does pause at the door. "I'm truly sorry about what Maddi did. It was cruel and unforgiveable. But I won't apologize for spending time with your mom."

His steps thud down the hall, and he slams his bedroom door harder than he closed mine. Soon as he's gone, I call Dad.

"Where were you Sunday?" I ask the instant he picks up.

"Hey, Pru. Everything all right?"

"No. You and Steve saw Mom on Sunday. Without me. Why?"

He sighs. "Steve plays an integral role in Mom's healing."

"And I don't? I'm her daughter, and he's—"

"Of course you do."

"Apparently not enough though, right?" I hate that I'm whining, but I guess it beats bawling or screaming. When I sit on the bed, the candy mountain shifts as the mattress sags, and a freaking bon-bon rolls to the floor. I kick it across the room. It hits the door with a thud, lying dented on the carpet.

"Part of Mom's program requires closure. That means talking with Steve about everything that happened. She's made incredible progress. And Pru? She's coming home. In a few days. She's requested a family gathering. An anniversary memorial honoring Davis."

Fabulous. Now, we're celebrating the Crap-iversary.

"I'm bringing you to the house on Friday, so pack an overnight bag. Everything's cleared with Mr. McKittrich for a sleepover. Exciting, right?"

"No. I don't want to sleep over. I want to move back home."

"It's only a few more days. Be strong, Pru. Things will be back to normal before you can say graduation." He chuckles at his joke, but he wouldn't be if he could see the pile of failed math tests on my desk.

Saying *graduation* is going to take a lot longer than Dad thinks.

And I have no one but myself to blame for that.

I'm nodding off in history class when Mrs. Pederman knocks on the door asking if she can borrow me for a minute. Mr. Luna hates interruptions. He scowls but nods. I'm all the school has been talking about since that appalling text yesterday, and now this? The whispers gnaw at my skin. Gossip-starved piranhas. After gathering my stuff, I rush out the door as fast as I can.

"Have a seat." Mrs. Pederman waddles behind her desk, firing up her computer. "We need to talk."

No good conversation ever starts with those ominous words. I choose to stand.

"I have good news and bad news."

Wow. I wasn't expecting any good news.

Peering at me over her glasses, she points to the dreaded seat. "Sit."

Ugh. I drop into the chair.

"I'll cut to the chase. Mr. Nolan has been suspended. Studying with him on school grounds cannot happen. At this late stage, and based on your teacher's calculations, it is impossible for you to pass."

"How is any of this good news?"

"The good news," she goes on with a glare, "is that there is an alternative."

Holy hell. I think back to the day she sprung tutoring on me. I already had the idea to fix this mess via virtual classes. If she tells me how that was possible eons ago, my head will implode.

She pulls out some colorful pamphlets from her desk drawer. "Online credit recovery courses are relatively new. None are affiliated directly with our school but with universal programs geared toward multiple school districts. Students learn at their own pace and participate only in the electives they need. They're based in the city, travel to a neutral, monitored location is required for exams, and they aren't free. Enrollment starts next month. With dedication, you'll complete the class over summer break and earn your diploma in September—"

"September?" There goes my summer. My plans to move to the city ASAP. I can't be stuck here until September. I can't.

"Yes. And without having to repeat your entire senior year. Which is your only other option." She slides the paperwork across her desk. "Talk it over with your folks. Let me know if you need assistance registering."

I don't know what to say. I don't know how to handle any of this. I know we can't pay for it, and I can't tell Dad when he thinks Mom will be coming home to some perfect reunion and a celebration of my success. Something he'd know didn't exist if he'd bothered to ask me how anything is going instead of taking Steve to see Mom behind my back.

With nothing else to do or say, I rise to take the brochures and leave, but Mrs. Pederman drums her red nails on the papers caught beneath her palm. "Hold on. There's more."

She waits until I sit again.

"Rumor has it you drew the prom posters hanging in the hallways. Is this true?"

It's like someone struck a match beneath my chin; my cheeks burn firecracker hot. "Um… technically yes?" Those posters are all anyone talks about. But God. Mrs. Pederman too? Fucking Maddison.

"I thought so. I took it upon myself to gather and print this information for you."

Great. It's probably some reform school she's suggesting I attend. But her doughy face softens as she hands the papers over. I take it in slow motion, but then I see what she's given me. It's a huge list. Colleges with top rated art programs. Contests. Scholarships. Links to online articles about building a successful artist life…

"Wow, Mrs. Pederman. I… I don't know what to say. Thank you."

"Well, hopefully it's motivating to imagine a brighter future." She winks and pats my shoulder before giving it a tender squeeze. "Remember us small town folks when you make your big debut."

"OK." The word squeaks out, rusty and raw. I thumb through the papers, pretending I'm reading them, but the letters blur and my hands shake. I drop half the stack.

"Hey there!" Mrs. Pederman reaches down to collect them. "Are you all right?"

"Butterfingers," I mumble and shrug, wishing I had one of those in my pack to eat right now.

She holds my gaze, frowning and totally not buying my phony grin.

All at once, it's too much. Maddi. The text. The posters. Living with the Nolans. Graduation, or the lack thereof. Mom, Dad, Steve. And now Mrs. Pederman's kindness. I crumple back into the seat. Words and tears gush out of me before I can stop them.

Mrs. Pederman rushes to her desk, grabbing her chair and a tissue box. Her knees bump mine when she rolls over to sit beside me, but she doesn't pull back. Her hands are warm as she folds a Kleenex into my damp palm.

"...and then Maddi sent that text, and I... I..." I hide behind the tissue, wishing it were a beach towel large enough to bury my entire body and not just my eyes.

"About that text. I want you to know the ramifications extend beyond the school's anti-bullying regulations. Distributing texts or images considered obscene, lewd, or indecent without consent carries consequences."

I sit up. "W-what do you mean?"

"I've been unable to reach your parents about the issue, but it's important for you to know that the police may be informed on your behalf. We would set up a meeting here in my office when it's convenient for you and your parents."

"My parents?"

"Yes. You're under eighteen. As a minor, they would have to be present. But Maddison wouldn't. It would be a safe space to share your side of events, learn your options. Harassment of this level could be considered a misdemeanor. My guess is that you're well within your rights to press charges. Especially if it continues. If she contacts you in person, sends you another text, or bothers you about this in any way, inform me immediately."

Press charges? What would *that* mean for Maddi? I entertain the split-second thought of Maddison all washed-out and pale in prison jumpsuit orange and almost laugh at the absurdity. The karma would be insanely great.

But I can't bear the thought of going through it all again. Thinking about the text. Reliving that moment from prom. I'm ready to forget it all happened. And if the stress of this is horrible for me? What would it do to Mom and Dad?

I shake my head. "No cops. Her suspension's enough."

"I am here to support you no matter what your decision. But I'm also here to inform the correct parties. Your parents will be informed... in due course."

She looks at me through her glasses instead of over them how she usually does, truly seeing me. Her eyes are fierce, yet kind. She's giving me time to bring it up myself.

"Thank you, Mrs. Pederman. Thanks so much. This... this has helped."

And it has. I feel a little lighter, a little less alone, even though my heart feels ten times too heavy. I clutch the art packet papers to my chest as the lunch bell rings.

"Go. Enjoy your break." She opens the door and pats my back as I leave.

I'm almost finished digging through my locker when I see Bruce pushing through the sea of bodies headed for the lunchroom. To get to me.

"Scooby Prooby Doo! How are you holding up?" Bruce points toward a prom poster.

Of course he does. 'Cause that's my loftiest goal. Getting over a poster. Is this to be the highlight of my remaining high school days? Perpetually rehashing all the most devastating, all the most traumatic moments of my life? "Don't remind me, Bruce."

I slam my locker, and he falls into step beside me as we move down the hall.

"What she did is beyond hideous. Everyone's talking about how great the posters are and how fucked up the text was. People aren't feeling her so much anymore. Oh, see!" He points to another poster, one with a curly green mustache painted across her lip and devil horns over her head.

I beam. "That's perfect. I should have drawn it like that originally."

Bruce blows on his knuckles, rubbing them across his chest.

I study him. "You didn't have something to do with that, did you?"

He waggles his shaggy eyebrows. "I'm nothing compared to Steve Nolan. He flat out leveled Ricky Morgan in the cafeteria yesterday, then turned on Maddi and ripped her a new one in front of everyone. It was epic."

Steve chewed out Maddi?

Before I can tell Bruce his poster graffiti is as good as anything else anyone has done for me, he loops his arm through mine, dragging me out the exit and away from the cafeteria doors. "Let's blow this joint and catch up with each other, yeah? Lunch is on me."

The overflowing line at Giallanza's spills out the door and streams down the sidewalk, so we make a beeline for the mini-mart instead.

Bruce nabs a slushy and a pastrami sub from the deli section while I stock up on the essentials—powdered doughnut holes, nacho-flavored chips, two packs of peanut butter cups, and a large bottle of cherry cola. "Lunch of champions right here!" I brandish my haul. "If you're lucky, I might share."

I'd rather return to school and eat on the front lawn than picnic in the park surrounded by memories. But Bruce, spotting a group of his friends, blazes across the street screaming, "Last one there loses those doughnuts!"

Damn. He's faster than he looks.

"Pru," Bruce pants when we arrive, "you know Logan, Poppy, and Marshall, right?" Stealing the doughnut bag, he grins at me before ripping it open.

"S'up?" Logan says to me as he holds his hand out to Bruce for a doughnut. Marshall nods.

"We walk to school the same way," Poppy says.

Her voice is a warm and raspy surprise, not squawky or bird-like as I always imagined. She's sporting new glasses— blue tortoise shell rectangular frames better suited to her round face than her oversized, golden John Lennon ones.

"You look great, Poppy. I love the new glasses."

Her small nose crinkles when she smiles. "Thanks."

"Sit. Join us," Marshall says, grabbing the doughnut bag from Bruce. He pops two in his mouth and hands them off to Logan.

"We'll eat them all otherwise," Logan says, dumping a quarter of the bag into his lap before passing it to Poppy.

Over half the bag is gone when Poppy hands it back. It's been an eternity since I had anyone to share anything with. It's… nice.

But as soon as I join them on the grass, Poppy scoots closer and says, "I love your prom posters."

It's like she's slapped me. My ears instantly ring and my cheeks burn. This is the last thing I want to talk about. To anybody. Ever again. I shove a doughnut and two chips into my mouth.

"Bruce is our coder; you could be our artist. Do you do commissions?"

I suck down some soda and shrug.

"We need art for our website. We're applying for our own local Amtgard chapter and drawings of our characters would be uh-may-zing. We'd totally stand out."

"Amtgard?"

"Live-action medieval combat," Bruce answers, swinging his half-gnawed sub through the air. Shredded lettuce flies from the makeshift sword.

"You know D&D, right?" Poppy asks.

I nod, swallowing the tang of memories.

"It's kind of like that. Live-action roleplay."

"But can you draw sexy beasts?" Marshall asks. "I need an artist who can handle capturing my dragonborn, heartbreaker rock bard!"

Logan smacks Marshall's arm. "Duranar slays it with the tavern wenches *and* cave trolls way better than Mihn!"

"Mihn?" I can't help but laugh. "Your big bad dragonborn is named Mihn?"

"Yes, Mihn Stryll, thank you very much." Marshall smiles.

I groan at the pun, but I'm smiling. "I'm curious, Bruce. Are you an elf?"

"You know me too well, m'lady." Bruce bows. "Temric, wood elf ranger at your service. But you can call me Tem."

Poppy giggles, and Tem/Bruce blushes.

"I'm Waia, halfling cleric," Poppy says. "There's six of us total for our usual campaigns, but thirteen of us also LARP. Which is what Amtgard's all about. With a sharp website, we can attract more members and build our own chapter. Then we could get into one of the big tourneys and earn a reputation for our crew."

"*Nossë Mellon* rules, biatches!" Logan fist pumps the air.

Bruce leans over to whisper in my ear. "*House of Friends* in Elvish."

"Davis used to join us sometimes," Marshall adds. "We enjoyed his company."

That totally doesn't surprise me. He and Steve loved pulling out Senador and Sumista, their dueling twin monks. An excuse to kickbox around the room and act silly. Pretend to be Jackie Chan. That was life BD. Laughing. Joking. "I know he loved it too, Marshall. Thanks. I used to play, too, but it's been a while." I immediately wish I hadn't said that last part, and shove more food in my face.

"Really?" Logan asks. "Spill it, Spellmeyer!"

I take my time chewing, swallow, and wince. "Siouxsie Sioux-Pendous, hex-slinging sorceress at large."

"Siouxsie Sioux like the singer? Oh my God, that's awesome. You have to play with us sometime." Bruce hugs me.

And I let him.

"OK. I'd like that," I tell him.

And I find that I actually mean it.

"So, you'll help?" Poppy asks. "We would pay you, of course. We budgeted thirty dollars per portrait for all thirteen of us, if that works? We'd only post them on our website. Of course, you'd also be free to put them up on your artist website too."

"I don't have a website. I actually have no idea how to sell art online, let alone get my drawings into a computer."

"That's OK," says Bruce. "I do. Meet me after school."

"Really?" I ask.

"Bruce! You're distracting her from the quest," Poppy complains.

They're all waiting for my answer. I add the numbers in my head. This would more than pay for my credit recovery course. I wouldn't have to ask Dad for a dime. I might be angry with him for taking Steve to see Mom, but I still don't want to burden him with more financial troubles when this whole flunking geometry mess is my screw-up to fix. And double bonus, working with Bruce would be a distraction from Steve.

"I'd be honored."

As we walk back to class, Bruce again joins our arms together. "See? Spellmeyer, one hundred; Wells, zilch. Success is the best retribution against your adversaries."

"Kernelless fusty nuts," I add.

"Scandalous wenches."

We continue the volley all the way to geometry hell.

It's the hardest I've laughed, the most fun I've had, all year.

At the end of the day, Bruce is waiting at my locker, ready to drive us to his place.

"We have to pick up my sister Bree on the way home." At his car, he doesn't hold the door open for me the way Steve does. I brush the thought away and climb inside.

At the junior high, Bree Baumgarten stands propped against a tree with her arms across her chest. Bruce slows to a stop and she stalks to the passenger side, tsking loud when she spies me through the open window. Her chocolate eyes darken to raisins. With her full lips, chestnut waves, and cinnamon dusted freckles, she's her brother's mini-me, minus the glasses and with longer hair.

The door slams as she slides into the back, then knees my seat. "You're in my spot."

"Bree, most people say hello when they meet someone." Bruce rolls his eyes and head my way and stage-whispers, "Thirteen-year-olds. Impossible."

"I can hear you."

Bruce shrugs, apologetic, and cranks the volume. It's an 80s new wave mix tape I gave him. BD, of course. Every song slaps me back inside the Gherkin. Me, Steve, and Davis, cruising and totally in tune with the music, with the car, with each other. Tightly bound and blissful.

Unlike Bruce and Bree. The car buzzes as they bicker, an inflamed hornets' nest. Sibling rivalries are ugly and brutal. I'm fortunate. And luckless. Listening to them argue, I'd give anything to fight with Davis one more time even though we rarely did.

We turn, and I shrink in my seat, grateful we are slinking silently along in a Prius. I only side-eye the Nolans' house as we go by, but still I notice Steve's truck in the drive.

Is he waiting in my room to apologize again since the last one got messed up?

I still feel the gentle pressure of his forehead pressed against mine. The warmth of his breath on my cheeks and lips. The way my heart soared as the song played… then shattered when he lied.

Shaking off the memory, I focus on the path to Bruce's house from the Nolans'—straight three blocks, right turn, left turn, right turn, two-story blue colonial at the end of the cul-de-sac.

Bree bulldozes between me and Bruce, shouldering her way to the door. "I'm telling Polly about your new girl."

"It's Poppy. And neither she nor Pru is my girlfriend." But he blushes, eyes glossing over as he mentions Poppy, and I wonder how much he wishes otherwise as we go inside.

"Whatever, nerd."

"You say that like it's an insult."

Bree rolls her eyes and runs up the stairs.

"Hungry, Pru?" Bruce asks, heading toward the kitchen.

I put my pack on the island next to his and pull out my leftover chocolate from lunch while Bruce pours two milks. Spiraling teal and orange blooms wind across the creamy ceramic mug in my hand. "Where'd you guys get this mug? It's beautiful."

Bruce grins. "I'm so glad you asked. That's my mom's art."

I swallow a mouthful of milk too hard. "Really?"

"Mom's an artist. Well, her day job's an RN, but she monetizes her hobby. Look." He pulls out his phone, bringing up a colorful art gallery.

"She has a website now, but she started with Instagram and an online store that converts her art to hanging prints, stationary products, even clothes."

"That sounds impossible."

"It's easy. Make the art, scan the art, upload the art. The manufacturer does the rest—including depositing royalties into your bank account."

"Tech hates me. I'm not good with that stuff."

"I'll help you get started. Takes seconds to set up your accounts."

"And the whole scanny/uploady part?"

"I'm sure Mom will let you borrow her scanner at first. Eventually, you can purchase a tablet and digital software that lets you paint and draw with your computer. No scanning necessary."

No joke, in a few impressive hours, Bruce has set up my Insta, store, scanned my favorite images from my journal, and priced them for sale.

"One hundred each? No one's going to pay that." I tug his phone out of his hand and ineffectually swipe at the screen to change the prices. He takes it right back.

"Value yourself, and others will too. Your art is good. Adjust it later if you want, but trust me. You're worth every penny."

Blushing, I change the subject. "I think I'll start off the commissions with a drawing of Tem. Can I come here again tomorrow? I'll bring my art supplies and sugar? You have your ideas and tech brain ready?"

"You're on it."

"Thanks, Bruce. See you tomorrow."

"See ya, Drew," Bree shouts as she clomps down the stairs.

"It's Pru," Bruce corrects her.

"Whatever, nerd." She pushes him as she heads toward the kitchen.

"Catch ya tomorrow, Flea," I sling at her, and Bree smirks. I think I kinda like her.

It's a quick walk to the Nolans' house. Steve's still parked out front, but so is Mr. Nolan, so I figure it's better to use the front door and not my bedroom window.

"Dinner is cheeseburger-mac with homemade cheese sauce," Mr. Nolan says when I walk inside. He and Steve are already sitting at the table eating. Steve smothers his perfect, cheddary noodles in sriracha sauce and doesn't look up when I walk past him and into the kitchen. He doesn't say a word when I sit at the table to eat. Two can play that game. I dip my head over my plate and shovel gooey cheesy noodles into my mouth.

Mr. Nolan looks between me and Steve and back again. "Let's not all talk at once."

He's smiling, but Steve walks to the living room, grabs the remote, and flips on the TV. Mr. Nolan frowns but says nothing. I hurry up and finish my meal as fast as I can, then hustle to my room. Once behind the safety of my door, I pull out my phone and scroll through my new artist store, falling asleep with my cell on my chest.

Wednesday afternoon is a glorious repeat of Tuesday. Bruce nabs me after school, we pick up Bree, and Bruce plays modern alternative in the car while he and Bree quarrel all the way home. We snack and draw in the kitchen, getting Temric fleshed out exactly the way Bruce imagined him. Things do turn out pretty cool, if I do say so myself. Wood elf zeal carries clear through to his pointy ears and drawn bow with concentration furrowed into his brow and all manner of trees and woodland critters surrounding him.

Everything clicks—Bruce, Bree, the gang, the art. It's all unexpected, enlivening. And frightening. What if this is temporary? People can't hurt you if you don't let yourself care. You can't lose what you don't hold close. But… I forgot how good it feels to be needed, to help. To be giving and friendly like Davis instead of doing nothing but missing him. Nothing but hurting all the time and hiding from the world. I want to learn how to be a good friend again. I'm not sure I know how. But this fits. It's a start I can live with.

Bruce and I work well together. I draw, and he scans, uploads, and prices. I manage to get Poppy's images done next, and half of Marshall's and Logan's before I begrudgingly leave.

My heart zings as Steve pulls into the drive when I'm feet away from the house. He's halfway out of the truck when his phone chirps. Even from here, I can see his cheeks redden as he checks the screen, and he pinches the bridge of his nose before answering.

Half of me wants to brush his bangs out of his eyes. To make sure he's OK and share my great art news with him so he stops frowning. I'm also dying to rocket past him into the house, lock him outside, and keep everything a secret. Same as he keeps important secrets from me. BD, we shared everything. No secrets ever.

Steve spots me staring and eavesdropping. When he slumps against the open door and shuts his eyes, it's all the dismissal I need. I'm unwanted company. With my head down, I push past without saying a word.

Mr. Nolan has made salmon burgers. The patties are full of orange and yellow pepper chunks and flecks of green dill. I load my burger with tomato and pickle slices, and I ask him if it's OK if I take it to my room. He frowns and looks like he wants to say something but sighs and nods instead.

Inside my room, I drop my plate onto the desk and pace the floor. Even though the food smells great, my stomach's fluttering too much to eat. I can't stop thinking about Steve's face at his truck. About how slumped and defeated he looked when he noticed me. About how he still hasn't spoken to me since our fight. Steve and I never used to stay angry at each other more than a day, but this year's been upside down and backward.

Flopping onto my bed, I shove a piece of candy into my mouth, but it's Steve's gifted candy, and sweet turns saccharine the minute I hear Steve's booming voice greeting his dad. Then his footsteps come down the hall and stop outside my door. I hold my breath, positive that if he put his ear to the wood he'd hear how loud my heart is crashing against my ribs, and wait for him to knock. Does he know how badly I want him to step inside?

But he doesn't. He goes to his room, then back to the living room. The front door slams, and his tires squeal as he peels out of the driveway.

The knock I wanted comes from Mr. Nolan five minutes later.

"Hey, Pru. Can we talk?"

The worry on his face when I open the door makes me take a step back. His eyes are wide, and his entire forehead crinkles as he chews at his thumbnail.

"Larry called. Said you were going to a memorial for Davis on Friday, and I wondered how you were holding up. I worry about you kids, what with Davis's... anniversary and all. That first year... it's always the hardest." Little red splotches form across his cheeks and the bridge of his nose as he speaks. "I know I'm not your dad and we haven't had much contact this year until now, but I wanted you to remember I've been through this before, and if you ever need to talk..."

He sighs and drags his hand over his eyes. "And maybe you could help me out with something too. Would you talk to Steve? I thought he was doing better, but now he's suspended for fighting in school and he isn't speaking to the one person who has kept him safe and sane all year. He says you two aren't talking either. I was hoping you'd consider taking the first steps to change this? Please?" he adds, voice shaking on the *please*, before gnawing at his thumb again. I notice all his nails are ragged now when a week ago they were neat and trim.

"OK. I'll try," I tell him, even though Davis was the fixer, the one who kept the three of us flowing. I'm not sure Steve and I know how to go forward together without him.

"All right, all right. Good, good," he repeats, and takes a shaky breath. But still his eyes are wild, and he doesn't stop chewing his nails.

I want to touch his wrist, remove his fingers from his mouth, but I grip the doorjamb instead. "He'll be OK, Mr. Nolan. We both will."

He smiles, but his eyes don't crinkle at the corners like they usually do. "I hope you're right." He sniffs, then straightens, pushing back his shoulders and shoving his hand into his pocket. "OK, Pru. Eat your dinner." He nods toward the untouched burger on the desk. "I'll be in the other room if you need me."

For the next few hours, I busy myself with finishing the drawings for the D&D group and pick at the burger, barely finishing half of it. My mind's on overdrive. Where is Steve anyway? Was it Maddi who messaged him and he forgave her? Is he with her now? Or is he alone, haunted and burning, missing everything that was. Lost in yesterday yet still aching for a fresh tomorrow.

Like me.

After Mr. Nolan goes to bed, I sneak from my room to trash my dinner remains and wash off my dishes.

It's late when Steve returns.

Not that I've been waiting or anything.

This time, his footsteps tread straight to his room, completely avoiding mine.

17

Drive ~ The Cars

My cellphone buzzes in my pocket in the middle of class on Friday. Mr. Roderick is facing the chalkboard, which means his eyes are not on me. Standing my math book open on my desk, I pull out my phone and dare to check the message behind the angled pages.

DAD: Running late. Hit traffic picking up Mom. Steve will drive you to the memorial, and Mom and I will meet you there. Sorry for the mix-up. Heart emoji, heart emoji, smiley face, thumbs-up emoji.

Of course they invited Steve. It shouldn't surprise me, but my hollowed heart sinks into the acidic depths of my gut all the same. Ugh.

My phone buzzes and rattles across the desk. Mr. Roderick spins around, hawk eyes peering down his hooked nose to look for the culprit. Stuffing my phone between my knees, I glance around the class too though I'm certain he knows it was me. His frown deepens when his eyes cross my desk. Thankfully he doesn't confront me though I hear him muttering something about passing or not passing class. When he turns back around, I dare to pull my phone out and read.

STEVE: Can't pick you up from campus. Meet me at your parents' house after school. Steve seems as unexcited about this as me. No encouraging, happy emojis. Not that I should be expecting them. But I do.

I push my phone back into my pocket and slouch in my seat, spying the fresh bag of Jolly Ranchers sitting at the top of my open backpack. Even though the only sweets I have left are the ones Steve bought me, I can't be bothered to open them. Everything to do with Steve leaves a bad taste in my mouth lately.

The rest of the day's a blur. At lunch, Poppy gushes over Bruce's new art, and Logan bribes me with powdered doughnuts to finish his next till Marshall one-ups him with promises of ice cream cake. I start to think I'm gonna enjoy this new art gig, but then my brain goes back to picturing the memorial for Davis: a picnic in the forest followed by a short hike up the road to plant a cross and flowers near the tree that took his life. It's the happy art thoughts that keep me moving forward on the walk home after school.

Steve is already waiting for me, engine idling, at the curb. When I rap at the window, he jumps and shuts off the radio before unlocking the door.

"Hey," he says as I slide into the cab.

"Hey," I answer.

Steve waits until the buckle clicks into place before pulling from the curb, but he doesn't say anything more and I don't offer to fill in the blanks. His jaw twitches as he focuses on the road, both hands on the wheel, his wide, square shoulders ramrod straight. He looks as tense as I feel, and I almost pull out that bag of candy hiding in my pack. But I don't. I can't eat his *apology* in front of him after our fight. It'd be like saying I accept it or something. Which I'm not sure I have yet despite my talk with Mr. Nolan about how concerned he is for Steve.

I fidget. Scratch my thigh. Rasp my nails against the denim then stop when it seems louder than the engine. In the silence, the temptation of the candy springs Roxy Music to mind, Bryan Ferry's voice crooning in my ears, the feel of Steve pressed close. The memory hits so hard and fast I groan.

When Steve brakes at the light and looks at me, a million questions jump to the surface. *Why didn't you take me with you to see my Mom? Why is your Dad so worried about you? Why'd you really break up with Maddi? Do you really think this memorial is a good idea so near to Davis's accident? Wanna turn around and drive to the city instead?* I don't ask a single one. All I see is my reflection in his mirrored sunglasses. I can't read his eyes or expression at all, but there's mine—the face Steve is seeing—cringing back at me: my eyes too open and haunted, my countenance too exposed and navigable. My cheeks tingle, and I turn my head and focus on the buttons that unroll the window. Laying my head back and closing my eyes, I stick my arm outside, catching the wind like Davis always used to do. The gentle pressure buffets my skin, the wind filling the cab with a hum that presses against my ears and gently squeezes my head. I let my thoughts scatter like dandelion seeds as Steve drives us through the windy forest hills.

Steve clears his throat when we arrive. "We're here. Wake up."

Dad's red sedan sticks out boldly—a bright and bloodied gash against the dark greenery of the forest and the grey of the cotton sky. Gravel crunches beneath the truck tires as Steve pulls into the turnout, parking behind him.

The trailhead starts wide by the side of the road. Steve stuffs his hands inside his front pockets, so I do the same. He walks next to me with his head down, staring at the undergrowth choking the sides of the path; again, I imitate his moves. When the trail narrows and we have to follow one another versus walking side by side, he lets me pass first. My shoulder blades itch as his eyes burn holes in my back all the way to the picnic table. Our march down the path is grave and uncomfortable. Everything about this day—this year—feels surreal.

Mom sees us as we descend a small hill and starts unloading food from her favorite woven basket, the same one that accompanied us on every BD Spellmeyer family picnic. It's the first time I've seen it, the first time we've used it, all year. A lump catches in my throat. Davis should be with us. It's so not fair.

Leaves crinkle as the wind blows. It feels like fingers in my hair, and I scan the treetops for signs of my brother. That magic, however, only happens in dreams. Still, I close my eyes and breathe in the smell of pine and impending rain. This is a day Davis would love. Food, family, and a good storm on the horizon. I think of the dessert he made me in dreamland and smile despite the pinch in my chest. Davis is everywhere. Maybe that's the point—feeling the pain but giving yourself permission to find some happiness anyway.

Dad spreads his arms, walking to meet us. Grasping me under one arm and Steve beneath the other, he pulls our heads to his chest in an achingly familiar Larry Spellmeyer bear hug. His flannel is soft beneath my cheek as he noogies the tops of our heads with his knuckles. Dad's hand bumps Steve's ear and his sunglasses slide down his nose, exposing bloodshot, puffy eyes. He blinks rapidly, the colors shifting from blue to green and back again. Steve looks more frightened than angry. I sway when Dad releases us, surprised by how much that hug felt like home, by how much I wish I could stay tucked away in that space, small and safe as a child again.

Steve coughs and runs his hand through his hair as his cheeks redden, and jams those damn sunglasses back into place. I wish he'd remove them, but he doesn't. Not even when he hugs Mom and helps her dish up the meal onto red checkered paper plates.

Mom looks… like Mom. Radiant and beautiful. Her soft pink cardigan brings a rosy glow to her cheeks and every hair is curled perfectly in place. She smiles when she sees me, tilting her head and clutching her chest, same as she always did BD. She's fidgety though. Nervous. Her fingers flutter around the table, setting plastic silverware exactly centered on the napkins. And I know that even while she looks perfect on the outside, she could be hiding a million different emotions on the inside. So while I should feel relieved that everything looks normal, better than it's been in forever, I don't trust it. Despite the spread before us, I don't think I can stomach a bite.

"We have some of Davis's picnic favorites," Dad says once we're all seated. "BLT pasta salad and fried chicken with more Parmesan than breadcrumbs. Sorry we don't have fruit cobbler—I'm not a baker—but we have blueberry muffins instead."

I stare at my plate but I don't even have the energy to pick up my fork. If I ate as fast as Steve, I'd bring it all back up. Still, he doesn't seem calm either. His knee won't stop jiggling beneath the table.

"Not saying I condone suspension," Dad says, "but I really appreciated your help in the kitchen today, Steve."

Steve shovels a hunk of rainbow corkscrew noodles into his mouth. "No problem, Mr. Spellmeyer."

Dad throws his head back and laughs so hard birds take flight from a nearby tree. "*Mr. Spellmeyer?* When have you *ever* called me that?"

Steve looks at me and flashes a half-smile, bumping my knee beneath the table with his. His leg stops bouncing and he leaves it there, pressed warm and trembly against mine. I feel his touch all the way to my heart, a slow warmth spreading through my chest.

I should feel angry at him still. At all of them, actually, for meeting up without me. For leaving me excluded and alone.

But Steve's leg touching mine feels like all the times he and Davis supported me all of my life. And Dad is laughing, and Mom is smiling, and the sun peeks out from a cloud to highlight her hair bright gold and angelic like Davis's. When I reach for the pain, the angry band that's encircled my stomach and chest all year, it's dull, blunted. Sanded down by the sharpness of all that's happened, good and bad.

"Steve... son..." Dad's forehead crinkles with worry, and his smile drops. "You've always meant so much to our family, to Davis—to *me*. I can't apologize enough for the way I treated you. For all the horrible things I said. It's been a rough year, but that's no excuse. Joyce and I couldn't imagine our world without you, and we are grateful we don't have to. You'll always be our second son."

Steve freezes mid-bite and drops his half-gnawed drumstick to his plate. Pulling his hands into his lap, he rubs his thumb along his wrist. He doesn't speak, only swallows the oversized bite in his mouth and nods, staring at his plate. When he finally speaks, his voice is rough. Scratchy and strained. "Thanks. I—I'm really glad that Joyce is healthy." He clears his throat a few times, picks up the chicken, then puts it back down. "Talking with her has really helped me, you know, sort stuff out."

"Nothing like a little chaos for sorting stuff out." Mom's laugh is high-pitched, and she fingers the buttons on her cardigan. "Davis used to say that. You know... he had that knack for turning the messiest situations into moments of clarity. Remember how he always used to say, '*Well this was an adventure waiting to happen*'? She grabs Dad's hand.

"He also used to say, '*Life's like an engine; sometimes it stalls just to annoy you.*'" Dad chuckles and pulls Mom into a tight hug, cradling her head against his chest.

"He told me Neil Armstrong's moon landing wasn't impressive because the cow jumped over it first." I don't know where that memory came from or why it shot out of me like that. The table is quiet, then everyone bursts into laughter. It feels like a heavy cloud suddenly releasing its rain. All the tension in my neck and shoulders dissolves at once, making my head spin a little. "Well, he was only six or seven." I shrug.

"Ohhh, I've got one better. Remember when we went sledding and I hit my head on that tree so hard I needed stitches? Davis kept telling me to swallow my blood to keep it inside my body where it's supposed to be." Steve lowers his voice to mimic the exact words. "*'Swallow your blood, Steve. You need your blood.'* I was glad he never dreamed of becoming a doctor."

"That's because he was fixated on pirates," says mom, her eyes growing dreamy. "Remember how he chose the same costume, year after year?"

"Yargh!" Dad growls the word. "And that stuffed parrot he'd insist must go trick-or-treating with him? Becky?"

"Beaky," Steve and I answer simultaneously. When Steve smiles at me, it feathers across my skin. After all this time, we are still in sync. It's a pleasantly surprising relief, like a tricky key finally sliding into a lock, opening what should never have been closed.

For the rest of the meal, we share our favorite memories. It's funny how many moments I had forgotten or had seen differently than Mom or Dad or Steve. How can people who were in the same space experiencing the same event all recall it differently? Even now, in this happier moment, it's happening. Tomorrow, all of us will recall something different about today.

Maybe this is what finally lets me see that while we've all been reeling from Davis's death, our living of it has been our own. Dad threw himself into work and adulting. Mom's unbearable pain dragged her underwater into a dark and soulless place she couldn't climb out of alone. I isolated myself, pulling away from everyone. I thought the blame and anger kept me moving forward, but really, it kept me stuck in place.

Not unlike Mom, I realize. And Steve? I steal a glance his way. Steve, relaxed and laughing, reaches out to take Mom's hand across the table. Dad rests his hand atop theirs, and my chest tightens.

I've missed this. All year, we could have still had *this*—a full if not ill-functioning family. I put my hand on top of Dad's, linking us all together the way we should have been all year.

Steve and I help Mom and Dad clear the table, packing up the garbage and carrying it all back to the vehicles. This is it. It's time. We are actually going to walk to that fucking tree that stole Davis's life. Mom clutches the white wooden cross to her chest, and Dad practically crushes the flowers in his fist. His periodic jaw twitch belies his calm visage as do Mom's wide eyes. Steve's are still hidden behind those glasses, his hands back inside his pockets. He looks up at me and shrugs. I take a deep breath. If Steve's OK with this, then so am I.

Single file, we march down the side of the street in the bike lane—Mom, Dad, me, Steve. Mom's pace is fast, hurried. She keeps her eyes down, focused on her feet. My eyes keep seeing Steve's old truck flying through the air, the tree branch impaling my brother. Soon the tree looms before us, and it's like I can still hear the low, keening cries from Davis's death loop—and then I realize Mom's stopped, and Steve has frozen in place about ten feet back, clutching his chest. The gasping, wheezing, choking cry is coming from the Steve standing here with me, not the one from my imagination.

The cross clatters to the asphalt. Mom bolts past me and Dad, catching Steve in her arms as he crumples to his knees. His sunglasses drop to the ground as she cups his face in her hands. "Look at me," Mom demands, voice strong and clear as BD times. "I'm right here. Look at me, Steve. It's OK, son. Look at *me*."

Steve is drowning. Gargling gasps jam his throat as he shakes, yet still Mom holds on. "Shh. I'm right here. I promise you, you're safe. We're all right here." She extends her arm toward Dad, toward me. Her intentions are clear. It's Spellmeyer family rally time.

My own heart is strangled in my chest as I watch Steve melt into Mom's arms. Dad moans, "Oh, Pru." And then he folds me against his chest, dropping the flowers before taking my hand and walking me toward Steve and Mom. Dad nods, and we drop to our knees beside them—Dad next to Mom, me next to Steve. Steve's muscles tremble beneath my hand as I rub his back. Sharp rocks bite my knees through my jeans. Dad's hand never leaves my sweaty grip as he squeezes Mom's shoulder.

"I thought I could…" Steve takes a shuddering breath and pulls from our grip. He rocks back on his heels, then sits, holding his head in his hands. "I'm sorry. You guys go put the cross and flowers in place. I'll… I'll wait here."

Mom and Dad share a look.

"I'll stay with him," I say when Dad starts to speak. "Go help Mom. I don't need to see." I've visited the tree enough in my dreams to know exactly what it looks like. Half dead, sloughing bark rotting in chunks along the trunk, upper branches thin, brittle, and leafless despite the spring blooms crowning everything else verdant and emerald bright. Rivulets of dark, crusty sap pouring down the sides as though blood spilled from knife wounds. A quick glance up confirms this reality is as haunted as my dreams. The tree waits ahead, a replica of the one in my nightmare.

Dad helps Mom up, they collect the cross and flowers, and both walk hand in hand to the killing tree. I sit next to Steve.

He still cradles his head in his hands. "I know you're still mad at me." He doesn't bother to look up, but a tremor runs down his back, shaking his shoulders.

"That depends on how much candy you have left." I nudge his elbow with mine to accent the joke. Any anger or betrayal

I felt shriveled when he collapsed, replaced by fear and worry instead.

Steve's head snaps up. "All year you've acted like you're the only one who lost Davis... who lost *everything*... when we *all* did. You have no idea what this year has been like for anyone but yourself." He doesn't look angry though his words kick the air from my chest. He looks broken and lost, the burgeoning tears in his eyes turning their vivid hue rheumy and watercolor soft. His lip trembles, but he doesn't look away; his tormented gaze stays locked on mine.

I try to swallow around the lump in my throat, but my mouth's a desert. My smile's broken too. My lips twitch, then droop. I nod and whisper, "I know. You're right. Maybe you could... tell me about your year?"

It's not the reaction he was expecting. His eyebrows shoot up beneath his golden curls, and his mouth forms this delicate O shape before it shuts again. His eyes narrow as he studies me, and he shifts, uncomfortable on the ground.

Afraid he will stand up and leave, I grab his left hand, grasping it between mine. "Steve, I'm so tired of being angry all the time. I don't want to fight with you anymore." He tries tugging from my grip, but I clamp down. "Please."

I run my thumb over his wrist, but my fingers find something odd. Both of us freeze. Steve sucks in a sharp breath when I flip his hand over to see what I felt.

The fresh scar is long, thick, and jagged. It tears across his palm, veering from the center of his wrist in a crooked path across the padding of his thumb. He holds his breath as I run my fingertips over it. "When did you... what is this, Steve? Is this from the accident?"

"No. It... it came after."

His hand shakes in mine. Ahead of us, Mom is hugging the tree, her cries drifting to our ears. *"My boy. My beautiful, beautiful boy."* She grooms dying bark from the trunk as Dad pounds the cross into the dirt near the roadside, marking the moment of Davis's final breath. Steve's eyes are on them, not me, as he speaks.

"I stole one of Dad's six-packs, sat beneath the bleachers at the football field, and... proceeded to get plastered. I mean, hey, if a little drinking killed my best friend, might as well take it all the way, right?" He laughs, but it's not a happy sound. "I was five beers in when I decided I couldn't... that I didn't want to hurt anymore..."

My pulse quickens, caught in the cross fire of anxiety and necessity. I'm unsure if I can bear to hear what he has to say next, but I know that I have to. I can't turn my back on his words. On him.

"I smashed a bottle against the metal stands." He closes his fingers around mine. Even though he squeezes hard, I still feel his tremors. Looking at his scar sends a burning flare flooding up and down my arms, his words searing my skin.

"I pressed the biggest shard of glass to the top of the vein, here"—he touches my finger to the scar, at the edge of his wrist—"ready to pull it straight back, right up my arm. To end everything..."

"Steve..."

He shakes his head. "I didn't hear Maddi until she touched my shoulder. And my hand jumped forward instead of back. I was so drunk, I didn't feel a thing. I've no clue how Maddi got me into her car by herself when I could hardly walk straight. She took me to her house, fired up YouTube, and stitched me up herself—all so I didn't have to answer questions at the ER. Probably not our smartest move."

I hold my breath, absorbing this new truth.

"After I sobered up and got things looked at by a doctor, they said I sliced through the tendons. I can hardly grip a foot-ball. I lost my sports scholarship..." He swallows and nods his head toward the tree. "I've been meeting with Joyce… to talk about it. She understands."

My mind flashes to that day with the pills. To the day my mom left for Oakmont.

He coughs. "So, now you're caught up on all the laughs. *Yippee ki-yay.*"

I can't stop staring at his scar. He lets me press his hand flat against my thigh and run my fingertips up and down the ropy veins bulging in his forearm. "I could have lost you…"

Steve shrugs. "You'd already tossed me away."

"But you could have died!" I imagine the glass moving the opposite way, imagine rivers of red staining the grass as Steve bleeds out, lost and alone. I shiver, grateful for the first time in recent memory for Maddison.

"We all die. It's the suckiest part of living."

I think of Davis cowering in the hall of his dreamland apartment, too frightened to let go and move on as the sun dips below the horizon. Ribbons of orange, magenta, and lavender wind between the clouds. It looks like the art on Bruce's mug, and I smile.

Mom and Dad walk toward us, arms linked, their faces tear-stained and puffy yet smiling. Mom, her head on Dad's shoulder, wears a white daisy in her hair from the flower wreath draped over the cross.

Maybe, I think, the suckiest part of living isn't dying. Maybe it's going through the hard parts of life alone, like we all have been until now.

"If you ever try to speed up the dying process like that again, I'll have to kill you."

"That makes zero sense."

"Hey, I've not had a single candy all day. I officially can't make sense."

"None? Now *that* is senseless."

Steve stands and holds out his hand. I entwine my fingers through his. His eyes search mine before he pulls me upright.

"I'm really glad you're OK," I whisper, and Steve smiles in a way that sends the butterflies in my stomach pole-vaulting.

I feel his eyes on me the entire walk back to the cars.

Once there, Mom gives us both a hug and a kiss on the cheek, then Dad gets Mom settled in the front seat of their car. "Coming, Pru?" he asks as he shuts her door.

"I can drive her."

Steve's offer surprises me. I think it's startled him, too, 'cause he roughs the hair at the nape of his neck in his signature *oh shit* move.

Dad chuckles and Steve flushes. "Sure. You two have some catching up to do. No rush, but don't be late. It's been a long day, and Joyce would still like to spend some time with Pru. Drive safe, son. See you both soon."

"Thanks, Dad." But Steve whispers it so soft, I'm uncertain Dad heard him.

Steve pops open my door before climbing behind the wheel and cranking the engine. The car vibrates and hums, but he doesn't start driving yet. Lightning cracks, and the clouds cry for Davis, blanketing the forest, the killing tree, and the road in tears. Steve unrolls the windows and closes his eyes, breathing in the sweet ozone, same as Davis always would.

I watch Steve's features glow in the dashboard lights. He's changed. From growing out his buzz cut into messy, curly locks to his thinner physique to his chiseled cheeks and jawline free of the baby fat that followed him into junior high. He's aged this year, his face more mature... and impossibly handsome. Despite his relaxed demeanor, two deep frown lines I don't remember him having rest between his shut eyes, their lashes so thick and lush I'm envious. They flutter open, landing on me.

"Are you staring at me, Spellmeyer?" His mouth twitches as he fights a smile, and he turns his head toward me in time to see the hot flush fill my cheeks. His teasing hasn't changed.

"Pfft. No!"

He chuckles, rolls up the windows, flips on the wipers, and pulls onto the street.

Before he can razz me more, I lunge and smash on some music to fill the cab with noise. The first notes of a song pulse, and Steve brakes hard, grabbing for the dash and twisting the volume down before the lyrics begin.

But I know every note start to finish. I'd know that song anywhere.

Roxy Music's "More Than This."

No station in Hicksville plays much 80s music. You need satellite streaming—which Steve never had BD—or your own mix tape.

I reach forward.

"Don't! Pruuuu!" His groan sounds painful. As though my name grew talons and ripped its way out of his throat. But I've already hit eject and snagged the CD. When he drives beneath a streetlamp, I can finally read the words scrawled across the shiny surface: *Dancing with Pru.*

"Come on, give it back. Please?"

"A CD? Not a cassette? Didn't Davis teach you anything?"

I mean it as a joke, but Steve winces. "Newer truck, newer stereo. I'll never own a pre–airbag era vehicle again." Steve turns off the stereo entirely. The steady *swish-swoosh* of the windshield wipers syncs up with my heartbeat. The silence sits heavy between us, filling the gap between our seats. Stretching it miles wide. Suffocating and soothing all at once.

I envision Davis in his nightmare death loop. The seat belt dangling limp beside him, no airbag to stop his flight or stop the windshield shards from pelting Steve. Dragging my dry tongue over my parched lips achieves nothing.

"Sorry," I finally say. Steve loved his old truck as much as Davis loved his Monte. No word in the English language sucks or is more inadequate than *sorry*. Sadly, it's the best I've got.

"Don't," he chokes. "It's my fault; you can't blame the truck. Just me."

"Wait, what? No! Dad told me the truth. You weren't even driving. Davis—"

"I was *there*. I think I remember how it went down. All of you were right to cut me out of your lives. I didn't drive, but I should have been able to." His eyes are locked on the road, knuckles white as they grip the wheel. A fat tear slides down his cheek. "Pru, can you forgive me?"

"Steve…" I yearn to reach for his hand, but watch him instead, drawn to the kaleidoscope of emotion and colors swirling in his eyes. "There was never anything to forgive. Sometimes, things just… happen. And even if you were driving, maybe Davis would have had a migraine behind the wheel a week later and died then. We can't know. Stop blaming yourself. Mom, Dad, even Davis in my dreams? They don't blame you at all." The words escape me in a rush, and I'm instantly light and airy against the seat. The cab beams bright even in the dark. Everything looks sharp and distinct. I take a deep breath and feel it fill my lungs clear to the bottom with ease. No stress, no strain, no constriction. My tummy knots are gone.

He rolls his head to look at me, his eyes a storm at sea, all glossy waves and roiling aquamarine tides. "That's the same thing your mom told me. She's the only mom I've ever really known. You guys showed me what family really means. And I blew it. I blew it all to hell, and I can't go back and fix it. I'll never get it back."

"You never lost it, Steve. You'll always be their son. You'll always be Davis's brother. Our brother."

"I don't want to be your brother. I never wanted to be your brother."

His words are a gut punch. They taint the air, and that pathetic squeaky cry I do bursts out of my lungs before I can stop it. Staring at the CD in my hands, I spin it around and around and around. I let the silence consume me like I should have in the first place, staring at the silver disc till it blurs into nothingness.

Steve can't drive me home fast enough.

Except when the truck turns and stops, I look up to realize he's pulled not into my driveway but into the deserted parking lot of the thrift store.

"This is where I come when I want to remember," he says.

He flicks off the engine but leaves the headlights on. They wash over the grassy side lot, illuminating patches of spring-time yellow dandelions.

"Do you love butter? Let's find out!"

The memory slams me against the seat, and I shut my eyes to see it more vividly.

Steve had pinned my shoulders in the grass while Davis laughed and scrubbed the dandelion under my chin. *"Yum! Butter!"* We squealed as my skin turned yellow beneath the silky petals. Then Davis and I tackled Steve and repeated the test on him. Dandelions are my favorite flower. They aren't weeds. They are full of dreams…

I open my eyes and let them drift to the double-door entrance. I've not gone near the thrift store since we shopped for my prom dress. My throat clenches, and I have to look back at the flowers. Davis still surrounds us, same as at the killing tree. It's painful yet… sweeter somehow.

"Here. Blow the seeds."

"What did you wish for?"

"Forever friends. With you."

I wonder what memories ambush Steve when he comes here, and I carefully sneak a glance. But he isn't daydreaming as he gazes out the windshield. He's watching *me*.

"Stop before you break it." He reaches over and eases the twirling CD from my grip. His fingertips trail over my wrist, and he pulls back as though burned.

My hands feel lost and empty without the disc, and I pick at my jeans instead. "What else is on it?"

Shadows dance across his face. I can't read his expression. His mouth opens and shuts a few times before he answers.

"Regrets."

He shakes the CD at me, slides it back into the player where it belongs, and hits stop before the song starts.

I understand. This whole year has been nothing but one colossal regret full of mistakes and blame.

"Assaholic!"

"We don't need you at all, Mom."

Shame burns my face and I'm grateful for the darkness. All my angry words tumble through my head. All my fragmented, pointless excuses and vile slurs. And the worst words yet, the ones that ruined everything forever.

"Davis, please come get me…"

"I never should have called you guys," I whisper.

"What?"

"That's what I regret. If I had never called, last year at prom, Davis wouldn't have died. I wrongfully blamed you, but everything's actually my own fucking fault. Steve, I'm so sorry. I'll be sorry forever." The words are out before I can suck them back, and the intense urge to escape, to race home through the dark, overwhelms me the same as it did that horrible night. Anything to outrun the pain. The memories. Myself.

I open the door.

Steve grabs my arm.

"What if I'd asked you to prom last year like I wanted to?"

The door slips from my hand and falls back into place with a heavy thud, plunging the cab back into shadow.

"Where would we all be if I had trusted my feelings? Ricky never would have touched you." Steve's voice dips to a dangerously low rumble as he spits the Dickster's name. "And then Davis wouldn't have…" He rubs the back of his scalp, ruffling his hair instead of finishing his thoughts.

My mind spins. My stomach churns. *Feelings? Prom?* I remember the heat of his forehead pressed against mine through the bedroom window, and my pulse flutters. "Why didn't you? You know… ask me?"

"I thought it'd be weird, that I'd lose… *us.* Turns out I did anyway. You hated on me so hard after Davis died, while I would have given anything—*anything*—for you to let me in even a little bit." He gasps, eyes wide, mouth slack, all secrets slipped.

"Anything?"

His voice is husky and his eyes darken as he answers. "Yeah. Anything."

The moment stretches eternal with his eyes on mine and my heart pounding frantically, screaming *Yes! Yes! Yes!* in response to his unasked year-old question.

I reach over and hit play. "Dance with me?"

He swallows hard, his hypnotic eyes shifting from blue to green and back again. "Wait a sec—don't move."

Slipping out of the truck, Steve runs around to my side of the car, crouching low in a dandelion patch before opening my door. His hand trembles in mine when he takes it, the only sign he's as nervous as I am.

He slips a perfect yellow bloom behind my ear. "Pru-Si-Q," he whispers, twirling an errant curl freed from my ponytail around his finger. His knuckles brush against my neck, making my pulse race as much as his deep gravely words do. No one calls me Pru-Si-Q but Steve. I've not heard this glorious nickname all year. "Your corsage."

Winding my arms around his neck as he pulls me close, I know this is how prom should have been. Steve's hands on my hips, his radiant eyes locked on mine. We sway gently in the shine of the headlights while pollen and tree blossoms float around us in glowing confetti swirls, the drizzle of rain a soft mist against our skin.

A breathy female voice glides through the air. It's a song I don't recognize, but the ache and warble in the singer's voice are beautiful.

Steve whispers the lyrics as his eyes bore into mine, the song turning personal, intimate, and deep—like all the words are his and meant for me and me alone. A slow burn flares low in my belly. I shiver. Not from the cool breeze but rather from the flush of heat engulfing my skin. Steve tightens his grip on my waist, pulling me closer. His stubble tickles my skin as he presses his cheek to mine, his warm sigh sending a zing down my spine.

"Who sings this?" My own airy breath hitches, matching the singer's.

I feel his mouth twitch into a smile, and his grip above my hips tightens. "You like it? It's newish. You don't usually do newish."

"Hey. I'm not afraid to try new things!"

"Yeah? It's Taylor Swift. 'Lover.'" He whispers *"Lover"* soft and breathy in my ear, a warm caress I feel everywhere.

"Not brother?" I tease, squeezing his shoulders playfully.

"Definitely not." His lips graze my jaw. "Not when I've wanted to kiss you practically my whole damn life."

My stomach somersaults.

He presses his forehead against mine. I grip his t-shirt in my fist, feeling his heart hammering as hard and fast as mine.

I rise on my tip toes to meet his lips and…

A phone blares from Steve's pocket.

He releases me, and I stagger.

"Crap." He flushes. "Just a sec. That ringtone is my dad."

I can't make out Mr. Nolan's words, but I hear the tone—tight and frantic.

"Yes, we are fine… Sorry I didn't text… We didn't mean to worry you… Yeah, I'm here with Pru… OK… I'll be right there after I drop her off… Yes, I promise we're fine. I'll see you soon."

He sighs and slides his phone into his pocket before closing the gap between us once more. "My dad needs me home, your folks want you home…" He rubs his thumb along my lower lip, parting them. "I guess we should…"

Blood rushes so loud in my ears it drowns out everything. Time slows as he drops his lips toward mine. Soft, deliberate, and tender, his mouth brushes my cheek, catching only the corner of my lips beneath his.

"…get going."

I don't mean it to, but a breathy groan escapes my tingling lips. Steve chuckles and laces his hand in mine.

He holds my hand the entire drive back to Mom and Dad's. It feels like home.

18

Mothers Talk ~ Tears for Fears

The front door creaks as it shuts. Crumpling against it, I press my fingers to my still pulsing lips and shut my eyes.

He almost kissed me.

He's always wanted to kiss me.

My head swims as I remember all the near misses we have had over the years, all of it taking on a deeper meaning now, and I smile.

"Mom? Dad?" I call. "I'm home." When they don't yell back a reply, my eyes shoot open. Even as I strain my ears, the house is so silent I can hear my shallow breaths and nothing else as my body tenses. A dreadful déjà vu jolts through me, and I yank the door back open, ready to climb back into Steve's truck and escape with him to his house, but his red taillights are fading as he turns the corner.

Shaking it off, I force myself to shut the door and move through the house.

The living room is spotless. All the quilts, pillows, and clothes previously strewn across the sofa, table, and floor are gone. The recliner—tucked together tight and neat—is a regular chair once again and not a makeshift bed. Every surface in the kitchen sparkles, smelling like rosemary, lavender, and freshly squeezed lemons. Shutting my eyes, I breathe it in, this smell of safety, of Mom, of our pre-disastrous world. I let its comfort and old familiarity seep inside my skin, calming my nerves, reviving my heart.

The clean, good house feeling stops at the dining room.

The carpet crunches, stiff and dirty beneath my sneakers. Decomposing streamers bleed from the ceiling, dusty and faded. China place settings dominate the tabletop. The room reeks of dust, decay, and despair.

Mom sits hunched at the head of the table, staring blankly at the mess before her. With a heavy sigh, she lifts the empty lasagna pan off the trivet and drags it onto her lap. She sniffles and puts it back. She repeats this move three more times, cheeks growing pinker, frown deepening with each pass.

"Maybe… I can help?" I whisper from the corner.

Mom's gaze is sharp and clear when her eyes lock on mine. More so than they've been every other AD day. She stands, bringing the pan with her as she walks toward me. Balancing the dish on one palm, she cups my cheek with the other, and I can't breathe. Her fingers are whisper-soft and warm, the sweet and soothing touch of steamed cocoa on my skin.

"I love the dandelion, Prudie." She smiles and hands me the pan. "Simply beautiful."

Blushing, I stroke the forgotten velvet petals above my ear. I think I get why Mom enjoys it so much when Dad adorns her in flowers too.

As I carry the pan to the hutch, she turns and begins separating china into piles in the center of the table for me to collect, then excuses herself to grab a stepstool from the garage to access the streamers. A garbage pail to trash them in.

When she returns, she hovers outside the room, watching me. Dust smudges her cheeks and coats her hair. She's shed her cardigan and rolled up the sleeves of her blouse. With the fabric rumpled and her perfect curls disheveled, she looks the same as she did prior to her Oakmont stay, and I'm slammed back inside the moment where I yelled at her. Called her a bad mother and damaged her so much she hurt herself. All my tension—the knots in my shoulders, the invisible spiked band constricting my stomach and burning my chest—returns in force.

She knocks over the stool as she runs to my side. Her fingers flutter at my temples and she starts this humming coo she used to do when one of us hurt—same as she did with Steve at the memorial.

When did I start crying?

I don't know the answer, but I know Mom's here, her delicate fingers floating around my face, wiping every tear as it falls and stroking my temples in small, soothing circles.

I'm seven and my knees are bloodied from falling off my bike until Mom bandages me.

I'm thirteen and Mom rocks me on the sofa, healing my stupid, boy-broken heart.

It's prom night and Mom does my hair and makeup, and I feel as pretty as she is.

Every time I've stumbled, she has caught me. And when she needed me? I let her fall.

"I'm so sorry," we both say at the exact same time, and she laughs, crushing me in the tightest of hugs. Her eyes, red-rimmed and glossy when she pulls back, bore into mine.

"Please. Sit." She gestures to the table and pulls out a chair next to mine, tugging my hand into her lap. "I want us to be good, OK? I know I was a terrible mother trapped in a terrible headspace. I wish so badly I had been there for you when we lost Davis. And I want you to know that the day I took too many pills, it was not to leave you and your father. And it was absolutely never your fault. Just mine, Prudie girl. Just mine." Her mournful smile makes her eyes swim with tears and regret, her expression mirroring Steve's, Dad's, mine.

We've all been clinging to *if only*'s as though they can rewrite the past. Billions upon billions of *what if*s… and not a single one of them matters. You can't reimagine your yesterdays, only divine new beginnings. Regret closes doors. I'm ready to open them. But before I can move forward, I have to know…

"Mom? Why did you take them?" I can't look her in the eyes, afraid of her answer. But her voice is so soft when she responds, I have to lean forward to hear her better.

"I've always had sleeping problems. Periodic bouts of insomnia. But it got worse right after Davis. I had some old prescription sleeping pills in the cupboard and I thought they would help. And they did. But then I started having these dreams. Vivid, electric, haunting dreams of your brother."

My mouth goes dry. I can't interrupt her to talk because I can't breathe.

She had her own dreamland.

"I'd wake up, realize nothing was real, remember that he was truly gone forever… The pain of that? Oh, Prudie. I was stuck in a loop. Sleeping or not sleeping, dreaming but not wanting to dream at all… I just wanted a reprieve. One dreamless night. I thought I needed to black it all out in order to escape when what I really needed was you and your Dad. But Pru, I'm here now, and I'm not going anywhere. If you can't forgive me right now, I understand, but—"

"I've been dreaming about Davis, too," I blurt. "Only if I sleep in the Monte Carlo though. I never see him when I sleep in my bed. I've been sneaking into the garage… even while I've been staying with the Nolans." I give a sheepish grin.

Mom pulls back, eyebrows up, forehead crinkled and concerned. "Yeah?"

"The dreams aren't always so good. But I will miss them when Dad sells the Gherkin." I swallow hard. I can't tell her about the dreamland apartment. Not yet. I'll share everything with her once I know Davis is safe. After I dream of him tonight. "I was hoping you would let me sleep in there once more?"

She nods. "Sure, sweetie."

"And Mom?" Her fingers flutters in my grip, a nervous butterfly struggling to break free, and I squeeze her hand reassuringly in mine. "We're good."

Mom grabs me in a hug. Pulls me closer than close. Kisses the center of my forehead. "I love you, Prudie."

"I love you too."

We hold each other for a while before finally Mom sighs. "It's getting late. You should get to sleep."

"No, I'll help. Let's finish this together, Mom."

Mom and I fall into an easy, silent rhythm as we work. I'm in awe of her strength. She doesn't sniffle and swipe at her nose and eyes the entire time like I do. Her hands barely shake when we pull down the streamers. She hums softly under her breath when she washes the china, handing me the pieces to dry.

I'm polishing the final plate, running my dish towel along the delicate scalloped edge, when I see Davis's face smiling at me from the creamy center. His eyes dart toward Mom, then back at me, his dimples popping. Mom rinses the last of the suds down the drain, shuts off the faucet, and dries her hands. The image of Davis fades, my own reflection superimposed over his. I watch as his smile morphs into mine, a part of my brother still alive in me.

"I'm so proud of my girls."

It's Dad's voice filling the kitchen. He coughs in the entryway, something clutched behind his back. "But, Pru? We need to talk."

He rocks on his heels, clearing his throat over and over as though attempting to reboot his voice box. His eyes glaze over. "The Monte Carlo's been sold. Buyer comes tomorrow. I am so sorry."

"But…" My brain screams a billion objections—that I need more time, that I won't ever be ready—but all I have to do is look at Mom, and all of them wash away. Trading the Gherkin for her soft smile is the most acceptable thing. "I understand," I tell him instead, swallowing hard.

"It's late. Get some sleep. They'll be here at 8:00."

From behind his back, he hands me my pillow… and Davis's letterman jacket.

Mom nods and squeezes my hand. "Go on. Go be with Davis one more time."

Dad closes the gap between us, grabbing me into a tight hug. Mom closes the space behind me, and together they hold me up. Squished tight against the softness of my pillow and the jacket smelling so much like Davis, it's as though he stands with us, hugging all of us back too.

19

World Leader Pretend ~ R.E.M.

Pru's heart raced as she entered the shattered remnants of dreamland. Discs of fragmented apartment spun through a starless, inky void. Jagged husks of misshapen floor and crumbling ceiling dotted the darkness like isolated islands lost within a sea of crackling static.

The long and skinny platform she straddled stuttered and jerked beneath her feet. Pru widened her stance and threw out her arms for balance. Around her, the destruction was overwhelming. Pru's heart stopped as she took in the sight. Gone were all the windows and doors. The walls, devoid of their cheery yellow paint, stood bare as skinless skeletons, the plaster flayed to expose rotted and splintered wood paneling. Charred carpet crunched beneath her feet, and smoke stung her nostrils. Pru ducked as the avocado-green refrigerator zoomed overhead with a heavy *whoosh*. The hinges screeched, and the fridge door tumbled open, raining gold foil-wrapped bon-bons. The dull glow of the interior light carved a subtle path through the shadows, and for a brief moment, Pru saw the flickering form of Davis ahead.

Pru carefully maneuvered through the maze of fallen debris, piles of garbage, and huge Swiss cheese holes peppering the decayed floorboards. Behind her, a hunk of matted shag peeled away with a loud snap, followed by a low whistle as it careened away into nothingness.

"Davis!" Pru dropped to her knees beside her brother. His tattered shirt withered under her touch, peeling away from his back. She pulled his hands from his head, and his body slumped backward, rocking the platform with a heavy thud as he slipped from her grip.

"Davis, can you hear me?"

His form flickered and wavered. Chunks of his hair floated up off his head, revealing an oozing scalp beneath. Pru swallowed hard and placed her hand on Davis's chest, expecting their usual dreamland connection to come roaring to life. The air buzzed and her skin sparked electric at the touch. A pale blue bolt heated her skin and opened her mind. For a moment, Pru saw a hazy vision of a panicked Davis racing toward a door at the end of an endless, blackened tunnel, reaching for but never grasping the knob. The spark fizzled. Her vision turned to shadow. And as their connection faded, so did Davis.

Pru watched in horror as Davis's already pale skin leached even more color, going grey and translucent. She sobbed his name as his eyelids fluttered open, revealing vacant milky orbs rolling sightlessly in their sockets.

The stove dropped from the sky onto a nearby platform. As it shattered, the faint smell of chocolate filled the air, and Pru thought wistfully of the grand desserts Davis had baked for her the first time she had visited him here. The bay window floated past, the ripped curtains billowing like sails. Pru closed her eyes, recalling how she'd watched Davis's uncoordinated dance moves through it. She remembered him clapping to the music as he decorated the living room. How everything sprang into being through the force of his imagination and determination alone. Same as he approached all things in life.

He had created this sanctuary to preserve their connection. But their connection was stronger than this.

Pru's eyes snapped open in time to see the sofa cushions implode in a mushroom cloud of fabric and foam.

"Please, Davis, please," she begged on repeat, needing him to take control of the apartment again. Needing him to recreate the guest room so that he could find relief. She tried clapping his listless hands together, wanting to summon something better, to save them from this mess...

But Davis was disintegrating, slipping from Pru's grasp, turning into the ethereal ghost Anne-Marie had warned her about. He had given everything, had risked his immortal soul, for her.

"You stupid, stubborn brother. I need you in the afterlife, not *here!*" Overwhelmed with fear, love, and gratitude, she cradled his head in her lap.

"Your apartment is beautiful," she whispered, smoothing brittle hair from his flaking forehead. Pru bit her lip and pushed on. "You've done everything for me that I've ever needed. And I'll always be grateful. Every time I think of you, I'll remember all of it. And this perfect apartment. I can totally see us living here. I can't believe you created this for me. I have cherished every moment spent with you. I've recorded it all in my journal, so I'll have this place forever."

Something deep in her jeans pocket vibrated hot against her thigh. Reaching inside, she tugged out her journal with a loud *pop.* Surprised, she dropped the book on his chest, and the pages blew open. Pru watched as every image she drew of Davis and the apartment lifted off the parchment. Hovering in the space between them, the images animated briefly before drifting onto Davis's arms. The ink swirled and seeped into his skin, transforming into vibrant tattoos that raced up his limbs and across his chest toward his heart.

As the tattoos spread, Davis's eyes fluttered open. His cheeks pinkened, and the clouds shrouding his cornflower blue irises cleared.

"Pru?" His voice crackled as he reached out his pinky finger, seeking connection and assurance. Glitter motes rose from the carpet as their fingers entwined.

A surge of hope flooded Pru's heart as he sat up and pulled her into his arms. "You're the best sister," he whispered in her ear, the smell of peppermint surrounding her.

Amidst the swirling ink and glitter, Pru and Davis held each other tightly, the motes of light dancing around them.

Pulling gently from his grip, Pru pulled the journal into her lap. Between the pages sat a marker from her tin. The tip sparked fire, small rainbowed firecracker flashes of color. Pru looked at Davis and smiled.

Hand trembling, she opened the book to a blank page. The pen ignited as it touched the parchment, and Pru drew the four corners of a door.

The platform stilled. The buzzing static changed to a gentle hum of tinkling bells and birdsong. Before the siblings, a glimmering door appeared, and Davis stood. He looked at Pru, his eyes wide and questioning.

"Go on. It's OK." She forced herself to smile even though her heart was breaking. "I'll be OK."

As he touched the knob, the last bits of the dreamland apartment swirled, faded, its broken fragments softening and slipping away into the void. The peppermint-scented wind lifted Davis off his feet, carrying him gently toward the threshold.

"I love you," Pru whispered as the world around her turned white.

20

The Power of Love ~ Huey Lewis and The News

Bright light floods the garage. Dad gently raps on the Monte's window, but I'm already awake. I've been glued to the bucket seat for half an hour, replaying the dream in my head over and over and over again. The apartment unrecognizable and broken. Davis limp, cold, and unresponsive. His skin flooding with tattoo memories. The peppermint wind ferrying him into the light.

Davis is gone.

Dad opens the door and pulls me into a hug, not fully understanding my tears. How can I explain my dreams to him when I don't even understand them myself? Still, it helps to be held above water when I'm drowning. I'm losing Davis all over again, but at least I've rediscovered my parents, and that feels better than I thought it would. I don't know how I managed all year without them.

Dad helps me clear the last of Davis's belongings from the glove box and the trunk, handing it all to me when we're done. But the only Davis things I really need to keep are already in my room. I get why the Nolans hang on to everything. It's a way to keep someone near. But in the end, love is the only worthy thing we leave behind—and the only thing we can ever take with us.

Together we wait, cross-legged on the cement, shoulders touching, knees knocking. I shiver despite the warm sun beating hot upon my chest. Despite knowing Davis is safe now, I feel anything but sunshine bright.

"That must be him." Dad points to the far end of the alley where a speeding tornado cloud of dust and gravel barrels toward us. Every cell in my body vibrates, and I bite my inner cheek hard enough that I taste the metallic tang of blood to keep from screaming my freaking head off. It's too soon. I'm not ready. I'll never be ready.

It's a hot minute before the dust settles and I can identify the flashy yellow sports car with duo black stripes painted down the hood. "Looks like a wasp."

Dad's eyes bug out. "It's a 70s Camaro." He drove a Camaro—and a motorcycle—before Davis and I came along and Mom forced him to downgrade to a child-safe sedan. "He's a collector from the city."

Wouldn't have needed Dad to point *that* out. The second the driver's shiny tasseled loafers hit the pavement, it is clear he's not local. Here in Podunk, if your jeans don't have holes, you're fancy. The ironed creases in this guy's khakis could gouge skin.

"1971?" Dad asks without preamble.

"Good eye, Larry," Wasp-man says, tugging his suit jacket into place. "My collection is all from my birth year."

A city tow truck pulls up behind the wasp-mobile, and Dad opens the garage, way more eager to get this over with than me.

Wasp-man whistles, pressing his hand to his chest, and I'm surprised to see his eyes water. "She's beautiful. Better than the photos. Do you mind?" he asks, but he's already running his fingers over her hood, circling her slowly, opening the doors, peering inside.

"You said it still has the original houndstooth lining?"

"It's patchy," Dad says and pops the trunk.

"It's fine," I say, offended on the pickle-mobile's behalf.

"This is unexpected!" Wasp-man laughs, running his fingers over my doodle in the trunk. "The B-52s were always one of my favorites."

OK. Maybe wasp-man's not all bad. Davis would approve of his taste in music at least.

"She's perfect. I can't tell you how long I've been looking for this exact car. I drove one just like her when I was a kid. My grandparents gave her to me when I turned sixteen. I had to sell her in my twenties, and I always regretted it. I've been looking to replace her ever since."

"The Gherkin's been in our family two generations, too," Dad says.

"Gherkin? Ha! Clever. I called mine The Green Machine. I see she was loved. I'll treat her right. Buff the paint job, fix the engine, get her purring. I'm keeping that art in the trunk though."

"I can make more." The words shoot out of me before I think better. Both Dad and wasp-man raise their eyebrows at me.

"The shack doodle. It's my art." Swallowing hard, I channel my inner Bruce. "I work on commission. If you want something else too. Something specific. Music based, or something original…" I shrug like it's nothing even though it's everything. I've never shared my art before, let alone encouraged some stranger to check it out or buy it.

"You got a website?"

I nod and catch Dad's eyebrow go up even higher.

Wasp-man hands me a business card. "Send me an email with your links. The trunk art would be perfect on my office wall with a pop of color. Red cabin door? The Gherkin parked out front?"

I smile at his use of our nickname. "I could totally do that…" I glance down at his business card. "…Mr. Perry."

All my proud feelings die when the Gherkin is loaded onto the trailer. It's Davis's funeral all over again. Workers in matching drab grey overalls flank the Monte Carlo like grim pallbearers easing a casket into a hearse. *Stop! My brother's still in there!* I wanted to scream as the processional ended and they drove him away.

I never expected to find him in the back seat of the Gherkin.

Dad stands with me, staring at the wasp-mobile and tow hearse until they turn the corner, vanishing from sight.

Now Davis is really and truly gone. For good this time.

Dad picks up the box of Davis's things and my pillow. "I'll take these inside for you. See you in a bit?"

He's looking down the back end of the alley instead of at me as he speaks. I follow his gaze and…

It's Steve. Butterflies soar in my stomach.

"Mom texted about the Gherkin," he calls over to me. "I thought you might… need me?"

It's a question, not a statement. After sucking in a breath, he holds it, and I swear he stops breathing. He doesn't budge an inch. Not as I stalk down the alley, not when I break into a run.

It's not until I throw myself against him, burying my face into the soft folds of his worn cotton tee, that he pulls me close, holding me like *he's* the one that's drowning, and *I* the life-raft.

"God, Pru that was as bad as the funeral."

"What?" I lift my head, searching his face. I don't know if he's in tune with my thoughts or if he means something else. "You weren't there."

Shaking his head, he shuts his eyes.

"But Dad—he told you not to—"

Steve's heart races beneath my palm, and his eyes fly open. I recognize in his face the same wistful expression from Anne-Marie's photo, and her words ring in my head: *"He always looked at you that way. Like you were better than pizza."* When he finally speaks, his voice dips thick and low.

"Your dress was black, lacy, long. Like nothing I'd ever seen you wear. The entire congregation sobbed and wailed, and you stood there with your chin held high the entire time, stubborn and stunning. When they loaded the casket into the hearse and everyone else left for their cars as it drove away, you stood there. You stood there long after it passed. When you thought you were alone… only then did you cry. And even though I knew you hated me, it took all my strength not to run to you."

"You were there!"

"I was there. I'm *here*."

"Steve, we've lost Davis, the Gherkin, dreamland. All that magic. It's gone."

"No, Pru. I believe we make our own magic. You're mystical, Pru. Not the car. *You*. It's always"—he drags his thumb along my jaw, dropping his gaze to my mouth—"been you."

His touch makes me gasp, and when my lips part, the softest moan escapes his. More throaty growl than actual words. "Pru-Si-Q."

And then, my whole world tilts.

Steve's lips are cinnamon. And fire. And like nothing else in the entire world. I'm soaring. Falling. Floating. His hands tremble against my lower back as he holds me, a full body shiver matching mine as I return and deepen the kiss. He's my tether anchoring me to the Earth, my rocket ship blasting me out of the stratosphere. My port, safely sheltering me through any storm. Same as always… only better.

Bonus Track.
This Is the Day ~ The The

I f you're wondering if I passed geometry and graduated…
Well, I didn't.

S'OK. I got to sit in the stands with my folks and Mr.
Nolan, totally skipping all that pomp and circum-crap, exactly
the way I wanted, rooting for Steve and my friends—even
Maddi. I may not be ready to forgive *all* of her crap, but I am
eternally grateful to her for saving Steve and being there for
him when I could not. She teared up when I thanked her and,
since then, said not one shitty thing to me any time I bumped
into her over the summer.

And now my diploma sits in front of me on the plaid
woolen picnic blanket. Sealed inside a thick manila envelope
along with all the official credit recovery paperwork.

"Aren't you going to open it?" Steve asks, snagging another
sprinkle-coated cupcake.

"Open! Open! Open! Open!" Nikki chants, dropping a
dandelion wreath around Anne-Marie's neck.

"Yeah, Pru, open it!" Tony's drenched in chocolate, sprinkles, and marinara, but I let him crawl into my lap anyway to press his gooey hands on my cheeks and plant a slobbery kiss on my nose. His sticky fingers slide down my neck, tugging at the shoulder of my shirt. Both kids have been fascinated with my tattoo ever since they first saw it peeking around the straps of my summer tank tops. It hurt like hell, but Steve held my hand the entire time and I didn't cry once.

I paid for it myself—in full—by selling my art. Thanks to Bruce. He gets all his art for free. I'll owe him for life 'cause he totally changed mine.

"That's your big brother! Like me!" Tony makes soft *vroom vroom* noises, tracing the mini-Davis driving his Gherkin above—and forever in—my heart.

Mom refills everyone's wine flutes with sparkling cider, and Dad taps his glass with his fork, smiling at me and shining a spotlight on why we're all here in the first place. BD, I would have hated the extra attention, but now? It feels good. I'm surrounded by family, and we're celebrating tiny Giovanni Davis as much as me, who impatiently came early. At only three weeks old, he's more perfect than anything else I've spent time drawing. I think I've got fifty sketches of his little feet alone. And I'll have John's commission done—a surprise Christmas gift for Anne-Marie—right before the holidays.

"Speech, speech." Dad's still tapping his glass, and Steve gently nudges my shoulder with his before slipping his pinky around mine.

"Congratulations, Pru," Mr. G's voice booms. "We know you're excited about the apprenticeship."

I glance at Steve and smile. He spent his entire summer tutoring my math-deficient brain so I could pass the recovery course. Geometry stinks, but he's a natural. So while he gets his teaching degree, I'll be starting a tattoo apprenticeship. I want to specialize in memorial tattoos, but I'll still keep going with my art commissions on the side. Already my posts sharing the D&D art has attracted other players—complete strangers—who want their characters captured. By me.

Anne-Marie's forehead scrunches despite her smile. "I can't believe you're moving next week."

"But we'll be close enough to visit a ton," I say. "You know we can't live without your pizza."

Mom leans her head on Dad's shoulder, and her shining eyes lock on mine, watching me the same way she always used to look at us BD whenever she was proud or happy or amazed. She literally glows—cheeks flushed, eyes damp. *I love you*, she mouths, tapping her finger against the dimple in her chin, the one that matches Davis's.

Reaching into my pocket, I finger my metal P, D, and S keyring: Pru, Davis, Steve. While the D and S were in the glovebox, Mr. Perry found the P crammed in the crevice of the back bench seat while detailing the interior—along with a crumpled handwritten list that made clear what the keyrings were for.

As his graduation neared, Davis had been searching for apartments between Podunk and the city. Ever the fixer, he had plans to secure a place for the three of us to share. He'd weeded out everything that didn't meet criteria that favored us all. He'd amassed quite an organized list full of addresses, prices, amenities, and pros and cons… with Steve and me at the forefront of every decision. He was focused on keeping the three of us together.

I squeeze the D on the keyring. Same as always, he continues guiding and directing me. Forever my compass, my brother.

It's kind of a scary thing… moving away from a small town where I know every street and person like the back of my own hand. Even if I'm not doing so alone and going with my BFF for life—who also happens to be the best boyfriend ever. I'm still a little freaked out.

WWDD?
The answer?
Take the leap, Pru.
So, I do.

THE END

Note to Readers

Can't say goodbye to Pru and crew? Newsletter subscribers have been writing in to say they cannot either. Stay tuned for book two: *Everything We Had*, a short story collection of perspectives from your favorite characters. Newsletter subscribers get to read these juicy tidbits first, and receive some author/reader interaction to help mold their creation. Want to be a part of the action? Subscribe to stay abreast of how the next story is progressing, future books, and the author life at www. krhansenauthor.com

If you enjoyed *Everything That Was*, I'd love to hear from you and hope that you could take some time to post a review on Amazon. Your feedback and support will help this author continue to create future works for your enjoyment. I want you, the reader, to know that your review is very important. If you'd like to leave a review, just go to my author page on Amazon or follow this direct link to the review page:

https://www.amazon.com/review/create-review/?ie=UTF8&channel=glance-detail&asin=B0CRSJBNPK

I wish you all the best, and thank you from the bottom of my heart.

Check out my website and blog: www.KRHansenauthor.com

Connect with me on social:

Facebook: www.facebook.com/KRHansenAuthor

Instagram: www.instagram.com/k.r.hansen_author_artist

TikTok: www.tiktok.com/@k.r.hansen_author_artist

Acknowledgments

Writing is solitary, but creating a book takes teamwork. *Everything That Was* would never have come to pass were it not for the following amazing people.

To my parents, Jim and Bon Fillpot, who always showed me the importance of following your dreams, the power of creativity, and cultivating perseverance in all things: I wouldn't be the person I am today without your loving guidance. Words aren't enough to express my lifelong gratitude for the support you have always shown me. Thank you.

To my husband, Kris, and my son, Tyler, who both had to live under the same roof as me during the production of this book, a span of years when I had little to nothing else to talk about: thanks to both of you for the countless hours of brainstorming. Tyler, thank you for reading *every* craptastic draft, and Kris, your belief in both me and this novel have been invaluable. Thank you both for constantly listening to 80s music with me—even though such amazing music is thanks itself—and for helping me choose the perfect songs for the chapter titles. I couldn't have survived the marathon of penning a novel without either of you.

Thanks to Noah and Caitlyn Richter, my niece and nephew, whose tight relationship inspired Davis and Pru in the first place, and to my sister, Alisa, for raising such exemplary young adults. They are two of my most favorite people on the planet.

Thanks to my amazing crew of beta readers and writing critique partners: Maura Boudreau, Jodi Gallegos, Hollie Park-Garcia, Doss O'Rourke, Sonja Phillips, Chad Richardson, Kristen and Alyssa Robertson, and Jerry Yon. Fresh eyes on a manuscript make all the difference. Your feedback, encouragement, and enthusiasm helped mold the characters into the best jump-off-the-page people they could be. Maura and Alyssa—a special thank you for being my teen slang/voice gurus.

Jodi Gallegos's developmental prowess during the beta reader stage opened my eyes to possibility and helped me see the inconsistencies I'd been missing. I appreciate your tough love—the kind of feedback many are afraid to give was exactly the kick in the pants I needed. It was an honor working with you.

Aimee Hill, your line edits took Pru and crew deep. Thank you for your insights, the countless questions that made me ponder everything and reach for something better, and for taking the dream chapters to new heights. Your contribution went beyond editing; it was a transformative experience that enriched the narrative in ways I could not have achieved alone. Thank you for being an integral part of this creative journey.

DJ Gann, I could have never written this novel without you. From that initial phone call when I excitedly told you, "I think I have an idea for a novel," to your help fleshing out the initial ideas and clear till the moment I typed "The End," your finger on the pulse of Pru's development has been exemplary. Thank you for all your book coaching and editorial skills, for the countless hours of video chats and phone calls, and for always taking the time to talk shop even when you had the busiest of days. My experience working with you surpassed my wildest dreams. Thank you for holding my hand (and heart) throughout the entire journey.

To Samantha Zaboski, your role in the final edits and polishing of the book cannot be overstated. Your innate ability to immerse yourself in Pru's world from the very first page— to grasp her unique tone and to encapsulate her vibe in every sentence—was nothing short of remarkable. Your meticulous work in perfecting every aspect of the manuscript amazed me. I was in need of someone who could step back and see the entire forest when I was deep in the undergrowth, able to see only the bark of one or two trees. Your discerning eye and dedication ensured that so many fantastic little details found their home in the novel—details that would have remained hidden without your expertise. Thank you for your unwavering commitment to this project and for breathing life into Pru's world with your exceptional talents.

To the team at JetLaunch: Debbie O'Byrne, you are a graphic designing, cover-producing wizard! Thank you for fashioning such an eye-catching, gorgeous cover that beautifully captures the essence of the story. Your creative talents have truly brought my vision to life, and I couldn't be happier with the result. Your dedication and expertise have added an extra layer of magic to this book, and I am immensely grateful for your contribution.

And Chris O'Byrne, thank you for all the work in launching the novel and getting it into the hands of readers. All of your hard work has been instrumental in making this dream a reality.

And last but not least, I want to extend my sincerest gratitude to all the readers of this novel. Your decision to embark on this literary journey means the world to me. Thank you for giving this story a home in your hearts and minds. Time and attention are the greatest gifts an author can receive, and

I'm deeply thankful to all who took the time to experience Pru's tale.

Everyone on this list—I am eternally grateful to each and every one of you.

Resources

If you are grieving or know someone struggling with great loss, please call the National hotline for grief—1-800-442-4673 (HOPE) to talk to a caring crisis hotline volunteer.

The World Health Organization lists suicide as a leading cause of death among youth aged 15-24. If you are feeling alone and having thoughts of suicide—whether or not you are in crisis—or know someone who is, don't remain silent. Talk to someone you can trust through the 988 Suicide & Crisis Lifeline. Call or text 988 or reach out on the web at 988lifeline.org to chat the lifeline. Additional resources are provided through the National Suicide Prevention Hotline: 1-800-273-TALK (8255).

Sexual assault and abuse can be disastrous for mental and physical health. If you have been sexually assaulted or know someone who is a victim of sexual assault, reach out to the National Sexual Assault Hotline: 1-800-656-HOPE (4673) or chat through online.rainn.org.

According to the National Center for Education Statistics and the Bureau of Justice Statistics, about 20% of students aged 12-18 experience bullying in the United States. Bullying can result in physical injury, social and emotional distress, self-harm, and even death. It also increases the risk for depression, anxiety, and sleep disorders. You don't have to suffer alone. Contact the Bullying Crisis Text Line. By texting HOME or HELLO to 741741 you can connect with a Crisis Counselor who can listen totally judgement-free and help you strategize ways to get through the day. For more information about the Crisis Text Line visit crisistextline.org.

About the Author

K.R. Hansen has been obsessed with stories—both reading and writing them—for as long as she can remember. With a deep passion for creating narratives that resonate on a profound emotional level, she delights in blending the ordinary with the extraordinary, infusing her tales with magical realism that invites readers to find enchantment in the everyday.

Based in the picturesque landscapes of Colorado, K.R. Hansen shares her life with her loving husband, adventurous son, and an ever-enthusiastic rescue dog. As a spinal cord injury survivor and a wheelchair-bound explorer, she understands that life's most magical moments often emerge from the everyday norm, a perspective that permeates her storytelling.

When not crafting tales or daydreaming about her next literary adventure, you'll discover her exploring the great outdoors, creating award-winning fractal art, experiencing the thrill of live concerts—especially 80s bands that resonate with her GenX spirit, and engaging in epic board game battles.